Under the Burning Clouds

MALIHA ANDERSON BOOK 6

By

Steve Turnbull

To my readers.

CHAPTER 1

i

The thunder was so loud and so close Maliha came awake with the idea that the world was exploding. She had dreamt she was falling forever through rain and the black of night.

It was night. The room was scented with jasmine, Amita always made sure of that wherever they went. Maliha rolled over onto her back. The night sounds were not India. She opened her eyes and stared up at a ceiling that she could not see. The night was very black. Rain hammered against the window. She sat up and discovered she was wearing a simple nightgown. The sheets were only linen but, from their feel, of the best quality and crisp with cleanliness.

Lightning flashed, illuminating the room in stark whites and thick black shadows. She took in the image and examined the memory of it as the light died. She did not know this room, though the furniture declared it to be British. There were windows on the walls opposite and to the right, so she was in a corner room.

The third wall, to her left, had two doors. The one furthest from her would lead out to an ante-chamber, perhaps a corridor. The other would be a dressing room. The ceiling had a rose with electric bulbs; there was a switch by the window and there would probably be another on the wall beside the bed.

There was no timepiece that she had seen.

Where was here? How had she come to be here? Where was Amita? Valentine?

The thought of her fiancé brought the previous few days crashing back and the events of last night in particular. She felt sick, as the memory of him tossing her from the slavers' Voidship returned to her.

Her hand went to her throat and she felt her skin almost as if it were not her own. He had dropped her from an open hatch hundreds of feet from the ground in the middle of a lightning storm. She had fallen for such a terribly long time and then nothing.

Was that last night? Or had more time passed? Just because there was a storm now did not mean it was the same night.

She pulled back the covers and slipped out onto the carpeted floor. She found that her muscles ached, as if she had been engaging in unaccustomed exercise. She ran her hands across her legs, searching for cuts and contusions. Her left side seemed a little tender; the ache intensified when she pressed the skin where it was swollen. She felt the scar on her thigh.

Her feet made no sound as she padded across to the window, dimly outlined by some light source outside. The curtain had not been drawn closed and she looked out into the black.

Some of the building's other windows had light behind them and cast their yellow glow into the night. She appeared to be on the third floor. Directly below her window a gravel path marked the edge of the house and the light revealed tidily kept borders and beds.

The interiors of the clouds above were intermittently illuminated from within by lightning. She waited. Her patience was finally rewarded as daggers of white crawled across the clouds in repeating sequences, casting their light on the lands below.

They were remarkably unrevealing. Beyond the gravel path were neat gardens—the inclusion of an acacia tree suggested she was still in South Africa. A wooded area began about two hundred yards away and blocked all further view. Just in front of the trees was a long lake, which extended as far in each direction as she could see, in a curve that implied it encircled the house like a moat.

She crept across to the window on her right. She did not have long to wait before the next burst of lightning. This side of the house must be the front as an avenue led away from the building to a bridge crossing the moat and thence into the trees.

There were British soldiers on the roadway. If she was still in Johannesburg then this must be the Consulate. She could not imagine how she had come to be here.

Maliha turned around and faced the interior once more. She took a seat in the chair by the window. The sound of the wind hissing through the trees filtered through the glass. Every now and then there was a shift in the wind direction and the panes were assaulted by the rain, driving it in rivulets across the glass.

When the next burst of lightning filled the room with light, she saw the tallboy with a clock perched on it. Three-forty. Next to it was a third door, which would lead to a bathroom and water closet.

It also revealed, draped across a carved wooden chest at the end of the bed, a dressing gown. She rose from the chair and put it on. She would feel more comfortable walking the corridors in this, rather than just the nightgown like some mad woman.

She went to the door she had decided was the way out and turned the handle. It was locked, which confirmed her thought. She was not surprised, though somewhat disappointed. This was a cage, gilded or not. She had hoped she might have been among friends.

Lacking any further purpose, she went to the next door. On the next flash she determined it was indeed the dressing room. It had no windows, but it did possess a dressing table with its own light. She returned briefly to the main room and drew the curtains; they had been made heavy enough to block the early morning sun, so would suffice for hiding a small electric lamp.

She returned to the dressing room and switched it on. She blinked against the intense brightness. The dressing room contained no clothes other than those she had been wearing when she was thrown from the ship. The clothes glistened and there was water collecting beneath them. She frowned.

Every item of clothing, including her underthings, was dripping wet. It might have been raining and she had been out in the storm, but for them all to be so utterly drenched she must have been submerged in water.

She sat in the chair opposite the mirror and looked at herself. There was nothing there she did not normally see. Skin almost white enough to be European—but not quite—and hair like a black waterfall, in need of brushing.

For the past year or so Amita had brushed her hair every morning, just as her mother had done until she was twelve when she had been packed off to boarding school on the South Coast of England by her Scottish father. She fetched the brush from the dressing table. She preferred it when someone else brushed her hair.

The state of her clothes meant two things. First, this was the same night as when she had entered the lion's den in her invasion of the slavers' ship—the same night Valentine had thrown her from it.

Second it meant she had landed in the Consulate's moat. That might not be a certainty, but if she had landed in any other water she would not be in the Consulate now.

Did that mean Valentine had intended for her to survive the fall? Or had she fallen into the water by accident when his intention was to kill her? She stopped brushing and looked at herself.

"I cannot believe he intended to kill me," she said out loud. Their parting, only hours before, had been very difficult. He would have to have been a consummate actor to fool her for so long.

Still, it was curious, since she did not believe survival, at least with nothing more than slight swelling, was possible from such a great height, even into water. She understood that water presented a hard aspect for objects moving at high speed.

That was a conundrum requiring resolution, but it was not of critical importance. It was clear that, however it had been achieved, she had survived the fall. Still, she did have bruises on one side of her body, so the landing could not have been soft.

With her hair in a better state she went back into the bedroom and checked the other door. It was a well-appointed bathroom with both hot and cold water. It also contained the water closet.

Maliha returned to the bedroom. There was little to be done until the morning, so she removed the dressing gown and lay down in bed again, favouring her right side.

There was a diffident knock on the door.

ii

The sun was pushing around the curtains and illuminating the room. The door to the dressing room was still open and the light was on. She must have fallen asleep the moment her head touched the pillow.

The knock on the door came again, a little stronger.

"One moment," she said. She climbed out of bed and slipped on the dressing gown, tying the bow at the front. She moved swiftly across the room, opened the curtain of the window that faced the door and stood beside it. It was not that she expected to be attacked—why go to the trouble of putting her to bed so carefully if they intended her immediate harm? She just wanted an opportunity to examine the person before they saw her.

"Come in."

The door must have already been unlocked while she slept because the handle turned and the door swung open. It was a maid, perhaps in her twenties, white enough that Maliha assumed she was English. She was carrying a quantity of clothes, dresses and undergarments on her arm.

The girl looked confused when she did not see Maliha, but then her eyes fell on the closed bathroom door. She nodded to herself and must have assumed Maliha was in there. She came in and went directly into the dressing room. Maliha heard her mutter something under her breath and guessed it was dismay at the dripping water.

She had left the entrance door wide open. Maliha could see out along a corridor. There were more doors off it, probably bedrooms. The sun shone in from the right, leaving alternating patches of brightness and dark. The furnishings were opulent.

Maliha could have walked out, but to have done so would have been foolish: she was in a state of undress and quite interested in discovering how she had survived such a tremendous fall. She stepped out from the shadow and across to the dressing room.

The girl was on her knees, mopping up the water, and she jumped when Maliha cleared her throat to attract her attention.

"God 'elp us—sorry, Miss."

"Are you here to help me dress?"

"Yes, mum," she said and scrambled to her feet. The front of her dress and pinafore were wet through. She bobbed a curtsy.

"I see," said Maliha. "What's your name?"

"Nessa, mum."

"You can call me Miss Anderson."

"Yes, mum."

Maliha waited a moment but it became clear that, in the presence of a superior, the girl became incapable of independent thought. She simply waited for the next instruction.

"Why don't you draw me a bath, Nessa?" she said. "And I'll see what I like among the clothes you've brought."

Nessa looked down at the thin sheen of water on the floor.

"Just leave that for now," said Maliha. "You can deal with it when I've gone downstairs."

"Yes, mum," said the girl. She curtsied again unnecessarily and hurried past Maliha to the bathroom. Maliha watched her go, wishing Amita was here and not on her way back to India.

But that part of Maliha's life was over now. There would be no return to Pondicherry. She felt empty. There was one thing she wished for even more than Amita, but he was even further away and getting more distant by the second.

She was not happy with Valentine. She had gone to a great deal of trouble, and considerable personal risk, to get aboard the slavers' ship, and he had thrown her off it. But if she could hold him and feel his skin pressed against hers, she would forgive him—at least after making him suffer for a while.

But he was not here and she was alone again.

The sound of water splashing into the bath filled the quiet room. Maliha went to the bedroom door, pulled the key from the outside lock and closed it, then locked it from the inside. She placed the key on the dressing table. She was not planning to run away. At least, not yet.

The bath eased some of her aches. She had Nessa check her skin for abrasions. Perhaps it was because her skin was not as white as it might be, but the girl was embarrassed to look. Maliha had no time for such silliness and insisted.

Apparently there were none, just the slight bruising.

Nessa was, however, good with a hairbrush. Maliha had her move a chair so that she could look out of the window while the maid ran the brush through her hair again and again. It was very relaxing for both her and the girl to perform something so commonplace and repetitive.

"How did I get here?" Maliha asked as she felt the tension in Nessa begin to dissipate. The brush hesitated.

"Don't know, mum."

Maliha closed her eyes. "Oh, come now, there's bound to be talk below stairs."

"Not sure I should say, mum."

Maliha smiled even though Nessa could not see it. "Did they fish me out of the moat?"

A moment of hesitation told her what she needed to know. "Yes, mum. Late yester-eve. There was a big fuss and all the soldiers were called out. And there was the storm, all the lightning and the terrible thunder. I was a-frighted."

"And I fell out of the sky."

"Yes, mum. Alfred says there was a splash and there you was."

"Alfred?"

"Oh, he's my beau, if you don't mind me sayin', mum," she said. Now that the floodgates had been opened it was going to be difficult to close them again. "He's not so very handsome, but he's an under-butler and one day he'll be a proper butler and I can be a housekeeper and we can work together in some nice house—"

"So they fished me out of the water?"

"Yes, mum." The girl did not seem put-out that she had been interrupted. "They didn't realise it was a person at first. They thought it might be a bomb, like they had last year. I wasn't here last year but there was all sorts of trouble with people shooting and bombing—that's what Alfred says. He's very brave. He says we'll get engaged very soon too—"

"But they did realise it was a person and not a bomb?"

"Yes, mum. They saw you floating there in the water and one of them went in and pulled you out. You were wearing those strange clothes but you were un-con-scious," she worked hard at the word but made it come out right, "so they brought you up here and put you to bed. But they should have hung those clothes over the bath or brought them downstairs to the kitchen to dry."

But this still did not explain how she had escaped with only slight bruising.

"If you don't mind me askin', mum…" she trailed off, waiting for approval.

"What do you want to know?"

"Where did you fall from?"

Maliha considered her answer. "Did Alfred not say?"

"He reckons you fell from a air-plane?"

Maliha nodded. "That's right."

"But you should be dead then, right mum?"

"Yes."

"Why ain't ya then? I mean, if you don't mind me askin'?"

Maliha did not reply at first; instead she thought about Barbara. She hoped her friend was recovering. But it was almost the last thing Barbara had said to her that Maliha had been unable to rid from her mind: the question of vengeance. She gave herself an internal shake.

"I don't know," she said, responding to the girl's question, "but I intend to find out."

iii

The clothes they had found for her were not a good fit. Maliha was slimmer than their former occupants, but they would do for now and Nessa had promised she would start on the alterations. Maliha had the girl find a shawl and place it across her shoulders so that it draped across her upper body and hid all manner of crimes against fashion.

Nessa had not been told that Maliha had to stay in the room—which begged the question as to why the door had been locked, perhaps as just an initial precaution—so, since she was not forbidden, Maliha decided to set out to find her captors.

Maliha retrieved the key and the girl let herself out. Maliha performed a last-minute check on her apparel and, when she emerged from the room, Nessa had vanished. No doubt she had slipped into the servants' passages through a hidden door. Maliha studied the inner wall and spied the door, disguised as a section of wooden panelling.

She locked the bedroom door and slipped the key onto a ribbon attached to the dress, and let it hang. The corridor outside her room ran along one of the wings of the building and ended in a sharp turn to the left. Her feet made no sound on the thick carpet. The place was silent as a mausoleum.

The rooms beyond the turn might have been more bedrooms, but there was rather more wear in the carpet. It was possible to see the tracks of many feet leading up to these doors. They were more likely to be meeting rooms or perhaps places for socialising. She was not sure whether the Consulate might be like a men's club. She had not had a great deal of experience with men's clubs and what little she did have was peppered with misogyny.

In fact, the building, with its long corridors and thick carpet, reminded her of the Guru's residence in Kerala, owned by the elusive Terence Timmons, the man she now pursued, if obliquely, for his crimes.

While it may not have been done by his hand directly, it was his people who had stolen the girl, Riette, from South Africa and brought her to India to be tortured by Maliha's uncle. It was his people who had abducted and killed children in Johannesburg as part of their nefarious experiments with the Venusian fungus. It was one of his vessels that had infected animals in the countryside to the south, which had killed a family of Boer farmers.

Timmons. A man with an industrial empire that exceeded the power of nations.

She paused at the top of the stairs. It swooped down in elegant curves to the next floor and thence the ground. How could she bring such a man to justice? What possible justice could be brought to bear against him when he could, at the very least, bribe his way out of any imprisonment and simply disappear? Even assuming she *could* find him and have him arrested in the first instance.

What was she doing? She was barely twenty years of age, not even reached her majority; she had no power against someone like him.

There was a movement below her, not on the ground floor but the one between.

"Is that Miss Anderson?"

The man who had spoken stood on the floor below, looking up. He was in a neat suit and had a small moustache, though that was the limit of the hair on his head.

"I am she."

"Excellent, do please continue down."

With her hand on the wide wooden rail Maliha descended the stairs. On the first flight she was facing away from him; the wall opposite was adorned with paintings of heroes of the British Empire, including a massive piece that featured Lord Wellington in full uniform.

Above the stairwell was a tremendous chandelier. She glanced at it as she made the first turn and noted that it had been converted for electricity. She estimated there to be upwards of fifty bulbs—the house must possess its own generator.

The second turn brought her into a position from which she could view the man who had accosted her. The *gentleman*, she corrected herself. He held himself with the relaxed confidence of a man who knew his place in society, and it was close to the top. An aristocrat of the first water, perhaps even noble.

He smiled with such affability as she descended that she did not feel she was being hurried. She reached the floor and he gave her a bow. She curtsied automatically. There was a movement in the corridor behind him and she saw a servant, a butler, hovering within hearing distance but not so close as to intrude.

"I do apologise for the informality," he said. "I am Sir Bertram Kingsley and you are, of course, the astonishing Miss Anderson."

"Mr Crier has spoken of you, Sir Bertram."

He laughed. "Has he indeed? Not in the most complimentary terms, I'm sure."

Maliha merely smiled. Valentine had indeed given mixed reports of the man who had at one time been his direct senior and, later, the person in charge of his 'freelance' activities.

"Are you hungry, Miss Anderson?" he asked, after a pause. Perhaps he had been waiting for a compliment. "I can have some breakfast put together in a trice. The kitchen is quite used to serving food at unexpected times."

Now that he came to mention it, she realised she was ravenous. She nodded. "That would be welcome," she said.

"Perhaps some coffee with a selection of bread and meats?"

"If it would not be too much trouble."

"Not at all."

He gave no orders but the butler moved back along the corridor and disappeared.

Sir Bertram offered her his arm. "It will take them a few minutes to prepare it. Shall we go down?"

She took his arm and he led her down the stairs. A majestic picture of Edward VIII in full imperial regalia dominated the final flight. They would have to replace it quite soon as the King could not last much longer. He had had very few years on the throne compared with his mother, Victoria, who had lasted for over sixty years. Both the next king and the generation after him were ready to take over.

Sir Bertram led her along the ground-floor passage, which was flanked by rooms on both sides. They passed one with closed doors from which leaked the murmur of voices. He brought her into a

bright and spacious morning room that faced in the opposite
direction to her bedroom. While it did have plenty of space, it was
home to rather more tables and chairs than one might normally
expect.

"All these rooms are used for meetings, conferences, parties and
suchlike," he said as if reading her mind. "Turns the place into little
more than an upper-class public house." He guffawed at his own
joke. Maliha smiled politely—he had said it as if the words were often
on his lips.

She took her hand from his elbow and negotiated the maze of
furniture to the wide windows. The gardeners had built up the trees
and bushes on this side to hide the outbuildings that stood about fifty
yards away, but smoke and steam issued from a chimney that still
topped the foliage.

She felt his presence next to her.

"You have your own generators," she said.

"Naturally. Can't risk being cut off by the native blighters."

While smoke poured from only one chimney, there were four in
a close grouping. Having one as a back-up in case of failure was good
sense, of course, but four was vastly more than one might expect.
Unless one were powering something much hungrier for electricity
than a house.

"You have a Faraday device under the moat," she said in a
moment of revelation.

"Mr Crier has a loose tongue."

"Mr Crier told me nothing," she retorted hotly. "I am perfectly
capable of reasoning it out myself. And that device," she continued,
"must be the reason I am still alive."

She thought of Valentine and his callous words as he dropped
her. He had referred to her as a "bitch" but, even while he was doing
so, he had known that they were above the Consulate and that she
would be falling into water in a Faraday field.

Still, she thought, it was a considerable risk. She was going to have words with him when she saw him again.

If he was still alive.

iv

Maliha perched on the edge of a hard sofa, with a platter of meats, biscuits and soft white bread, and coffee. Sir Bertram also had a coffee. She had tried to give up meat, but her years in England had ruined her Hindu upbringing.

When she had first arrived at boarding school she had refused to eat the meat they served at almost every meal. She had been punished mercilessly and forced to sit facing it for hours. In the end, after what had seemed like months but was only a single week, she had given in. She was only eleven and the combined force of punishment from a dozen teachers and catering staff was irresistible.

She had been sick but had become used to meat and eventually learnt to enjoy it. And now she could not do without it. She ate delicately but steadily to fill the void.

Rather than have her companion simply stare at her as she ate, she paused to ask a question.

"What can you tell me about Terence Timmons?"

"You as well, Miss Anderson? Bill was quite obsessed with the man."

"With good reason, sir," she said. "It is obvious the fellow is not acting with the best interests of the British Empire at heart."

"Who does, Miss Anderson? Oh, we may sing 'God Save the King' and all that malarkey, but who truly acts for the greater good? Everyone is out for themselves in the end. Any benefit that leaks out is the result of accident, not intent."

She looked at him with surprise. "I must say", she said, "I did not expect such an extreme view from a British peer."

"Altruism is a deceit, Miss Anderson. It is nothing but a lie to make one feel happy with oneself. But giving to the poor ultimately benefits no one."

She took a sip from her coffee and enjoyed the way it invigorated her. "You are saying that no one acts except in self-interest?"

"That is my experience."

"Perhaps you're right," she said. "Although it does make the world a rather dismal place if that is the case."

They continued in silence for a while. She noted that he had side-tracked her question and said nothing whatsoever about Timmons. There was something else, too, but that could come after the Battenberg cake that awaited her.

*   *   *

She brushed imaginary crumbs from her skirt—she had caught them all in her plate—and sat back.

"Thank you, Sir Bertram. That was just what I needed. It has been a trying couple of days."

"Perhaps you'd like to take a turn about the gardens?"

"That would be delightful," she said. "But I'm sure you have more pressing issues to deal with than escorting a surprise guest about the place. I will not be offended if you wish to get back to them."

She got to her feet and he stood up with her as etiquette dictated.

"Most thoughtful," he said and affected a sad face. "You are quite right, of course—my duties are calling me. You can wander any part of the grounds but do not cross the moat."

"Am I a prisoner?"

"Good heavens no, dear lady. It is for your own safety."

From what? she thought as he took his leave and headed back into the depths of the house. She turned back to the outer wall, the centre of which was a French window. She turned the handle and it opened. She stepped out into the warm and humid air.

The storm had long since passed and the sun had evaporated the moisture from the ground into the air, where it hung in the increasing heat of the day.

There were convenient paths, wide enough for two people walking side-by-side, winding in and out of the flower beds and trees. It looked haphazard but she was able to divine the pattern.

Each path was suitable for two diplomats or businessmen to walk about and discuss matters in complete privacy. Each path was hidden from the others except at the junctions. It was a garden designed for negotiation.

She followed a winding trail away from the house. The various twists and turns made attaining her goal tricky, but within a few minutes she was at the edge of the moat.

Her suspicions, if they had not been confirmed by Sir Bertram himself, were revealed plainly here. Cables in wooden conduits— painted green to blend in—ran along the shoreline and emerged at intervals to plunge down into the earth.

It must have been a massive piece of construction, not only building the sizable Faraday grid itself but laying it out underground and proofing it against the water that would undoubtedly try to leak into it.

And what a folly of a concept. It could hardly be of much more benefit than the simple fact of the moat. What difference could it possibly make in the event of an attack? It might provide some disorientation but no more than that.

But it had saved her life.

And therein lay a matter of extreme interest: she had twice given Sir Bertram the opportunity to question her about where she had fallen from, but he had taken neither opening. He was a skilled diplomat; if he had wanted to know, he would have used those chances to their best effect.

But he had not asked. And that could only mean he was part of it. Part of what? A conspiracy? Would one of the nobility lead a revolution against the government of his own country?

He might if he did not believe that Society was a real thing, if he believed that personal gain was the only thing that drove a person. A revolution backed by the might of a major industrialist, perhaps?

She looked out across the water. Perhaps Valentine had been right to throw her from the Voidship. It was clear that, in his estimation, her chance of survival aboard the ship was nil. So tossing her from the ship was an improvement, no matter how dangerous.

It seemed he did not suspect Sir Bertram would be in league with Timmons. She was indeed a prisoner here. She had been thrown out of the frying pan and into the fire.

v

"When is your day off, Nessa?"

"I get Sunday mornings so I can go to church, mum," said the maid as she cleared away the breakfast things the following day. "And Thursday mornings."

"Tomorrow morning?"

"Yes, mum."

Maliha stared out of the window at the overcast day. She did not want to wait a week before escaping. It needed to happen sooner.

"And the church, is that far?"

Sunday morning at a Christian church was another British custom Maliha had been forced to endure. She could sing 'Jerusalem' with the best of them and probably knew better than most what it really meant. Blake had always appealed to her.

"No, mum," came the reply. "Just a short ways down the road. Half hour of walking."

"No chapel on the grounds?"

"No, mum."

Maliha considered her options. If she suggested that she might attend the service, she would either be denied outright or be given an escort. If she remained here, the staff would be reduced and she would have more freedom.

That settled it.

In the meantime she should make herself familiar with the layout of the house and gardens, and see whether she could discern a pattern in the movements of the guards. There was bound to be one.

She dressed for walking and, now that they had dried out, she used the sturdy shoes she had been wearing when she arrived.

"Might rain, mum," said Nessa.

"Perhaps you could find me an umbrella?" Maliha said. "Just in case."

Her coat and hat had also dried, so she wore those as well. They did not suit the dress, which was of a far older style, but she was not overly concerned with appearances. The overall effect, once Nessa had returned with the brolly, was not the woman of sophistication she had originally intended.

She began her reconnaissance by wandering the entire upper floor from one end to the other. There was little enough to see, just bedrooms. She noted the position of all the entrances to the servants' passages. At the far end of each wing there was another staircase, far less elaborate than the principal one in the centre of the building but still intended for guests and residents.

The next floor down was much the same, except here all the rooms had been pressed into service as offices and rooms for meeting. She received curious looks from the few staff she encountered, but she moved briskly as if she knew what she was about. As a result, no one questioned her or barred her way. The servants' entrances mimicked the upper floors except in places where the rooms were of different sizes.

She had already seen most of the ground floor rooms, but she still made sure of the location and purpose, where it could be seen, of each area. Doors led out of the building not only through the main entrance and at the far ends of the wings, but also through several rooms which had their own exits, both into the atrium and out towards the moat.

The east wing differed most from the rest—it was almost completely occupied by the ballroom. As she pushed open the door and stepped into this empty space, her heels clicked on the herringbone-patterned wooden floor. Electric lights in the form of small chandeliers were arranged in a pattern of diagonals across the ceiling. The walls were panelled with dark wood. To the right of where she had entered were stacked tables and chairs.

The sound of something dropping to the floor echoed around the room. She saw a movement by the wall; an Indian in overalls was gathering his tools.

"Many apologies, *sahiba*," he said. "I will leave."

"*Don't go*," she said in Hindi and pressed her palms together at her waist, giving a slight bow. He stopped and perhaps realised that her skin was not as white as he had thought at first. He returned her greeting but indicated his lower caste by moving his hands to his face and casting down his eyes.

"Can I help you, *sahiba*?"

"I am Maliha Anderson."

She had hoped he would recognise the name, but apparently not—his expression remained respectful but unmoved.

Maliha straightened her posture and said in Hindi. "I am the avatar of Durga Maa."

He fell to the floor and prostrated himself. She sighed inwardly. This was why she had no desire to use the title: they would treat her like a goddess and nothing good would come of it. Of all the nine incarnations of Shiva, that fool of a priest had had to choose this one. Still, she might need this man's cooperation and Durga Maa was most likely to compel it.

The mere name was enough; she did not have to enter riding a tiger. In fact, if she told him that's how she had arrived he would probably have believed it.

"You fell from the sky," he said into the floor. *On a tiger.*

"Yes."

"Do not bring vengeance on me, Durga Maa. I will no longer steal from my masters."

Maliha almost laughed. If she had known it was this easy to get confessions out of people, by simply pretending to be a goddess, she would have done it long ago.

"What is your name?"

"Nedumaran."

"Very well, Nedumaran, I accept your promise," she said. "It is possible I may need you. How can I get them to send you to me?"

"If an electric light does not work, they call for Nedumaran, Goddess."

"Don't call me that," she said. "And get up. I am in disguise. You must call me Miss Anderson and not," she could not think of the word for a moment, "not cower or prostrate yourself when I'm around."

Reluctantly he climbed to his feet, but he would not look at her. That was less of a problem.

"And don't tell anyone you met me."

"Yes, Goddess."

"Miss Anderson."

She left him and went out into the garden. She was not entirely sure of the punishment for representing oneself as a goddess. *Still, he did appear to be very gullible*, she thought and headed for the moat.

She passed under the trees and realised that she had done the man an injustice by considering him gullible. People needed hope and perhaps that was what she gave them. It was a different way of looking at it.

As she circumnavigated the Consulate, checking the paths and committing the layout to memory, she considered simply attempting to leave. After all, she might be wrong; perhaps she was not a prisoner after all.

She approached the bridge, with its guard of three infantrymen. Before she had even moved to within twenty yards they had noticed her and stirred. She decided not to press the point and gave them a wide berth, clearly signalling that it was not her intention to attempt to cross.

A little further on she paused at the water's edge to watch some ducks. Pretending to sneeze, she glanced back. They had resumed their previous positions, but one of them still looked in her direction.

That settled the matter.

vi

"You are Miss Anderson." It wasn't a question.

The Consulate had a communal dining area for its staff, but to call it a refectory was to do it an injustice. It was probably on a par with the very best restaurants and offered an extensive menu, though not *à la carte*.

Maliha was in the middle of her evening meal of trout with a mix of vegetables when the fellow simply walked up and began to speak. She swallowed what was in her mouth, though it was not fully chewed, put a smile on her face and looked up.

She was not impressed by what she saw. He was middle-aged and quite portly. He had a bold moustache and had tried to disguise his partial loss of head hair by combing long strands of what remained across it. His suit was a very good fit for his frame but, all physical attributes apart, he leered and his eyes were not on her face but her *décolletage*.

"You have me at a disadvantage, sir," she said. In the periphery of her vision she could see heads turning in their direction. Apparently his behaviour was noteworthy.

"Geoffrey Penn," he said. His face bulged as if it were packed with pillows beneath the skin, and his eyes disappeared into the folds. Maliha could not help but imagine a frog. She knew he had been in the room when she entered and, if she was not mistaken, he had been consuming his dessert by the window.

Now that she recalled it, he had spent an inordinate amount of time looking at her. Others had looked up—after all, this was a preserve of masculinity—but they were polite enough to look away once normal curiosity had been satisfied. Mr Penn, however, had watched her in the mirror.

In the time she had taken to be seated and have her order delivered, he had finished his dessert, had a liqueur, a coffee and a cigar. The air was thick with the smoke of cigars, cigarettes and pipes; it floated in layers and streams through the room. It seemed a requirement of the male staff that they breathe the fumes of burning tobacco.

"I do apologise, Mr Penn, but I seem to be in the middle of my meal."

"Yes, appalling manners, I know," he said with an unctuous smile. "But I had to talk to you."

"Perhaps when I've finished?"

"Too kind," he said. "I'll be in the library."

She nodded and glanced at the clock standing in the corner. "As you wish. Perhaps nine o'clock?"

"Nine o'clock then." He gave her a hint of a bow and left the table.

Frowning, she returned her attention to her meal, ignoring the glances from the other diners.

She lingered over the coffee, watching the men go in and out, listening to the murmur of their voices. It was Saturday, but the staff was always on duty. A pity.

It was not just a matter of getting out of the building and back into the city, it was how she was going to get to the *Sigiriya*. But she understood the problem: she simply needed more information and, as soon as she had everything she needed, the plan would fall into place. For now it was sufficient just to have a goal.

But time pressed.

The clock chimed the three-quarter hour. She stood and made her way out into the passage. Taking it at a leisurely pace, she made her way round the front of the building to the library, situated in the other wing. It took her less than five minutes, so it was well before nine when she pushed open the door and entered.

The walls were lined with shelves and stacked with the books one would expect. There were several armchairs and sofas suitable for reading, as well as three tables and two writing desks. Other than that, it was empty. She preferred to arrive early—it meant that she could choose where to stand or sit.

Of course, it was completely inappropriate for her to meet a man in a secluded place without a chaperone. However, she doubted anyone would care; the colour of her skin meant she was not considered a lady.

She chose to examine the bookshelves near the window. These were occupied by volumes of maps and encyclopaedias. She ran her fingers along the books, feeling the rough texture of the spines. She stopped at a slim volume entitled *An Atlas of the Known Regions of Venus.*

She slid it from between the others and laid it on a table. It cracked slightly as she opened it, as if she was the first. She went through the pages, studying each for a moment and then moving on. It was her skill and her curse, the ability to recall anything she saw with perfect clarity.

Not that the atlas revealed a great deal. The greater portion of Venus was still unexplored and the constant mists and clouds made the mapping process very slow. There was only one major landmass—which was at least the size of Europe, Asia and Africa combined—stretching in a bent ellipse around three-quarters of the surface.

The rest was occupied by one major ocean, except this was dotted with islands large and small. One page noted that all depth-soundings suggested the sea was no more than a few fathoms deep across the entirety of its surface.

The major British population centre, the city of Regina, was located near the north pole, that being the coolest part of the planet. The lowest temperatures exceeded a typical day in India and the humidity was like a constant monsoon.

The atlas included plates of the flora and fauna: the great fungus forests; monstrous creatures like the giant reptiles dug from the ground at Whitby; smaller, wolf-like animals that ran in packs; and so many more. It was said that nothing native to Venus was not inimical to human life.

And yet we still colonised it.

As did Terence Timmons and his fleet of vessels, which carried naïve African farmers who thought they were going to Australia. How could she possibly find them with an entire planet to search?

The door opened and the bulk of Geoffrey Penn negotiated the gap between door and frame. He shut the door behind him. She took the opportunity to close the atlas and return it to its place.

vii

Geoffrey Penn's walk was almost a waddle, there was so much mass he had to move. She concluded that she would be completely safe, since she would have no difficulty outrunning him if she should be called upon to do so. He made his way between the furniture and stopped opposite her across the table.

"Kind of you to agree to meet with me, Miss Anderson," he said. She recognised a hint of Yorkshire in his voice, but it had been smoothed out by years in the Civil Service.

"Not at all, Mr Penn," she said. "Being trapped in the Consulate means that nothing that can fill my time is unwelcome. Shall we sit?"

He did not so much reply as grunt.

"Trapped?"

"I am prevented from leaving," she said. "So yes, I feel the term 'trapped' is valid, and it is less provocative than 'imprisoned'."

She was not entirely sure whether this was the correct approach to take with a man she did not know, who might even be working for her adversary, when she was not aware of his position.

"Yes, well, can't say I know anything about that," he said, shifting his weight uncomfortably. "It was you I was interested in, you see, Miss Anderson, and your cases."

"My *cases*?" she said. "You mean like Conan Doyle's fictitious detective, Sherlock Holmes?"

"Yes, exactly so, you see." He hesitated. "I am an admirer."

"Well, Mr Penn, for one thing I have not had many cases, and I am not fictitious."

"Precisely, Miss Anderson." His delight leaked through the layers of fat in the form of a childlike smile. "You are real, your cases are real—does that not make it so much more interesting?"

"Honestly, Mr Penn, I'm afraid you may have misunderstood. I do not enjoy what I do." Even as she said it, she knew it to be a falsehood. "What I mean to say is that they involve real people, death and horror; they are not some intellectual game in the mind of an author."

She could see from the look in his eyes that her words were having precisely the opposite effect to what she intended. He was not put off by their truth—it excited him.

She sighed. "What is that you want from me, Mr Penn?"

"Call me Geoffrey."

"I do not believe I will. It is not personal but I do not think we should become intimate."

"Are you really prevented from leaving?"

She nodded her response.

He looked thoughtful and his eyes kept dropping from her face to her chest. It was quite uncomfortable; she could not imagine what was going through his mind. Or worse, she was quite able to imagine.

Something occurred to her. "To what extent are you privy to the facts of my encounter with Guru Nadesh?"

A look of embarrassment came over his face which told her all she needed to know about that. Both Detective Forsyth and Valentine had made private reports which were not included in the general files about the death of the Guru. Those reports contained details of how she had persuaded the man to confess his crimes.

It seemed that Geoffrey Penn had used his position to read those reports and, while neither of her friends would have been prurient in their descriptions, they would not have omitted the fact that she had gained the Guru's confidence by becoming one of his students, being naked with him and letting him touch her.

Here was a man she did not know, who knew her history in intimate detail.

"What is it you want from me?" she said again. "And what will you do in exchange?"

"I cannot help you escape," he said quickly.

"Let me know your demand first, Geoffrey," she said, trying to suppress the aggressive tone that Valentine had told her she adopted all too easily. "But be aware, I will not do anything that might be considered indelicate."

He looked horrified, though possibly a little disappointed as well. He did not respond. If she was not mistaken there was a battle going on inside the man.

"I said 'nothing indelicate', Mr Penn."

"No, of course, I would not suggest such a thing."

His words belied the look in his eyes, and the location to which they were directed said quite the opposite.

"Are you married, Mr Penn?"

"I do not have that pleasure, Miss Anderson." The look of sorrow in his face was enough to break a woman's heart. But clearly it never had.

"I am going to be completely honest with you, Mr Penn," she said. "I know what you most desire and I cannot give that to you. Nor anything even close to it."

He appeared horrified that she might be able to see into his soul. But she had seen true horror and there was little he could imagine she had not either seen or experienced. Saying these things did not embarrass her.

"But I will permit a kiss."

"A kiss?" His voice caught in his throat and the words barely emerged whole. "What do you want in return?"

"You have access to records?"

He hesitated sufficiently for Maliha to think he was going to deny it, but not admitting that he had seen the private records would have made him a liar. He nodded.

"I want to see every record you have on Terence Timmons."

He nodded.

"And I need them tonight."

"I don't know—"

"Tonight, Mr Penn," she said. "I am going to retire now, but I will find that I cannot sleep at about two o'clock and I will return here to find something to read. I hope I will find something very interesting on this very table."

He nodded again. "And the kiss?" Once more it was as if his voice had deserted him and the words came out as barely more than a croak.

"If you are here then, it will be possible to bestow the favour."

She knew that would guarantee he carried out his half of the bargain. After all, she was not going to get dressed to come down; she would be wearing only her dressing gown. He would see her feet, her ankles as well, no doubt, and a more interesting version of her upper torso.

As she headed upstairs she wondered what she had become that she would sell her body to achieve her aims. Was she any different to Amita, or Riette's mother, Akua? *It is only a kiss*, she thought to herself, *with a man who will always lack for female companionship*. But even as she thought it she knew it to be no more than a rationalisation. She was prostituting herself.

viii

She had no alarm clock, so instead she spent the night sitting in the dark or pacing. The lights of Johannesburg faded out one by one, save for the electric street lights that burned through the night.

She had the window open to allow cooler air to circulate. Night sounds filled the room. The voice of what may have been a fox called in its penetrating shriek. Owls of different types made themselves known.

The sky was clear and brilliant with stars shimmering against the black. Here in the Transvaal, the Victoria Voidstation that hung above the Fortress in Ceylon was not visible, even though her windows were facing the right direction. If she could have looked to the east, the now-defunct Albert Station would be hanging motionless above the horizon. The third station in the triangle that enclosed the globe, Elizabeth, sat above the Pacific Ocean. She had never seen it.

The clock chimed the half hour. She realised she had been dozing and looked at her watch to see the hour, but it was too dark. She stood stiffly and went into the dressing room. She closed the door, turned her head away and switched on the light. Even behind her shut and averted eyes she was dazzled by red.

She waited for them to adjust and then opened them cautiously. It was half-past one. Leaving the light on, but with the door pulled almost shut to provide minimal illumination, she made her way across to the bathroom, where she washed her face and applied a light dusting of sweet-smelling talc to her neck and under-arms. Finally she freshened her mouth with tooth powder. If she was going to repay him with a kiss, she would make it as pleasant an experience for him as she could.

There was a sound from the bedroom, something slapping gently on the exposed wooden floor near the walls. It could have been bare feet but it sounded too light. She looked around for a weapon, but there was nothing of any size except the loofah.

She pushed the bathroom door shut and slid the bolt into place as protection.

"Who's there?" she called.

There was a pause then a small voice said, "Goddess?"

Maliha pulled the bolt and flung the door open, taking care not to let it bang noisily against the wall. In the half-light, two shadowy figures stood near the window, one half the size of the other.

She almost ran across the carpet and threw her arms around them. She found her eyes tearing up, though she had no idea why. She crouched and hugged them close. They were both wet, but Maliha did not pull away. Lilith returned her hug, clinging to her neck. Izak did not, but neither did he pull away.

"We've come to rescue you, Goddess," said Lilith in a whisper.

"Mama Kosi said we should come. See if you want to leave," Izak said. "She said you were caught by the crushers." He glanced around. "If I was in this prison, I would stay."

"We can talk later," she said, still clinging to them as if they were her only lifeline. She could not quite understand it. "I have to meet someone."

"Mr Valentine?" asked Lilith.

"No, Valentine is gone," she said. "This is a man who has information."

"We should come," said Izak. "Mama Kosi said we should protect you."

Maliha let them go; she noted Izak stagger a little as she released him. "What's wrong, Izak?"

He said nothing. Lilith gave him a moment and then answered. "The bad people shot him in the leg."

"Scratched me is all."

"Izak, you should have let someone else come."

"We told Mama Kosi we are your people now, only we can come."

Maliha sat back on her haunches. *What have I done?*

"You can't come. I will be safe," she said. "I may be a prisoner but they won't hurt me."

Izak looked at her though in the dim light his face was unreadable. Pinpricks of illumination reflected in his eyes. It reminded her of the infected child in the diamond mine. She shivered.

"But as soon as I have learnt what he can show me, I will return." She stood up and straightened her dressing gown, which was damp from hugging the children. The wetness had soaked through to her skin and tightened the belt. "Just wait here. I will be an hour."

She left the room as the clock chimed the three-quarter hour.

The corridors of the Consulate were dark, but there was sufficient light filtering through the windows to guide her. The library was in the opposite wing and two floors below. She navigated to the other side of the building and then took the smaller set of stairs down.

The place was quiet as the grave. The only guards were outside; after all, there was no reason to think there were any threats inside. She did not relish the prospect of swimming the moat as the children must have done. *What possessed Mama Kosi to send children?*

There was no light showing beneath the library door. She turned the handle and pushed it open. She slid inside and shut it behind her. The place was pitch-black. The curtains must be drawn.

She could smell his sweat in the room, overlaying old tobacco smoke.

"Mr Penn?"

"Miss Anderson." His voice came from the right. It sounded drowsy; perhaps he had been sleeping in a chair.

"Do you have what I asked for?"

"I have what I could gather."

A gas lamp went on. It was a good choice, since it would throw the least light but still allow her to read. She gathered up a rug and placed it against the bottom of the door to prevent any light leakage.

She headed over. Her clothes were still damp and she was aware the material clung to her skin in a fashion that emphasised her contours.

He made no comment, but as she came into the light his gaze was glued to her upper body. She sighed—his payment would be even greater then.

There were three files stacked on the table. Two of them were thin, while the third was two inches deep. She would not have time to absorb it all now; she must employ the trick of simply looking at the pages and 'reading' them later.

"I will have to concentrate, Mr Penn," she said as she seated herself. "If you would be so kind as to keep still and quiet that will help."

"You're going to read it all?" he asked. "That will take hours."

"I won't be too long," she said. "If you could move the light closer I will begin."

He slid the slightly smoking lamp closer. She removed the first folder from the pile and opened it. Then she simply turned over each of the handwritten reports and filled-in forms, looking at each one. She did not hurry but endeavoured not to notice any distracting detail.

This was how she had absorbed so many volumes on such diverse subjects over the years, though she shivered when she remembered the bookshop owner.

Focus.

She finished the first folder and changed it for the second.

"I thought you were going to read them," he said in a tone of annoyance.

"This is how I do it," she said. It would have been easier to lie and say she was looking for something specific, but she did not like to lie.

She finished off the second folder in as little time as the first and moved on to the third. She opened it and stared long and hard at the first page. It was written in Valentine's untidy hand. This was his report and analysis of Timmons' trading empire, the one that showed there was something odd about the fleet and its connections. She ran her finger lightly across the page, as if touching the letters he had written would somehow connect her with him.

"Found something interesting?" asked Penn.

She shook her head and forced herself to turn the page. It took her a few more pages to return to the previous rhythm and a good ten minutes to work her way through the whole report. It would take her hours to read it thoroughly. It was not that his conclusions were incorrect, but she was sure there would be more useful information buried within.

She turned the heavy folder back and re-tied the ribbons that held it, thinking that *he* had probably been the last person to tie the knots. Finally she placed the three folders together in a pile and neatened them up.

"Thank you, Mr Penn," she said.

"You owe me a kiss," he said, his voice a little hoarse.

She put a smile on her face. "Of course, I am a woman of my word."

Pushing back the chair, she stood up and moved around the table. Penn was considerably taller, as well as significantly overweight. He would easily make four or five of her, she thought.

The light from the gas lamp turned him into a planet with a light and a dark side, the mountains of his suit creases and edges casting long shadows. She was acutely aware that the same effect was occurring across her body.

She knew she had made the wrong decision when his hand enclosed her upper arm in a painful grip. But there was still a part of her that insisted on carrying through her promise even though he intended harm to her. She did not protest.

His other hand wrapped around her other arm and he pulled her towards him. With the violence of barely reined-in lust, he leaned down and crushed his lips against hers so hard their teeth ground the flesh of their mouths together.

Her part of the bargain was fulfilled.

He released her right arm and grabbed at her breast. His fingers dug into her tender flesh.

"This was not our bargain," she said, trying to prevent the pain from being reflected in her voice.

"I love you," he said. "I want you."

She could try to reason with him, but she knew there was little left in his mind to reason with.

Twisting slightly, she slammed her knee as hard as she could into his groin. He spasmed, driving more pain into her arm and breast. But then his grip loosened.

In the dim light she could see the excruciating agony spreading through him, almost too much for his nerves to comprehend. She pushed him away and he fell back, nearly missing the chair and landing on its arm instead, then tumbling sideways.

"Thank you for the information, Mr Penn. I am sorry you were unable to resist your baser instincts."

He groaned in agony. She forced herself to breathe normally, but her blood ran hot in her veins and her heart threatened to pound its way through her ribs.

She made her way from the room, closed the door on him and ran.

CHAPTER 2

i

Izak and Lilith were still in the room when she returned. They looked up in alarm as she dashed inside.

"We must go," she said. "Quickly."

Penn might not raise the alarm once he had regained some control, but she could not rely on it. She threw off her dressing gown and hurried into the dressing room, pulling off her night clothes.

The clothes she had had Amita make for her were designed so that she could put them on without requiring a maid. It took less than three minutes for her to return fully dressed and pinning her black hat to her hair.

"Let's go," said Izak as he headed for the window.

"I cannot go that way," said Maliha. "We must go through the house."

"We may be caught."

"It will be quicker."

She went directly to the open door, where she paused and listened. The house remained quiet. She turned left immediately and opened the door to the servants' passages. She tried not to think of the moat—she had no desire to get wet again, but there seemed to be little option. The bridge was not going to be available for their use.

She heard one of the children close the door behind them. Dim lights shone along a short passage to the stairs. These routes had no external lighting, so the electric lights were kept burning at all times.

They headed down the circular staircase; her shoes clicked, while Izak and Lilith's bare feet barely made a sound as they descended the wooden steps. They passed the next floor.

It was then they heard shouting. Distant at first but growing. Maliha paused.

"Should have gone out the window," muttered Izak.

Marching but muffled feet moved through the carpeted corridors beyond the walls. They might have some leeway—Maliha was aware that those used to being out in the main corridors of a house failed to think of the servants' passages, just as they failed to consider the servants at all.

She moved forward and continued down. They reached the ground floor. The stairs continued into the cellars. Maliha hesitated. The cellars might provide an excellent way past the guards, but she did not recall seeing an exit.

Where they were now was close to the ballroom. She turned to the right and headed towards it. As she had expected, there was a servant's passage that ran the length of the hall. They hurried along it.

On the other side of the wall she could hear a squad of soldiers searching. They were moving pieces of furniture to ensure she was not secreted behind them. They spoke in low tones which were hard to make out through the wall, however she was certain they were not English. Punjabi, perhaps.

Maliha and the children came to a door; it lacked the ornamentation that marked those in the public parts of the house. She listened but could make out no sound beyond it. She pushed it open—it was a kitchen. There were several tables with cutting blocks, as well as a fireplace with metal warming shelves near to it.

Across on the other side of the room a door led out into the grounds, and artificial light gleamed on the glass from the outside. The three of them made their way across. Maliha peered out through the glass. She knew exactly where they were in relation to the rest of the building: the bridge was on the far side, the moat was not far from the house at this point, and the trees on the other side grew close to the water.

If there was a good place to cross, that was it.

The door was bolted top and bottom but had no keyhole. She reached up on tiptoe and slid back the upper bolt. Izak knelt down and wiggled the lower one to make it move.

"Stop."

The man's voice came from behind.

Maliha felt her blood run cold. She could not remain here, there was so much that had to be done. There was a man to bring to justice. If they caught her now, they would never let her go.

She put her hand on the doorknob.

There was the click of a well-oiled gun being cocked.

"Please release the handle. I do not wish to shoot you."

Maliha turned but did not let go. The door was unlatched. If she pulled it, it would open. Izak remained by her feet. Lilith was on the other side of her and might not be visible.

The soldier was Sikh, but his uniform was British. She could see other turbaned heads behind him.

"Release the handle, miss."

"I cannot stay."

"And I cannot let you leave."

"Then you must shoot me."

"No!" shouted Lilith. She jumped out and stood as if her body could be a shield, even though she barely reached Maliha's waist. "You cannot shoot the goddess."

Izak chose this moment to emerge as well. He too placed himself between the gun and Maliha.

Maliha released the door handle, but not before she had given it a slight tug. She stepped to the side to allow it to open and also to get the children out of the immediate line of fire. The soldier turned the gun away.

Maliha felt the cool breeze on her neck and cheek as the door swung open.

"Foolish children. Out with you, outside now." She shooed them through the door but made no move to head that way herself. They went reluctantly and stood just outside.

"Goddess?"

"They are children," said Maliha.

"Durga Maa," called Lilith.

"Hush, Lilith. They're Sikh not Hindu."

"You are Maliha Anderson?"

The Sergeant took a step forward into the room. Two of his men came forward as well and the others crowded behind, peering over shoulders and between heads.

He holstered his weapon. "You drove away the ones killing the children."

Maliha frowned. "What do you mean?"

"We all saw it, last night," he said. "The ship from which you fell. We thought we were under attack, so we activated the moat Faraday when the ship appeared from the north. Then you fell from it."

"I was pushed," Maliha corrected.

"Then the reports came in today of the old diamond mine."

"That was where the slavers were based."

He nodded. "You drove them away."

Maliha nodded slowly. "Yes."

It certainly wasn't Valentine who had made them leave. She had made it impossible for them to continue their experiments. And completely misjudged it, so many natives had died because she had not realised the scope of their activities.

She brushed away a tear. At least Izak had only been slightly hurt. That would have made her as bad as the scientists who thought nothing of killing babies in pursuit of their answers.

"Go."

She stared at him.

"Go now," he repeated. "We have not seen you."

His men went back into the ballroom. He bowed and closed the door behind him.

Maliha did not hesitate. "Stay behind me," she said to the children.

She ran.

ii

Using her perfect memory of the paths and the positions of the soldiers' outposts she had studied earlier, she headed towards the moat. She kept under the cover of the trees and behind the larger bushes.

They got further than she expected before the hue and cry was raised.

She abandoned all attempt at secrecy and took the most direct path towards the moat. The cries to stop became background noise and the order must have gone out not to shoot because no one was taking pot-shots at them. To the left and right soldiers were heading in their direction, running to intersect.

She could hear the panting breaths of the children behind her and was satisfied they were keeping pace. Izak's injury could not be serious. They were probably more accustomed to running than she was. She also noted with a certain satisfaction that her attire allowed her to run, which had been a consideration in its design.

Until a few moments before, she had hoped to get across the moat without drawing any attention. That had been a long shot and the swim across the moat would have been difficult; it was at least twenty feet from one side to the other.

But her plans had changed as soon as the alarm was given. In some ways she was glad that Penn had been unable to keep his mouth shut. Perhaps glad, too, that he had been unable to keep his hands off her so that she had had a reason to abuse him.

The alarm was important.

They rushed out onto the open grassy area that ran down to the edge of the moat, along with the bump that paralleled the shoreline on both sides. There were three soldiers coming in from the left and two from the right, running pell-mell along the moat-side path.

She allowed herself a smile. She and the children were running directly at the moat. But the water—black under the electric lights that shone from the eaves of the building lighting up the entirety of the gardens—was no longer moving normally.

The little ripples that should move across its surface were gone, replaced by low waves that rolled sluggishly along its length and across its width. These combined and grew to a foot in height before falling back.

Water under the influence of a powerful Faraday field.

"Take my hands," she called and splayed out her arms. Two small hands grabbed hers and she clasped them tightly. "Get ready to jump, hard!"

In the distance, she heard someone shouting to cut the Faraday. Someone clever had divined her purpose. She smiled even more.

They reached the bump in the ground and Maliha jumped onto it, feeling her skin prickle as they entered the edge of the field.

"Jump!"

With all the strength she could muster, she launched herself, pulling Izak and Lilith as hard as she could. They sailed into the air and soared across the moat. She estimated they reached a height of at least twelve feet. The Faraday might reduce their weight, but they were already travelling fast and it did not reduce their speed.

She realised they would overshoot the Faraday on the other side. "Hard landing!" she shouted again as they passed the opposite shore at a height of three feet and the bump on the far side at two feet. Normal gravity reasserted itself and pulled them to earth with a heavy thud. Still holding the children, Maliha lost her balance and stumbled onto the ground.

There was a series of splashes. Maliha clambered to her feet. There was no time to look, but she knew precisely what had happened. The men coming from the left and right had also jumped, but they had been running along the moat and their angle was too shallow. There was no chance they could cross, so they were guaranteed to end up in the water.

The order to kill the Faraday was bound to take time to reach the ears of the person who controlled it, and they would take even more time to react. They must have switched it off after Maliha had reached the other side, just in time for the soldiers to hit the water in its normal state.

Maliha ran for the trees, Izak and Lilith ahead of her. The lights from the house made shadows between the trunks that seemed to shift and move. They were not safe yet since they were still on consulate property.

A shadow moved out from a tree in front of her. "This way, Goddess," said a man's voice. He moved off into the trees at an angle to her original route. Izak had Lilith's hand now and pulled her after him. Maliha followed.

More and more shadows moved among the trees.

There was gunfire behind her, but it was getting further away. She kept stumbling on roots she could not see. Someone came up beside her and put a strong arm around her waist. It pulled her back up to a walk.

There was a fence with a hole in it and they climbed through. They walked a while longer. Apart from the man beside her and one who walked with the children, Maliha could see several more spread out, keeping a watchful eye on the surroundings.

Twenty minutes later they reached the outskirts of a residential area. The houses were dark and silent. They moved through the streets in silence. Finally they turned into a *cul-de-sac* and Maliha was hustled up an overgrown path into a brick-built house at the end.

The building was small and of simple design with two rooms on each floor. The man with her knocked. The sound was surprisingly loud. The door opened moments later and the light from oil lamps filtered out into the night, making a silhouette of a woman, who gestured for them to enter. The man gave Maliha a gentle nudge on her arm and she went in alone.

The possibility that they were in danger did not cross her mind; Lilith would have been very vocal if she thought there was any danger.

The interior had not been decorated recently. The walls and wood were scrubbed clean, but the white of the paint had been rubbed through in places, showing a dull grey sheen beneath. The floor was linoleum with the occasional threadbare rug.

The short passage inside had a door to the right leading into the main room, but it was closed. Directly ahead a flight of stairs led to the next floor.

"Use the bedroom at the front," said the girl in a strong native accent tainted with South African. Maliha recognised her as Nkechi who attended Mama Kosi. Did this place belong to either of them?

Maliha nodded. Izak and Lilith were behind her and she stood back to let them through. She gave Izak a gentle push as he brushed past and ran her hand across Lilith's hair, then she plodded heavily up the stairs after them. Having arrived, she felt a wave of exhaustion go through her.

Pressed against the wall by the door was an iron bedstead with a thick mattress covered with a threadbare satin eiderdown.

Maliha found herself on the verge of saying, "Take off your shoes," but neither Izak nor Lilith possessed shoes. "Lie down but leave room for me," was what she finally said. Lilith climbed into the bed and closed her eyes. Izak hesitated for a moment.

"Thank you for rescuing me, Izak," Maliha said.

"And me," Lilith said, though the words were slurred with sleep.

"And you, Lilith."

Izak lay beside Lilith with his arm over her protectively. It made Maliha think of Valentine. She may not need protecting, but that did not mean she did not appreciate his touch.

There was a steaming pot of tea on the dresser but no milk. She sat in the chair and poured herself a drink. She sipped and felt its potency relax her.

She yawned. Her muscles ached from the unaccustomed running. She unpinned her hat and laid it on the dresser, then unbuckled her shoes and slipped them off. She took another mouthful of the black tea, stood up, removed her coat and put it across the back of the chair.

She lay on the other side of Lilith, balanced precariously on the edge so as not to disturb the child. The dark of the night engulfed her.

iii

Something wriggled in her arms like a dog wanting to avoid being picked up. But she was lying down.

Maliha opened her eyes. Lilith's black face was inches from hers.

"I need to piss," said the girl. "Will you let me go, Goddess?"

Maliha realised she was holding the girl tight in her arms. She lifted her left arm and let her right relax back onto the bed. Lilith scrambled free and jumped off the bed. Izak was missing.

Lilith ran from the room. Maliha wondered why she didn't use the chamber pot, then she realised that, brought up on the streets, she might not even know about them. Even assuming there was one.

It was no longer night and the light from the sun shone in from a high angle. It was late, perhaps ten o'clock. Lilith must have lain there trying not to disturb her for as long as she could. Maliha smiled. It had felt good holding Lilith. It was a different kind of pleasure to holding Valentine; some parts were the same but she felt … motherly?

Not that Lilith would think she needed protecting, though there were so many dangers in her world for one so young that it did not bear thinking about. At least Lilith had been spared the horrors poor Riette had had to suffer at that age.

At least, Maliha *thought* she had, but what did she really know of the girl's life?

Maliha sat up and put her feet over the edge of the bed, facing the window and the thin curtain that hung across it, through which she could see the street beyond. The homogeneous imprint of the Europeans made itself felt everywhere—if she had not known where she was, and ignored the shapes of the trees, she could be in any part of the British Empire. It was all the same.

The British were not the law here. There was an uneasy truce whereby they gave the Dutch autonomy of rule and justice in return for the right to own everything. This would be to her advantage because it meant that the British could not, themselves, call out the Dutch police to search for her. They might be able to encourage it, but the Dutch were unlikely to be cooperative.

That meant the British would need to mount their own search, using limited resources. And all they would know was that she had information about Timmons (though Mr Penn might have hidden that detail) and that she had escaped in the company of two children.

But she should not underestimate them. They were not stupid. With more limited resources they would gather information first and then attempt to locate her through intelligence. It was not that she expected Mama Kosi's people to betray her, but knowledge of her whereabouts was bound to leak out. She needed to move quickly to stay ahead of Timmons' wolves.

There *was* a potty under the bed.

Ten minutes later, having washed and put her shoes back on, she briefly checked the other bedroom: there was a wardrobe containing two dresses that were out of style and did not look as if they had been touched in years.

The scents of cooking drifted up from below as she descended the staircase and pushed open the door to the front room.

Mama Kosi sat in a rocking chair, which moved slightly as she adjusted her position. She was old but her eyes were bright.

There were sounds of cutlery and stirring in the kitchen to the left. Maliha glanced in and saw Nkechi with Lilith and Izak who was eating a hunk of black bread.

"Mama Kosi is glad you are safe," shouted Nkechi from the kitchen. "When she learnt you fell from the sky vessel and became a prisoner of the English, she knew you would need help to escape."

Maliha looked back at the old woman, pressed her palms together in front of her face and bowed. "Thank you for your gift, Mama Kosi." She held the pose for a few moments to emphasise her gratitude.

Mama Kosi said something so quietly that Maliha did not think Nkechi could have heard. She was wrong.

"Mama Kosi says you cannot carry the weight you are destined to bear if you are a prisoner."

There she went again with her fortune-telling.

"I am grateful to Mama Kosi for her help," said Maliha. "But I must get to the Fortress in Ceylon by the fastest possible route. Can she help me?"

Nkechi came through with a bowl and set it down on the table. She moved a chair over to it. "Mama Kosi will help you all she can. You must eat."

There had been no translation that time, Nkechi had just answered Maliha directly. Maliha sat and tried the soup. It was hot but thick and nourishing, with vegetables and several different types of meat. Maliha glanced into the kitchen, where the children were digging into their own bowls.

"The ports will be watched," said Nkechi, "as will the air-dock. You will go to Mombasa on the atmospheric and meet with someone we know who will carry you to Ceylon."

"Won't the atmospherics be watched as well?"

"No one will see you."

"I need to go soon," said Maliha.

"You will be on the three o'clock train."

Four hours.

"I need clothes."

"They will be provided."

Maliha glanced at Mama Kosi, who rocked gently in her chair. It squeaked as it moved on the floorboards.

"Is this Mama Kosi's house?"

Nkechi put her head on one side. "The British do not understand us," she said. "For our people the only thing one can own is what you can carry. We were not meant to live in huts like this. Nor the places the Europeans build for us."

Maliha nodded.

"I am indebted to Mama Kosi for my very life," she said. "I do not know how I can repay her. In my life in India I am wealthy, but she does not value those riches."

Nkechi did translate this time. Mama Kosi spoke briefly and Nkechi nodded. "Mama Kosi says your future deeds will be repayment enough."

Maliha did not hide her annoyance. "I am sorry, but I am not interested in Mama Kosi's predictions," she said. "If there is anything of value I can do now, I would rather that."

Nkechi smiled. "The goddess does not believe in predictions?"

"I am not a goddess. I am just a woman like you."

"And I am not a goddess?"

Maliha hesitated. "I really wouldn't know. Is there anything I can do?"

"There is something," she said and Maliha sighed with relief; she was tired of playing word games. "There is a thing Mama Kosi wishes you to see. She does not know what to say, she believes you will."

iv

Maliha watched from the downstairs window as a two-wheeled cart arrived outside the house. The half-caste driver pulled the rein to make the donkey turn into the alley between the houses. As the cart trundled past she saw something furry lying in the back.

A wave of cold ran through her.

"Don't let him bring it into the house," she said to no one in particular and everyone in general. She turned as Nkechi headed through into the kitchen. Lilith jumped from her chair, ran to the door, opened it and stepped out.

"No!" screamed Maliha. The girl turned, her face a mix of surprise and fear. "No, Lilith, Izak. Don't go outside. Nkechi, stop!"

Nkechi came to a halt and looked back.

"Lilith, come in now and shut the door."

The scared child did as she was told. Maliha stared at the air around Lilith as if she were seeing invisible demons. She licked her lips. How long would it take for the spores to settle? Was there anything she could do? The door had only been open for a moment, Lilith had only been outside for a short time and the cart had only just arrived. How bad could it be?

"If this is what I think it is, you mustn't go near it. It is the disease the kidnappers brought with them, the reason they took the children."

The voice of Mama Kosi filtered through from the other room.

"Mama Kosi says I must do your bidding," said Nkechi. She looked down at Lilith and Izak. "Do what the goddess says."

Maliha gritted her teeth. She allowed the children to call her that mostly because it seemed impossible to break them of the habit. She was not happy with adults doing it too.

"Does he speak English?" Maliha asked, nodding to the back door.

"Yes, his name is Tinashe."

Maliha went to the door. Tinashe had stopped the cart and climbed off. He glanced up at the door and went to the back of the cart. Maliha did not open the door but raised her voice to speak to the man.

"Is it dead, Tinashe?"

He stopped. "You are Goddess?"

She hesitated then forced herself. "Yes."

His eyes widened and he did not seem to know what he should do next.

"Do not touch the animal, Tinashe, but tell me exactly what it is you have in the cart."

"My dog, Goddess."

"Is it dead?"

He nodded.

"How did it die?"

He did not reply but wiped his arm across his eyes. "I kill it."

"What happened?"

"It is possessed by demon, attack me. I smash its head with my stick."

"Are its eyes black?"

"Yes."

"Wait there."

Maliha felt rivulets of sweat running down the scars on her back. She could fight a man when he tried to force himself on her, trick a man into revealing the truth, or persuade the man she loved to whip her until she bled, but she could not defeat a thing she could not see.

She pressed her back against the door and her heart pounded with fear.

Nkechi, Izak and Lilith were staring at her.

"The goddess is afraid," said Lilith. It was not the recognition of frailty in her voice—instead the words were spoken in awe of whatever could scare the goddess. Maliha suspected that Lilith had not the slightest idea what a goddess was, apart from someone brave and strong.

"What is it?" asked Nkechi.

Maliha shook her head. She turned and saw the door had a bolt; she drew it, knowing it could not keep out the airborne spores of a fungus.

She took slow steps through to the front room. She sat back down in the chair and faced Mama Kosi, whose face fell at the sight of the terror in hers. Maliha looked up at Nkechi. "I am going to tell Mama Kosi what I know. If there is anything you do not understand you must ask me to explain. It is very important that you all understand the danger."

Nkechi nodded and stood waiting. Maliha gathered her thoughts.

"The planet Venus has fungi like our own mushrooms and molds. But on Venus they are more powerful and they can infect animals to be carried to new places to grow. Some of these fungi can infect our minds and be used to control people—perhaps. That is what some people want to do.

"The men who kidnapped the children were experimenting on them, trying to make the fungi live inside them. I saw a child that had been infected. Its eyes were black. It was no longer human—it was as if it had been possessed by a demon.

"I spoke with the scientists. I learnt that if a possessed creature is killed quickly and violently, the fungus sends out its seeds to survive. These seeds are so tiny they float in the air and cannot be seen.

"But if the creature dies slowly, perhaps from being starved, the fungus does not think it is dying and does not send out its seeds."

Nkechi had interrupted her to clarify some points and Mama Kosi had had her repeat herself and change the wording so she understood.

Mama Kosi looked at Maliha, her eyes filled with tears. She spoke and Nkechi translated.

"They starved the children to death?"

"Those that survived the initial infection, yes."

Mama Kosi made movements with her hands, as if she were pushing away an attacker. She muttered words that Maliha could not have made out even if they had been in a language she understood.

"Tinashe will die," Nkechi said without prompting.

"I don't know," said Maliha. "Perhaps he was not infected, but we cannot be sure."

"How long before his illness shows?"

"I don't know," she said. "Hours? Days?"

Mama Kosi spoke. When she had finished, Nkechi said something that sounded like agreement.

"We will make sure Tinashe is looked after until we know," said Nkechi. "If he is ill we will starve him until he is dead. What should we do with his body?"

"Once they have been dead for a while they should be burned in the hottest fire you can make, perhaps in the furnace of a steam engine. But anyone who comes into contact with them must be careful—they could still become infected."

Nkechi nodded.

"If it infected his dog then it must have come from somewhere," said Maliha. "My man found infected hyenas to the south."

"I understand," said Nkechi. "We will do what we can. This will not be the first time disease has stalked our lands."

Mama Kosi spoke again.

"It is time for you to go," said Nkechi.

"I will take Izak and Lilith," said Maliha. It would be easy to explain two street urchins; it was not uncommon for rich British women to take in strays just to show what decent people they were. The 'why' was possibly more difficult to understand—perhaps it was simply that she cared for them. And the possibility Lilith had become infected.

It would do. She turned to the children. Izak looked as if he had been hit by a train, Lilith was simply confused.

"They will need clothes," said Maliha.

Nkechi communicated Maliha's requirements to Mama Kosi, who nodded without any apparent surprise or concern.

"You want to take us with you, Goddess?"

"Yes, Lilith," said Maliha. "But you must not call me Goddess when other people are around. They won't understand."

"What do I call you then?"

Maliha barely hesitated. "Mother."

The atmospheric slid down its tube and out of Johannesburg station. They had a first class compartment to themselves that Mama Kosi had arranged. Boarding had involved entering the station grounds through the staff entrance and making their way onto the train via the crew cabins.

It was simple. There were people around, but no one looked in their direction. And no one close by was European. It was an easy thing to understand: when one invaded a country and took over, but employed the natives in every walk of life, the most outrageous acts could be committed under the nose of authority and they would never be the wiser.

Even the Dutch, who held the natives in contempt—many thinking them little better than apes—were not immune to this. They were still in the minority. The British might have built the atmospherics, but it was the natives who ran them.

The flashing display through the window, alternating blank metal with scenic views, changed from the outskirts of the city, through the mine workings of the gold and diamond works, and eventually gave onto the cultivated fields that surrounded and fed the city's population.

As the atmospheric picked up speed—it would reach almost two hundred miles per hour on some stretches—the view blurred. The hills to the north grew apace.

Maliha turned her attention to Izak and Lilith. They still had no change of clothes even though it had been promised. Izak sat by the window and stared out. Lilith was bouncing on the bench seat. She had never experienced reduced gravity like this before and had taken to it.

"It is like flying," she said as she jumped from the bench on one side of the carriage to the other, flapping her arms.

Maliha felt as if she ought to admonish her and tell her to sit quietly, like every teacher she had ever had, her grandmother and even her mother. But, she thought as a smile grew on her face, never her father. Though, he had not been there much of the time, which meant an exuberant child was not as great a trial to him as she must have been to her mother.

But that wasn't it, she thought to herself. It wasn't that she had been an exuberant child full of energy. That was not the reason she had been constantly admonished to be still. It was because she was female and it was not appropriate for a girl to behave in such a way.

Lilith threw herself to the other bench. She landed with a bump and collapsed into a sitting position facing Maliha with a grin on her face. Maliha smiled back. "It is just like flying, Lilith. You should practice until you become like a bird."

The girl jumped up again and launched herself at Maliha, who had to jerk her head out of Lilith's path as the child crashed into her, knocking the wind from her. Lilith hugged her.

"Thank you, Goddess."

Maliha could not say anything, since there were no other people around.

Izak sat back from the window. His expression was serious. "Where are we going?"

"Mombasa and then to Ceylon," said Maliha. "Then I'll put you on an airship to Pondicherry where Amita can look after you."

"Your maid."

"She is not my maid anymore," said Maliha. "She is my friend and I have put her in charge of all my affairs."

"If you are going to leave us, why did you bring us?"

The warmth of Lilith pushed away from her. "I don't want to go to 'Meeta, Goddess. I want to stay with you."

Maliha sighed. "I can't take you where I'm going."

"Why not?" said Izak.

"It will be very dangerous," said Maliha. "I don't want you to get hurt."

"If you leave me I will be hurt," said Lilith. Maliha smiled sadly and tried to hug her, but Lilith kept her distance.

"That's just blackmail," said Maliha. "With emotions."

"What's blackmail?"

"When you threaten to make someone feel bad so they do what you want."

Lilith thought about it.

Izak looked at Maliha. "You wanted to get us away so what happened to that man won't happen to us."

Maliha nodded. "He might not be ill."

"But others will be."

"Yes," Maliha would not lie to them. "I believe it will become very bad there. I don't think there is anything that can stop it."

"Then everyone should leave."

Maliha smiled and shook her head. "That's not possible—and people can be very stupid. They would never believe it until it was too late. Have you ever heard of the Black Death?" she asked, not expecting they would have. It had been taught in her school, though she learnt the real truth of it in her other reading. They shook their heads.

"Hundreds of years ago a disease struck the world and killed many people. If you took ten people and stood them in a line, this disease killed seven of them."

"And this will kill seven people?"

"No, this will kill all of them and their animals."

"Will it kill me, Goddess?" said Lilith in a very small voice. She crept under Maliha's arm.

"I will do my best to keep you safe," said Maliha. *Because there is nothing in all my knowledge that tells me how to prevent this.*

Izak frowned. "You told Mama Kosi it comes from Venus."

"Yes, it does."

"You are going to Venus."

Maliha sighed. "Yes, there is something I must do."

"Will you stop the disease?" asked Lilith.

"No, Lilith, I cannot."

"If you go to Venus will the disease kill you?"

"I do not think so."

"But," said Izak, leaning forward, "if you are not going to stop the disease why are you going?"

"There is a bad man who must be stopped." *And a good man I must find if I can.*

Maliha found her back was pressing into the padded back of the seat—the atmospheric was decelerating.

"Is this Mombasa?" asked Izak. Through the window came fleeting glimpses of mountains with farms on their green foothills. Bulawayo was the first scheduled stop, and this was not Bulawayo.

vi

The carriage of the atmospheric jerked to the side as it shunted off the main line and onto another. The railway signs said 'Polokwane'. Maliha dredged the name from the depths of her memory—it was a small community that happened to be in a good position for a station. The doors of the tube on the platform had to line up exactly before they would open.

Maliha was on her feet with her hand on Izak's shoulder and the other holding Lilith's. She was not sure whether she did this to comfort them or to give herself additional security.

The door to the compartment opened and the train conductor who had brought them on board appeared. He glanced along the carriage corridor and then gestured for them to follow.

"This compartment occupied from Bulawayo," he said as they followed him forward. They passed through the pressurised rubber tunnel that linked this carriage to the next one, which was intended for food preparation.

He led them to the outer door and poked his head out. "Is safe." He stepped out. Maliha and the children followed. There was an abrupt change of feeling from light to heavy. Izak stumbled.

"Other doors not opened, you see? Quite safe," he said. "You go outside." He pointed at an exit into the station's concourse and waiting area. "Someone coming to meet."

Maliha stared for a moment; there was no one around. She turned back. "How will I—" The door to the atmospheric snapped shut in her face. She pulled back as the outer ones closed too, though more slowly.

The conductor grinned, waved and pointed again to indicate they should leave the station. There was a roar of steam and the whoosh of pressurised air as the airlocks inside the tube opened and the pneumatic forces were let loose on the vehicle. It slid away, accelerating as it went.

They were already a long way from Johannesburg but still over a thousand miles from Mombasa. Maliha sighed—she disliked being subject to the whim of others. Gathering Lilith and Izak to her, she walked out onto the concourse. They were hit by a wave of hot air. It was midday and nobody went outside at a time like this.

There was a railwayman behind the ticket counter. He seemed absorbed in whatever he was doing and did not even look at them. Did Mama Kosi's influence extend this far? Why not? She had been able to start a riot and, more importantly, bring it to an end with just her word.

The invention of the atmospheric had created an anomaly in the way nations grew. Once upon a time they had grown along waterways and extended into the hinterlands of countries along the rivers and streams, because man needed water to survive and to grow crops, and because the river provided transportation. Now it was along the routes of the atmospherics—where they went and where they stopped—that civilisation grew.

Maliha and the children stepped out onto a verandah along the front of the station building. The roof kept them in shade as they squinted out into the reds and browns.

"This is not a busy place," said Lilith.

She was right. Although there were many buildings, including shops, a hotel and a post office, there was a lack of people. Still, it was the hottest part of the day—no reason why anyone should be out.

Maliha sat down and licked her lips; they were dry. If she needed water the children would too. There was a slight breeze, but it brought no comfort.

"What's that?" said Lilith. Maliha glanced around but saw nothing unusual. She looked at Lilith, who had her head cocked on one side. She was listening, not looking.

Maliha listened. Something.

"Big engine," said Izak. Lilith nodded. Maliha could still barely hear it, but it was growing in volume. They were right: a powerful propeller was churning the air. There was a movement to the north. A black dot detached itself from the sky and grew, fast.

It was coming straight towards them. It was not as big as a Sky-Liner, in fact it appeared to be not much larger than Valentine's *Alice*—the vessel he had named after Maliha before he discovered how much she disliked the name—but its wings were much shorter.

The sound it made became a constant drone.

Maliha looked up and down the street. There was insufficient flat space for a fixed-wing vehicle to land and this one did not appear to have rotors that could turn. She did not, for one second, assume the ship was there to do anything but pick them up.

The drone of the propeller dropped in volume and pitch, indicating that the pilot had cut the power. Maliha frowned. She was not an expert flyer, but she had read many manuals and technical specifications. Cutting power meant that it was coming in to land but was still far too high. Never mind the lack of space, it would either overshoot or stall into a crash, depending on what the pilot did next.

The black dot resolved into a real shape. It had a blocky, solid body, unlike the slim fuselage of the *Alice*, so it would be able to carry several passengers. The propeller was rear-mounted, as was often the case, and it had a chimney above, which was releasing remarkably little smoke.

The wings were curiously shaped: they were shorter than she expected and wider, and they appeared to be composed of … she stared … feathers.

"It's a *bird*," shouted Lilith in delight.

The wings suddenly came to life. They bent and folded as the plane back-winged. Its horizontal speed dropped to nothing. The wings beat powerfully and the vessel simply hung in the air like a hawk above the grass, ready to swoop on its unsuspecting prey.

The wings paused and the metal bird dived. It looped around, almost standing on one wing, then fluttered to the ground blasting dust all around. It landed without a jolt. The wings folded in along its body, as if it had come to roost.

Maliha knew what it was now: a Clayton & Shuttleworth 'Iron Pigeon', nearly twenty years old. Nobody made ornithopters anymore, as they were simply too hard to fly. This one, however, appeared to be in perfect condition and whoever was at the helm was extremely competent. She saw through the large windows someone moving inside.

Two machine guns were mounted in the lower fuselage—Maliha knew they were not original to the plane. In addition, as far as she recalled, a vessel like this was not capable of hovering. Even with the advances in Faraday technology in the last twenty years, she did not think such a heavy machine was capable of performing the aerobatics she had just witnessed.

She studied the vessel. Beside the hatch in the side was a worn painting of the winged horse, Pegasus, drawn in the Ancient Grecian style. Her breath caught in her throat—she knew what this ship was, she knew who owned it and who flew it. She jumped to her feet.

"Come on children," she said excitedly. "You are about to meet one of the greatest pilots that has ever flown."

She hurried forward as the hatch opened and the stairs of the *Iron Pegasus* were kicked out.

vii

With Izak and Lilith in tow Maliha hurried out to the vehicle. She knew she had a grin on her face. She wondered what on earth she would say to the pilot when she appeared. There were pulp magazines dedicated to the adventures of this ship and the sisters who flew in it, and Maliha had read every single one of them.

As she approached, a woman in a loose jumpsuit stepped out and down to the ground. She placed her hands on the small of her back and stretched. Her hair was tied back with a scarf, which had a pair of flying goggles around it.

"Khuwelsa Edgbaston!" said Maliha in astonishment, and suddenly she could not think of anything else to say. The black woman was in her thirties, her arms were bare and well-muscled. She ceased stretching and turned her attention to Maliha.

"You're Miss Anderson?"

A man wearing a stoker's apron appeared at the hatch. His hair was neatly trimmed. He looked a similar age and was peering at them, almost owl-like.

"Are these the passengers, Khuwelsa?" he said. His English was perfect, but Maliha recognised a German accent.

"Think so," she said still looking at Maliha but loud enough for him to hear. "Were we expecting children? If I'd known we'd have brought our three."

Maliha felt as if her world was being held upside down and jiggled about.

"You *are* Khuwelsa Edgbaston?"

"Of course."

"You're married to … Johannes?"

The older woman regarded Maliha with solemn eyes. "You mean why aren't I Harry, and how can *I* be married to Johannes instead of her?"

The rude nature of her enquiry brought back to her thus, Maliha had the decency to look embarrassed, but she nodded anyway.

"You have an unseemly interest in my personal affairs, Miss Anderson, since we have barely been introduced," she said. "You read the books, didn't you?"

Maliha nodded.

"Let me explain, then. I am happy enough to do a favour for Mama Kosi, but I do not expect to be cross-examined about my personal life." She took a step to the side and gestured with her hand. "Now, I believe we are in a hurry, so if you would care to step aboard we will be on our way. Then we can talk and, if I decide I like you, perhaps we will get to know one another a little better."

Maliha walked to the ship. When she put her foot on the step she stopped and shivered.

"Problem, Miss Anderson?"

"I just wanted to apologise for being so familiar, Miss Edgbaston—"

"Mrs Schonfeldt," she said and then smiled. "But you can call me Sellie, almost everyone does."

Maliha climbed the steps and went inside with Lilith and Izak behind her. The furnace and generators were smaller than she had imagined them, but she recognised that the current units were modern replacements. There were seats welded to the floor. The pilot's area was separated from the main cabin by wooden panelling, as was the engineering section. The portholes in the fuselage were larger than the design and there was a small kitchen. The entire vessel had been remodelled.

"So we're going to Ceylon?" asked Sellie, standing at the small door that led through to the pilot's area.

"You can go straight there?"

"It won't be entirely comfortable," she said. "But we can be there in under twenty-four hours. Speed is of the essence, I understand."

"Yes", said Maliha, "it is."

"Well, take a seat and make sure the children are strapped in properly. And you too. It can be a little bumpy until we reach cruising speed."

Maliha sat Izak and Lilith in chairs and helped them do up their belts. It wasn't possible for them to see out, but that could not be helped. She strapped herself in. The connecting window opened for a moment as Sellie checked they were ready.

The disconnect between the stories and the reality continued. In the stories it was always Sellie who was in the back, stoking the engine. She did not fly the ship—that was her sister, Harry. And it was Harriet Edgbaston who was sweet on Johannes, the German army officer.

But now Sellie was married to him and, apparently, they had children. Three of them.

Maliha wondered where Harriet could be and whether something had happened to her. But surely there would have been something in the papers if she had been killed. And if it had been written down, Maliha would have read it. She would know.

A red electric light lit up in the wall in front of them; it was labelled, 'Going light'.

"We're going light in a moment, like the atmospheric, Lilith, Izak. Don't be scared."

The light flashed and went out. Maliha gasped as she lost almost all her weight. This was nothing like the atmospheric. But it was exactly like Timmons' vessel.

The *Pegasus* leapt into the air.

After a few minutes their flight stabilised and Johannes came through from the back.

"There is not a great deal for me to do once the steam is up," he said and sat down on one of the chairs. He pulled off a gauntlet and held out his hand.

"Johannes Schonfeldt, Miss Anderson. I am pleased to make your acquaintance."

She took his hand; his grip was firm.

"You do not seem entirely well," he said. "Shall I make a cup of tea?"

"Do you have any food?"

"Oh yes, plenty. We are going to Ceylon, are we not? Lots of time."

Moving lightly in the very reduced gravity, he almost appeared to waft to the galley area. He engaged an electrical device connected to what looked like a kettle.

The *Pegasus* flattened out and a few moments later Sellie came into the cabin.

"Fifteen thousand feet at three hundred and fifty miles per hour," she said with pride in her voice.

"And, I would guess, over ninety percent gravity reduction," said Maliha. "May I enquire how that has been achieved?"

Sellie stared at Maliha for a moment and then looked at her husband. *Her husband?* Maliha still could not quite imagine it. In the stories of Harry and Sellie in the 'Astounding Stories of Adventure' magazine—which she had eaten up when she escaped from school to the bookshop—Johannes sometimes appeared and he was always Harriet's love interest. Unspoken, true, but it was always very clear.

This seemed wrong.

"Did you ever read 'Harry in the Desert', Miss Anderson?"

Mrs Schonfeldt's words brought her back to the present.

"The last one? Yes, of course, I read them all. Several times," said Maliha, then she blushed. "I found them … inspirational."

Sellie smiled. "It wasn't entirely truthful."

"I didn't really think any of them were."

"Oh, they were, for the most part. The publisher and the writers were quite good really, not too much embellishment," she said. "But not that one. We lied."

She pushed off gently and floated down to Maliha's side. It was like an aerial ballet in slow motion.

"I want to fly!" said Lilith.

"When we land, little one," said Sellie kindly. "I cannot allow you to float around when we are in the air. You might hurt yourself."

"I don't care."

"You might hurt the *Pegasus*." To which Lilith had no answer.

"To put it simply—"

"Khuwelsa, you should not tell her."

"If I'm not mistaken, Joe, she already knows." She turned to Maliha. "Don't you?"

"I know it's possible to achieve this level of nullification, though I do not know how. I have experienced it before."

Sellie became serious and looked at Johannes again. He bounced over. Maliha realised with horror that he had a revolver in his hand. He was not pointing it at her, but he looked as if he might at any moment. Sellie put her hand over his and pressed the gun down to his side.

"No," she said. "Let her tell us what she knows first."

What has Mama Kosi thrown us into? Maliha thought. *How could the heroes of my youth be so ... dangerous?*

"What have you to say?" Johannes asked, the harsh burr of his German ancestry coming to the fore.

Maliha composed her thoughts as best she could with the threat of the gun hanging in the air. She turned to look at Izak and Lilith; they clung to one another. It was all very well for them to be excited by these new experiences, but to be so trapped was terrifying.

She turned back to their captors.

"There is a fleet of vessels belonging to no country I know, of a design used by no one else, which can do this. They are huge and they are slavers. They trick people into taking ship with them and then carry them off, certainly to Venus and possibly elsewhere.

"But they also trade in slaves here on Earth. I have an adopted daughter who was born of one of their slaves, a black African girl called Riette. She was raped and murdered after being separated from her beloved—" she looked at the two of them, black and white, and married, "—a Boer farmer."

Maliha paused. Their stern looks had not changed. "The reason I am here is that I am in pursuit of the man who runs this fleet and, on behalf of Riette and her daughter, and all the other lives he has destroyed, I am going to exact the vengeance that is their right."

Sellie turned to her husband and kissed him on the cheek. "Put it away, Joe, you're scaring the children." Without another word he drifted off into the rear of the machine.

viii

Sellie sat down beside Maliha.

"The problem with the traditional means of producing gravity nullification is that there is a limit to how fine we can make the copper wires and how closely we can pack them together.

"It is not that we do not know *how* to achieve greater efficiency, it is simply that we lack the ability."

Maliha nodded—she understood the theory even if she did not have the practical engineering skills of the great Khuwelsa Edgbaston, the first woman to graduate from an English university with a Science degree.

"However, it turns out there is a naturally occurring crystal that is able, on the atomic scale, to nullify gravity when a current is passed through it. You are familiar with Bohr's model of the atom?" Maliha nodded. "That is a much finer grain than we can achieve hence the stronger the effect. Harry and I managed to retrieve a quantity of it from that last adventure. I stripped down the *Pegasus* and rebuilt it with what we had."

Maliha nodded. "Where is it mined? How has it remained such a secret?"

Sellie shook her head. "It is not mined. It is discovered. My understanding is that it is not naturally occurring on Earth but occasionally falls in meteorites. The people you are pursuing, however, do seem to have a limitless supply."

"But surely it would burn up or be shattered if it were to fall...? Oh."

Sellie smiled. "You are an exceptionally bright woman, Miss Anderson," she said. "Harry and I wrestled for weeks over the answer to that question."

"It is energised by its rapid passage through the Earth's magnetic field and lands gently," said Maliha.

"Well, not exactly *gently*, judging by some the craters I've seen, but they do not consume themselves in a fireball." She glanced back at the rear of the ship for a moment. "I do apologise for my husband.

I love him dearly but, while he has certainly relaxed in his attitudes, he can't quite lose that Germanic sternness he was born with."

"I'm not offended," said Maliha. There were things one said as small talk among women, she knew, but it was not a skill she practised. "You and Johannes have three children?"

"That's right," Sellie said with a smile. Maliha was pleased she had asked the right question. "Two girls, Mary and Esther, and a boy, Johannes."

"Are they in Mombasa?"

"Yes, with their grandfather."

"He's retired?"

"He no longer works." Her answer was abrupt and Maliha decided that might not be a good line to pursue.

"Can I ask where your sister is? I must admit I was very surprised to find that you are the pilot. It quite upset my preconceptions."

Sellie looked uncomfortable for a moment. "Oh, Harry's off somewhere doing something adventurous." Then she grinned. "She'll be back, no doubt, when she's done with that project."

"Is—" Maliha was not entirely sure whether this was an appropriate question; it wasn't clear whether the camaraderie that had existed between the sisters in the stories still existed.

"What?"

"Is your sister married?"

Inexplicably, Sellie glanced into the back again. Was there some love lost over her marrying Johannes instead of Harriet? Maliha heard Johannes coming through from the back. Sellie turned back to Maliha and smiled again. "Oh yes, Harry's married."

Johannes coughed suddenly.

"I'd better check up-top," said Sellie. "Wouldn't do to head off course."

Maliha sat back in the chair. There was something very odd here, but she had no idea what it was. It was not that she did not trust Miss Edgbaston—she could not imagine her with a different surname—it was just something behind the scenes. And when she spoke about Harry there was no malice or ill will, just that underlying strangeness.

She sighed. It was very difficult to suppress her natural desire to know everything. She glanced out of the porthole; the sky was darkening. That couldn't be right, she thought, and looked at her watch. No, they had only been in the air for a couple of hours.

Sellie had said they were making three hundred and fifty miles per hour, so they would already be passing Madagascar. Then she realised: they were travelling so fast into the East the day was being compressed.

"How are you two?" she asked, turning to Izak and Lilith. She was greeted by a pair of scowls. She sighed. This was difficult. She knew only too well that trips of this nature could be very boring even when you had an entire Sky-Liner to wander about on, but being forced to sit in a chair without a view outside for hours would be intolerable.

"I'll see what I can do," she said.

She unclasped the belt that held her to the seat and stood, keeping a firm hold of the back of the chair. She glanced fore and aft and decided she would try to engage Johannes. She had been quite taken with him in the books—always so thoughtful and kind to both sisters. Was he really so different in real life?

With the changes to the equipment, the space in the engine room was much larger than she had expected. As she entered, the temperature increased noticeably.

Johannes was sitting near the back, smoking a pipe. He rose to his feet with the natural care of someone used to this fraction of normal gravity; he did not go flying up to the ceiling. Maliha, on the other hand, had to keep a firm grip on the door frame. The sensation of falling was disconcerting—it reminded her of being thrown from Timmons' ship.

"I wondered whether you might have something that could keep the children occupied?" she said without preamble. "They are very bored."

"I understand, Miss Anderson. Children are a delight and a trial also. Our five are always getting into trouble if we don't keep them busy." He looked around. "I may have some paper and pencils—do they draw?"

"I have no idea," she said. "They have only recently come under my responsibility. I seem to collect waifs and strays."

"You are engaged?" he said looking at the ring on the third finger of her left hand.

"Yes, to Valentine Crier."

"And he is not with you?"

"He has gone on ahead."

"Ahead?"

"To Venus."

He paused and looked at her, as if trying to understand her. "I see." He rummaged in a box underneath a worktop; the area was completely clear and all the tools properly stowed. She admired neatness.

"Five children must be a handful," Maliha said carefully, in case she had misheard.

"The boys are the worst," he said absently as he removed a rug from the box and set it to one side. "But only by a fraction."

Maliha's heart stopped. *Boys*. It was none of her business. She felt breathless, but it was not as if it changed anything. These were just people she had met who were helping her. *It's none of my business.*

Yet she was desperate to know how such a thing could possibly work. Still, it did satisfy one thing in her mind: she had never imagined how the sisters could possibly be separated. Or how Harry could not have married Johannes.

But it was none of her business.

"Here we are," Johannes said and pulled out a sheaf of paper. He held it up with a grin. Maliha smiled and took it. "One moment," he added and located two pencils, which he passed across.

Feeling as if she had been knocked to the ground, she returned to the main cabin and gave the paper and pencils to Izak and Lilith. Lilith had no idea what to do with them. Izak understood about writing and drawing, but it was not something he had ever done. Maliha spent the next hour showing them how to draw, using a simplified version of what she had been taught in school and getting them to copy her.

By five o'clock they were in complete night.

"It's best to sleep when you can," said Sellie. "These fast, long-distance trips can be very upsetting if you try to keep to your normal schedules."

"What about you and Johannes?" asked Maliha.

Sellie shrugged. "We'll be flying back directly so there's no point in us adjusting to the new time."

Maliha had the children lie along the chairs and she settled down to do the same. It would only be a few hours.

CHAPTER 3

i

It was her sudden increase in weight that brought Maliha awake. She was stiff from lying on the chairs and it took her a moment to remember where she was.

The hatch had been thrown open and warm, moist air flowed in to replace the used and smelly atmosphere they were in. She knew she was filthy again.

"It's three in the morning," said Sellie. "We're on the outskirts of Colombo—I guessed that might fit your plans better."

Maliha sat up and rubbed her eyes. She felt muzzy and was not thinking straight. The children had not woken.

"What's the time back in Africa?"

"We have shifted about six hours," said Sellie, "so it's early evening as far as your body is concerned, but it's confused."

"We were promised a change of clothes," Maliha muttered with more annoyance than she intended.

"Can't help you there," said Sellie. "Have you got any money?"

Maliha shook her head. "I was expecting to sort it out in Mombasa."

"Joe, give the girl some money, enough for a hotel and a change of clothes for her and the children."

"Are you sure, Khuwelsa?"

Maliha smiled to herself; she had always noticed in the books how he used their full names.

"Quite sure," said Sellie without any rancour. "Miss Anderson is not the enemy."

Maliha suddenly became serious. "I need to tell you some things. You probably won't believe them, but you must because your lives may be forfeit if you do not."

"Is that a threat, Miss Anderson?" said Johannes.

"Oh hush, Joe. What is it you need to tell us?"

Maliha ran through what she knew of the Venusian fungus. Sellie questioned her on a couple of points but did not scoff, though Maliha could feel the animosity from her husband. From *their* husband. Unless they had others. That was also possible.

They woke the children and gave them some water to refresh them. Izak was *compos mentis*, but Lilith was simply grumpy and hung on to Maliha's skirt with a face like thunder.

They went outside. The *Pegasus* had landed behind a copse with the sea on one side and the lights of the city along the coast about a mile away.

Sellie embraced her warmly.

Maliha could not stand it any longer. "How does it work?"

"The gravity-nullifying mineral?"

"You, Harriet and Johannes."

"Oh," said Sellie. Johannes made some sort of strangled noise. "What gave us away? Joe doesn't like people knowing."

"You need to keep your stories straight about the number of children you have."

"That again," said Sellie. "I have three children, Joe has five. I suppose I'll have to say five—he's never going to remember."

"Does your father know? And what about the children?"

"It's always been this way for the children, they don't know it's unusual," she sighed. "And Dad, well, he hasn't really known anything for a long time."

Maliha went numb. "Oh, I'm so sorry."

"It's all right," said Sellie. "He's happy enough, though he has no idea who he is or who we are from one day to the next. The doctors say that, while it's unusual for someone of his age, it's not unheard of. It's hardest for Harry really."

"And her mother?"

"Not supportive."

It sounded as though she wanted to say a great deal more, but propriety and the presence of Johannes prevented it.

There was a long silence. Then Sellie sighed and said, "You asked how it works? You were referring to the sleeping arrangements, I take it?" She glanced back at Johannes, who appeared to be in the centre of his own storm.

Maliha nodded and felt embarrassed. They probably thought it was prurient curiosity, but for her it was just about knowledge and nothing more.

"It's not that strange, really. Harry and I always slept in the same room, sometimes the same bed, and we still do. When she's around, anyway. With her away so much it's better for her children to be able to call me mother as well."

"She wants to know about the copulation," said Johannes, his voice filled with disapproval. "The sordid details."

"Yes, well, people always do, Joe, but those who find out about us are usually too embarrassed to ask," she said. "I think I prefer honesty over decency. Is that what you want to know, Miss Anderson?"

"I want to know it all," Maliha said.

"We don't engage in that sort of thing when both of us are there," said Sellie. "Some things are meant to be private. I know women can take pleasure in each other's company, but Harry and I don't feel that way about each other. She may be my wife, so to speak, but she's my sister first. Even if we're not related by birth." She sighed. "And to most of the rest of the world, Joe is married to Harry and the children are all hers, even the dark-skinned ones. I'm just the nanny."

"I understand prejudice," said Maliha. "I'm sorry."

"No need to apologise, it's always been that way," said Sellie. "I've always been seen as Harry's companion and not a person in my own right. I've stopped waiting for the world to change."

Johannes moved forward and enfolded her in his arms from behind. He stared at Maliha, daring her to object. Sellie leaned her head against his shoulder.

Maliha fumbled for more words of comfort and sympathy but she was not very good at them and nothing came. "Thank you for your help, and your honesty," was all she could think to say.

Sellie smiled. "If you want someone to feel sorry for, you might be better addressing any condolences to Joe." There was a hint of playfulness in her voice. "After all, he has to suffer the nagging of two wives."

"You never nag me, Khuwelsa," he said, squeezing her. "Harriet is the one who nags."

Maliha suddenly felt uncomfortable, as if she was intruding on their privacy, which was curious since that was all she ever did with people. But on this occasion they were showing her how much they loved one another, without any prompting.

"I should be going."

Sellie shrugged off Johannes' arms and came forward. She held her hand out before her. Maliha took it. Sellie's grip was firm and her skin was hardened.

"Well, that's another favour Mama Kosi owes me," said Sellie. "*Bon voyage*, Miss Anderson. I hope you succeed in your quest."

She turned and headed back to the hatch. Johannes placed his hand on the small of her back as they returned to the vessel. The hatch closed and sealed behind them.

There was a shimmer in the air above the vessel as the Faraday engaged, and Maliha backed away, pulling the children with her. The iron bird flapped its wings once and leapt lightly into the sky.

Despite their sleep during the trip, and the fact that their bodies still considered the time to be early evening, Maliha found herself quite tired. Izak said nothing, but Lilith complained about every little thing.

Colombo was on the west coast of Ceylon, facing out into the Indian Ocean. It took them twenty minutes to reach the outskirts. The city had once been the capital of Ceylon but no longer. It had been replaced by the Fortress, which had no other name except when referred to by its Sinhalese name.

Sigiriya was a granite outcrop that rose six hundred feet above the plain, in the centre of the island. For thousands of years it had been home to kings, queens and emperors. They had turned it into a labyrinth of tunnels and chambers, with great buildings on its flat summit.

The British had decided it was the perfect location for their military base in the East and had set about converting it to their use. As time went on it grew, and the residential buildings for the officers required shops and municipal buildings. So the gentry flourished and a great wall was built to keep out the natives. And Colombo became a shadow of its former glory.

There were lights further into the city, but the buildings they reached first were dark and empty. Maliha considered using one for the night, but she was not convinced they were unoccupied. She pressed on with her charges.

After traversing more than half the distance into the centre and finding most of the buildings still deserted, they came at last to streets lit by electric lights. From her time in the Fortress, she knew the city was still used for holidaying by the sea, so she steered them towards the seafront.

The sound of the waves grew filling their ears with its rhythmic thundering and background hiss. The children were in awe as the ocean came into sight—Johannesburg was over a hundred miles from the nearest sea.

"It's so big," said Lilith. The moon's light glinted from the waves, which stretched into forever.

Maliha had grown up by the sea, both in Pondicherry and in Britain but its majesty never failed to impress.

However, there were more important matters. The buildings set back from the seafront were all hotels to cater for the tourists. It was now a matter of choosing one. She considered the options: her skin was almost white, but she was still clearly Indian and accompanied by two black children. She did not want a repeat of the events when they had arrived in Johannesburg with Riette's daughter. Then again, perhaps she did.

The small hotels may or may not take non-whites, depending on the preferences of their owners. Medium-sized ones were likely to feel they had appearances to maintain and might be difficult. The biggest would be happy to take Indians and were the least likely to make a fuss.

She looked along the front. There was a gap in the buildings; if her memory served, that would be the Grand Metropolitan, set back from the others. They should not arrive on foot, but there was a line of taxicabs near the station. The fact that she and the children were not very clean and had no luggage would be dealt with by her best British accent and the money they had been lent.

She hired a cab, which conveyed them along the front and into the grounds of the hotel. The doorman looked askance as she paid the driver, but the haughty angle of her chin, along with the unusual but clearly expensive cut of her clothes—even if they were dirty— gained them access.

The look they received from the desk clerk might have cowed a duchess, but Maliha was used to it.

"A small suite for myself and my charges," she said.

He shifted his weight from one foot to the other and fiddled with one of his buttons.

"Come, come, do not waste time. I have had a most trying day."

"One moment, madam," he said and fled into a room in the rear.

Moments later the night manager emerged. His dark suit was impeccably cut. He had a wide but neatly trimmed moustache that declared him a man to be reckoned with. Maliha met his gaze. She was relaxed, he was not.

She took the initiative. "A suite, if you would be so kind. And, if you have someone available, a maid. My luggage and fiancé are both lost at present."

"Lost?"

Maliha glared. "I am not about to discuss my personal affairs in public," she said, rummaging in her bag. "However, I'm sure you would like to know that I can pay, so here."

She tossed four white fivers onto the counter. "Now, a suite if you would be so kind."

Forty-five minutes later she was luxuriating in a bath, with Lilith at the other end sitting upright and nervous amid the warm water and foam bubbles. Izak had been given a bowl and instructed to wash thoroughly. Maliha was not sure how he would cope, but it was a start.

"Here," said Maliha and she tossed a sponge to Lilith. It landed on the foam and stuck there. The girl took it between thumb and finger. Her eyes showed her confusion. Maliha picked up another one, dunked it into the water and set about scrubbing her skin with the rough surface. Lilith copied her.

"It scratches."

"It's supposed to. It will make you cleaner than you have ever been."

Lilith pulled a face.

"Come here and I'll do your back."

"I don't want to, it's slippy. I might fall."

"Then I'll catch you."

Lilith moved gingerly along the bath, holding tight to the edges. Maliha sat up, crossed her legs and had the child sit down, facing away from her. Lilith's hair was in dense, plaited ringlets that were thick with dirt.

The bath water was turning cold by the time Maliha had them all undone. Dead insects dropped out of Lilith's hair as the process continued, but thankfully Maliha did not notice anything living.

She scrubbed the child's scalp and back. Lilith was ticklish and squirmed. Maliha took the opportunity to examine Lilith's skin closely. It was problematic; since Maliha had not studied it before, there was no way of telling whether it was abnormal. However, it seemed to be healthy and there was no sign of any infection at this point.

Finally Maliha got her out of the bath and drained it. Considering the state of it—lined with grime and dead insects—she wondered whether she should have another one. But it was getting late, or early.

The suite comprised the main bedroom, a smaller one for a child and a bathroom. She would put Izak in the small room and Lilith in the big bed with her. For now, all three of them were wrapped in large towels. She called the kitchen for food, which arrived with a seamstress and a small selection of nightwear.

There was a nightdress for Lilith, pyjamas for Izak, and a nightdress with matching dressing gown for Maliha. She put them on in the bathroom while the seamstress measured the children and then took her measurements when she emerged.

"Can you take these to be washed as well?" asked Maliha, indicating her clothes. They would not bother washing Izak's and Lilith's. They were better burned.

With everything settled they went to bed, but Maliha spent a long time staring at the ceiling while Lilith's soft breath murmured beside her, mingling with the distant sound of the breakers on the rocks.

iii

The time it took to organise matters preyed on Maliha's mind. Each day was another one lost, but it was impossible for her to move things along faster without revealing herself.

Once she was settled in the hotel it did not matter how much expense she incurred, since it was simply added to the bill. This was just as well because she had thrown almost all her money at the concierge that first night. The first step had been to visit a bank and set in motion the process of claiming her money.

It took two days for the message to return from the Fortress that Alice Ganapathy did have money in the bank. Clearly Amita had acted swiftly, as Maliha had instructed in her letter. She had created a bank account under the new name and transferred funds to it.

Maliha relaxed. The next stage was simply to book passage through a travel agency to Venus. This did present something of a difficulty—it was not expected that a woman with children would travel unaccompanied. However, it was not forbidden and was arranged.

The cost was astronomical even without purchasing a return ticket. She was advised that a bank draft for all the funds she would require was the best way to take her money to Venus, since it would be light and easily hidden. This seemed reasonable, but she arranged three drafts instead, stored separately, any two of which could provide her with what she needed.

While Colombo possessed all the services a tourist might require for their stay on the coast, it lacked the shops that could outfit a trip to Venus. Those establishments were at the Fortress, so she was forced to arrange matters by catalogue and letter. She was concerned about being recognised, so her plan was to ensure all her baggage had already been transferred to the station. They would then arrive at the last moment and board the shuttle-craft that would take them up to the Victoria station with as little delay as possible.

The whole process troubled her as so much of it was out of her direct control. There were pamphlets available that explained Venusian necessities and there was a great deal of nonsense published as well. She found it necessary to acquire various publications and compare them.

The difficulty came when a document published by, say, Ventris 'Stays-Lit' Venusian cookers over-emphasised the need for their company's products, while completely failing to mention storage facilities for the food that one would take to cook.

In fact, the most reliable sources, such as those produced by the Army & Navy Stores, indicated that all food taken on an expedition should be pre-cooked and sealed. Most raw foods became inedible within a day and food preparation was difficult due to the high humidity. It was also mentioned that while many of the native species were edible most others were toxic.

The Ventris pamphlet was discarded.

It was only a week after she had landed in the Consulate's moat that she departed the hotel, having paid in full, with minimal luggage of undistinguished quality filled with a fresh wardrobe appropriate to her new role as a professional escort for young children.

Her charges also wore new clothes. Lilith in particular had protested at the layers of white and blue clothing she was forced to wear but, while Maliha sympathised, they were a necessity. Izak's discomfort in his purple velvet travelling suit communicated itself as surliness appropriate for a young boy of his age.

A carriage transferred them to the station and Maliha took a long last look at the waves crashing on the beach in fountains of white.

She had taken walks along this beach with Izak and Lilith. She did not begrudge them the opportunity to splash in the water. Simply playing was not a skill they had learnt on the streets of Johannesburg. Lilith found it easier than Izak.

It had not required much persuasion to get him to remove his shoes and stockings—he had never owned any before and he disliked them—but the feeling of the wet sand ebbing and flowing beneath his toes upset him. So instead he walked with Maliha on the dry sand and pebbles further up the beach while Lilith played tig with the waves.

"Are there monsters in the ocean?" he had asked.

"Who's to know?" said Maliha. "There are always tales of monstrous fish and squid with tentacles that that could envelop a ship. But they are probably falsehoods created to make the speaker sound important, or to explain the disappearance of an experienced crew.

"Besides," she said. "No one but fishermen sail the seas any more. Any passengers and cargo are taken through the sky."

"But no monsters."

"Not here, perhaps, but on Venus they have great creatures on the land. I think it's safe to believe they also exist in the one sea that Venus possesses."

And we may yet get to see them, thought Maliha as she settled Izak in the seat by the window and herself along the aisle, with Lilith between them.

She ran her fingers through Lilith's hair. Even if she had not seen the alteration in the child's skin during one of their baths, she would have changed her mind about taking them to Venus. But something was growing under the girl's left shoulder blade. A slightly spongy patch had developed and it was not the only one. Lilith did not seem to notice. Maliha did not mention it. But she could not abandon the girl now, nor could she separate the two of them.

The atmospheric was not busy. Thursday was not a day for going home. They were not travelling first class, as that would be inappropriate in her new guise. She had bought first-class tickets at the hotel, to keep up appearances, but exchanged them for second-class tickets at the station.

The carriage had three commercial travellers, of whom two were reading the *Times of India* and the other a book.

It was barely an hour later—though the children were already getting restless—that *Sigiriya*, with towering buildings of stone, glass and iron perched on its summit, came into view.

"Is it Heaven?"

"Not at all," said Maliha, "though perhaps it might be called the gateway to the heavens." Her play on words was lost on them, which was perhaps just as well since it was not particularly clever.

For about a mile the tube housing the atmospheric was carried on pylons thirty feet above the ground, above the unnamed city that had sprung up around the wall. The buildings leaned one against the other and were built from anything that had come to hand. Most did not exceed a single storey above the ground, but one or two were higher and single-minaret mosques pierced the irregular surface of roofs at regular intervals.

The atmospheric plunged through the wall of the Compound and emerged into the organised perfection of the British Empire with its wide clean streets, lines of identical residencies and majestic civil buildings. The area within the outer wall contained, manned and supported the administrative offices for hundreds of trading lines, as well as for the British Army and Navy Far Eastern forces.

Control of the Void was given over to the Fortress itself.

The atmospheric came into the station and jerked sideways as it was shunted off to a platform. It slowed and came to rest. Through the window they could see the cathedral-like ceiling of the great hall. At the end of each platform stood a colossal furnace and boiler that generated the pressure to begin an atmospheric's journey. And each of those great engines depended on a valve designed by Maliha's father.

It was then Maliha noticed three men loitering on the concourse. They had no baggage and, though they stood in what might be seen as a friendly group, she could see them studying every person who disembarked. Particularly the women.

They might be looking for someone else, but it was a risk she could not take.

There was no Mama Kosi here to help them. She might be able to delay disembarking for a while but, unless she could find another way out from the station, the prospect was hopeless.

"They after us, Goddess?" asked Lilith. She too was looking at the men and so was Izak. Living on the streets gave them a sense of when things were not safe.

"Just me," she said. "And if they take me, you two should run."

Maliha pulled out one of the cards she'd had made up with her new name and wrote an address on the back. Barbara Makepeace-Flynn—she should be in Pondicherry with Amita, but there had been no time to sell the house yet.

"Get someone to take you to the address on the card," she said. "The people there will help you. They'll send you to Amita."

"We won't leave you, Goddess," said Izak. "We'll fight them."

Maliha's attention was caught by a movement on the concourse. Between the disembarking travellers, she caught sight of half a dozen policemen surrounding the group of three men. There was considerable gesticulating and possibly some shouting since passengers paused to stare before moving on.

There was a brief scuffle and the three were taken away.

"I'd say that makes us about even, Miss Anderson." The coarse Glaswegian accent rolled across the carriage. "Wouldn't you?"

iv

Maliha turned and could not suppress the smile on her face. "Inspector!"

"He's a crusher?" said Izak.

"He's a friend."

"Friend, is it, Miss Anderson?" he said. "I seem to recall you interfering with my investigations and robbing me of my perpetrators."

"I think you'll find that was Valentine."

Inspector Forsyth drew closer and glanced at her left hand. "Making an honest woman of you, is he?"

"I was always an honest woman, Inspector."

"Aye, that you were," he said. "And who are these ruffians dressed in finery?"

"Izak and Lilith, Inspector—my wards."

"And you have the documentation to prove it?"

"Of course."

Forsyth bent down and looked out the window. "All right, the lads have removed them. There's a car outside that will take you directly to the Fortress, no messing about."

They disembarked. Their luggage was already in transit. No one bothered them as they crossed the concourse.

"It seems rather quiet," said Maliha.

"I applied some pressure to the station staff and insisted on them delaying any further incoming atmospherics."

"Why?"

"I don't like being indebted, and the way you've been going, Miss Anderson, you'll be dead before I could pay."

"You know about Johannesburg?"

"I have a vested interest in staying up to date with the waves you're causing. I don't intend to be caught napping when one of them rolls in my direction."

Rather than exiting through the main entrance, Forsyth guided them through a door marked 'Staff only', along a passage and out into a narrow cobbled street that ran down the side of the station.

A steam police carriage puffed quietly. The driver turned and grinned, Sergeant Choudhary.

Forsyth opened the door and ushered them all in, then followed and closed the door. When they were settled he banged on the glass to the front.

The curtains were pulled closed on all the windows. The carriage moved off along the bumpy road, its rubber tyres and suspension failing to improve the ride.

"How did you know?" she asked.

"Oh, not much detecting needed for that," he said. "An order came from on high, alerting all divisions to be on the lookout for Miss Maliha Anderson, last seen in the company of two negro children. Well, there's only one Maliha Anderson."

"What did it say I had done?"

"Escaped lawful custody."

"For what crime?"

"It was a little vague on that precise point, but it implied you had incited a riot against the civil government."

"She *stopped* it," burst out Izak.

Forsyth turned his attention to the boy. "You have big ears, young man. Wise to keep them open, wiser to keep your mouth shut."

"Well, she did," said Lilith. "She's our goddess."

Forsyth looked back at Maliha. "That business in Pondicherry?"

Maliha frowned. "Your obsession with my affairs could be considered worrying."

Forsyth shrugged. "It was a bad business. You have my condolences."

"Thank you."

"Anyway, I didn't believe a word of it and I remembered that little affair with the Guru and Timmons. The toffs are all best pals, so I put two and two together and found you first."

"You got hold of the French police reports, then the South African police reports, realised I might be going to Venus, so you checked the passenger lists. You know my full name and the name of my family back home."

Forsyth smiled. "If I had a daughter, Miss Anderson, I would be happy if she grew up to be half the woman you are."

"Won't you get into trouble for helping me?"

"Only if someone finds out." Forsyth leaned back and filled his pipe without looking at it. "Someone reported those men at the station for being shifty, so picking them up was routine. There will be apologies if it turns out they were official, otherwise they'll spend some time in the cells. Either way, they'll get out long after you're gone. And there's only one other person who knows you're in this carriage."

As he spoke the carriage slowed to a stop and there was the faint sound of discussions outside.

"Goddess, I'm tired," whined Lilith. "And my head hurts."

"Hush, dear heart. I'll deal with it when we're safe."

The carriage moved off again. Forsyth peeped out through the curtain.

"We're inside the perimeter of the Fortress. You'll be getting out in a minute or so." He turned in the seat and faced Maliha. "Once you leave the carriage I can't help you any more."

She put her hand on his. "Thank you, Inspector. I don't know what I would have done if you hadn't been there."

"And there I thought you had it all planned," he said.

Maliha frowned. "Had what planned?"

"Solving the murder on the *Macedonia* so you would meet me and I'd get promoted and brought to Ceylon, then all the rest of it. Just so I would owe you a favour and deliver you to *Sigiriya* when you needed it." He kept his face straight.

Her frown deepened for a moment and then she laughed. And found she couldn't stop laughing. She flung her arms around him and put her head on his shoulder, holding him tight. He did not return the gesture. Izak and Lilith laughed too, though they did not understand the joke. Finally she let him go and pulled back.

"Yes," she said between heaving breaths. "Yes, I had everything planned right from the very beginning."

It took her several moments to compose herself, during which time the carriage came to a final stop.

The door opened and Sergeant Choudhary peered in. "Miss Anderson, we have arrived at your destination. If you would be so good as to come along?"

She looked at the inspector; he shook his head. "I'll stay here. I am not very good at goodbyes."

Maliha shooed Izak and Lilith out of the car, then returned her attention to Forsyth.

"Thank you for your help, Inspector," she said and placed a kiss on his cheek.

"You're not the same woman, Miss Anderson," he said and held out his hand.

His words brought her back to reality. "No, Inspector, I am not."

He looked as if he wanted to say something, but instead he patted her hand and nodded towards the door. She paused for a moment, giving him a little more time, but he closed down.

"Be off wi' you."

She almost said goodbye but caught herself and smiled once more. Then she climbed from the vehicle and out onto a flagged surface. She reached out and pushed the door shut. It clicked with finality.

v

Choudhary stood there holding the hands of Izak and Lilith. She thought he looked very natural like that. She did not even know if he was married—in fact, she realised how little she really knew about the people she had met. People she might think of as friends.

She took Lilith's hand—the girl looked very unhappy—and Izak took up a position on Maliha's other side. Choudhary escorted them across the flat and barely worn surface. In front of them the massive bulk of *Sigiriya* loomed.

At its base was a set of doors constructed from iron and big enough to accommodate a small flyer if they had been open. There was a smaller door beside them and soldiers guarded that entrance. The British were bound by their love of commerce to permit the transportation of civilians and goods to and from the Victoria station above, but they also had secrets within *Sigiriya* they were desperate to protect.

She scanned upwards, studying the ancient fort and the changes its new imperial owners had imposed upon it. Hammered out of the granite, fifty feet up its side were openings from which protruded the long barrels of powerful artillery. And below those, other gaps with machine gun mounts.

Other constructions of metal and glass clung to the sheer sides like tumours, defacing what had once been a triumph of the ancient world. This is what the British Empire did to the world. It was a fungal growth creeping across the surface of anything foreign, consuming and transforming it.

And yet they were not the enemy, though they carried its semblance. There was no us and them, there were only people and their decisions for good or bad.

"How is your dilemma, Sergeant?" she asked.

He hesitated and she wondered if he had forgotten their previous conversations. She had not, but that was no surprise.

"I have decided that order is better than chaos, Miss Anderson."

She nodded. "And does that work?"

"It serves for the time being," he said. "I need to thank you for your wisdom. It has brought calm to my heart and my soul."

"It was only the truth."

"That is a rare thing in this world, Miss Anderson. There are few who can see it."

"It is a greater skill to see it for what it is and then follow it, Sergeant."

They reached a low fence with a gate and guards. One man came forward; he was in uniform but, rather than carrying a gun, he had a clipboard. Choudhary walked up to the guard. "Alice Ganapathy and her charges."

The man checked his list. "She's late."

"But not too late."

"No."

Maliha moved forward with the children. The barrier was raised and she passed through. She turned back.

"Thank you for your help, Sergeant."

"I am pleased to count you as a friend."

She noted he had not used her fake name in their exchange. She pressed her palms together and bowed. He saluted in return.

"This way, Miss Ganapathy," said the clerk. "The shuttle lifts in ten minutes."

He led the way towards the single door.

Maliha found it an alien notion that she had friends. The years at school, before she returned to India, had been filled with loneliness and abuse. But now she had Barbara, Amita, Inspector Forsyth, Sergeant Choudhary, even Françoise Greaux, and Ray Jennings, as well as her charges: not just Izak and Lilith, but Riette's baby too— sweet little Barbara who had stolen her heart.

But no family to speak of, since they blamed her quite thoroughly for the events in Pondicherry. If she had left it alone, things could have been different, but the truth would have come out eventually and been a hundred times worse. But they chose not to see that.

And there was Valentine.

Lilith clung to her arm harder as they passed through the passage and into the interior. It was not dark; the electric lights shone hard and bright, banishing any shadow. Maliha did not fail to notice the modern loopholes and ancient sluices from which could issue death if any invader got this far.

The corridor they passed down was so narrow they could only walk in single file. Lilith still clung to Maliha's hand even though she walked behind. The temperature dropped significantly and she felt Lilith shiver.

They passed four metal doors and came out finally into a cave. The walls had been painted by the original occupants, but the British had given the designs no consideration and had drilled into them and chipped them away to build their machines, which included a set of four lifts running up through the ceiling.

Their escort opened the doors to a lift. Lilith and Izak were reluctant to enter what appeared to be a metal cage, but Maliha stepped inside and encouraged them. Even Izak held her hand tight.

"Is it a Faraday lift?" she asked the fellow before the doors closed.

"Of course."

"You will feel the lightness like in the air-plane and the atmospheric," she said quickly, though the words were hardly out of her mouth before it came upon them and they shot upwards.

Lilith whimpered.

They traversed the distance to the apex of *Sigiriya* in less than twenty seconds, with acceleration and deceleration smooth enough to prevent bumps. Maliha glanced at her watch. Five minutes.

The summit resembled Verne's *City in the Sky*, she thought. It was almost unreal with its towering modern buildings built more from steel than stone. The guard ushered them into a small atmospheric designed to take a party of up to twelve. He had them sit in the red leather seats before entering a code. The inner and outer doors closed together and the vehicle shot away.

The atmospheric came to rest less than a minute later on the far side of *Sigiriya*. They disembarked onto a wide open space, in the centre of which was the shuttle. She had seen them launch and land frequently, and had even employed binoculars to study them more closely.

This was a vessel that employed the secret *complete gravity nullification* that Valentine had been horrified to discover she knew about. But, as she had pointed out, it would take a complete fool not to realise what they were seeing when they launched.

The surface of the launch area was metal and, no doubt, hid the secret of the process. Each panel of metal was one yard square with a metal loop in its centre. The vessel itself had very small wings and large thruster ports at the rear. It did not have a funnel.

A steward stood at the door and several crew waited around the vessel. They had ropes attached to belts around their middles; the other ends were attached to the loops on the ground. As she got closer Maliha saw that the vessel itself possessed a clamp, which held tightly to one of the loops.

The complete nullification meant that any person or object in its field would simply float away until they reached the edge, where full gravity would reassert itself and they would fall. Possibly over the edge of *Sigiriya* itself.

Their escort gave her name to the steward. He smiled at Maliha with the outside of his face. He must have made this trip so many times any passengers warranted no more attention than an inanimate piece of cargo. Or he took objection to the skin tones of the three latecomers.

It did not matter one way or the other.

There were airlock doors both outside and in. Maliha understood their significance and was glad the children did not. Once they had reached sufficient altitude the only breathable air would be what the ship carried.

It was a terrifying thought.

The passenger cabin was full. The seats were arranged in rows of four with an aisle along the middle—two on each side. And there were perhaps fifteen rows. These were the second-class seats; the first-class seats were towards the front. There was no third class, at least not on this type of vehicle. The vessels of Terence Timmons were a different matter.

Maliha and the children had seats halfway down the cabin, so they had to bear the stares both indifferent and malign from the passengers who were already seated. As there were three of them, they had two seats together and one across the aisle. Maliha debated over the best arrangement.

The fourth seat in their row appeared to be occupied by a middle-aged businessman. He was one of the ones who had watched them with indifference, as if their entrance was simply a distraction that passed the time.

She had Izak sit next to him and she quickly showed the boy how to operate the seat restraint. She put Lilith by the window and then sat in the aisle seat so she could reach and speak to both of them easily. She tied Lilith into her seat and tightened the belt, although it was not designed for a small child.

"Going light," called the steward from the front. He did not appear through the curtain, so Maliha guessed he was already in his seat. A red light went on at the front of the cabin. It flashed three times.

There was a chance to breathe in before all weight went from her body. Maliha gasped and Lilith cried out in fear, but their sounds were hidden amidst all the voices that expressed their surprise at the sensation in a dozen different ways.

Someone was weeping loudly.

Maliha felt as if she were falling, yet she could still feel the seat beneath her and the restraint across her. She reached out to hold Lilith's hand. Her arm moved normally and she grabbed the girl by the wrist.

On her other side another hand grabbed hers. She turned to see the face of Izak trying to suppress his terror, and perhaps his lunch. She smiled at him.

"This is a tremendous experience," she said in an attempt to lighten the mood. She was not sure if she was successful. An unpleasant smell permeated the air. She hoped it was not one of the children.

She looked back at Lilith, but as her gaze crossed the window she stopped and stared out. All she could see was ocean. They were already at high altitude, though there was no reference to indicate how high.

"Prepare for thrust," called the steward.

Maliha could not think what effect this would have and she had no words of comfort for the children. "Hold on to me," was all she had a chance to say before a thunderous roar filled the vessel and they were slammed back into their chairs.

vi

The pressure lasted for five minutes and in that time the sky went from porcelain blue, through deep purple to complete black, and the stars came out. They did not flicker and jump, as they did when seen from the surface of the Earth, but were hard and sharp like diamonds.

And there were so many more of them. The firmament was thick with stars. Maliha knew they were not all white, though that was the impression one got on Earth. But here, without the blanket of atmosphere to hide their true colours, they shone red and yellow, blue and orange. The Milky Way became a thick band stretching around them.

It was breathtaking.

The vessel rotated slowly as it rose. At no point could she see the Earth itself—they must be flying directly away from it—but she caught sight of the Moon regularly. Its seas (not filled with water, of course) were clear, as were its huge craters.

Lilith and Izak took their cue from her and, while others continued to suffer and wail, they relaxed, though they did not let go of her hands.

The steward floated through and tended to those who were in need of it. Some sorts of personal facilities were provided in the rear and Maliha imagined they would have to use them at some point, but not yet. Perhaps they could last until they reached their destination. It would be so embarrassing otherwise.

The man next to Izak had closed his eyes and gone to sleep. A seasoned traveller, no doubt.

The Victoria station was located at an altitude of seven thousand miles and the brochures said the travel time was only four hours. They would have to reduce their velocity once they reached the station, but for now they must be travelling in excess of two thousand miles per hour. So fast that their journey from Africa to Ceylon would have taken an hour.

"Try to sleep," she said to Lilith.

"I'm scared."

Maliha turned to Izak. "I need to comfort your sister. Can you manage without my hand?"

He looked uncertain, but then nodded and released her.

"Thank you." Maliha leaned over Lilith and put her arm around her. "There now, you go to sleep."

Lilith closed her eyes but remained tense. She was trying, but Maliha could tell she was not sleeping.

Outside the vessel, nothing changed. The ship continued to rotate and the view was always the same, constantly repeating. The only way she knew that time continued to tick away was by the changes in the passengers as they quieted, and the settling of Lilith's breathing.

No meal was served; the overall travel time did not balance against the difficulties the passengers would have. Easier to let people become a little hungry than force them to attempt to eat in this weightless condition.

She sensed the change.

Something in the rotation of the ship altered and through the porthole she saw an elegant, sparkling stream of ice crystals curve into the Void—the residue of a steam-thruster on the side of the vessel.

They were manoeuvring for their approach to the station. She peered out. The stars were no longer simply circling them but were now engaged in a more complex dance. She breathed in suddenly as the Earth came into view: an enormous blue, white and brown ball filling the sky. She could see the shape of India, the islands and land masses to its east, and the coast of Africa in the west with the island of Madagascar off its coast. Great swirls of white cloud hung above the surface.

Maliha tried to grasp the idea that only a week before she had been an invisible dot on the surface of Africa. Cloud covered the southern regions of the continent, hiding Johannesburg from her sight.

But she could see the place where Pondicherry was located on India's coast. Her vision blurred as tears filled her eyes but did not run down her cheeks. They clung to her eyelashes and she had to wipe them away with the back of her hand. She was not even sure why she was crying.

The Earth rotated out of view to be replaced by the velvet black filled with gems, and then her first glimpse of Victoria Station. It resembled a Fabergé egg enclosed by five great cartwheels. It turned about its own axis and reflected sunlight from its seemingly jewelled surfaces, which were no more than glass and steel.

She knew from her reading the central 'egg' contained the docking ports, Spanish furnaces and boilers, along with the gardens and administrative offices. The rings—accessible through any of the eight spokes which were not currently visible—had been given sufficient rotational velocity to provide a low level of artificial gravity.

The various residential quarters for crew and visitors were located in the rings, along with shops and other amenities, including a small theatre. The two outer rings (upper and lower depending on how one looked at it) were not yet complete, but even now the station could house fifteen hundred passengers.

The station was a colossal construction and a testament to the engineering abilities of the British Empire—and Nikola Tesla, who had defected to the British camp after his American laboratory was destroyed over ten years before. Maliha did not doubt that it was Tesla, in collaboration with Rutherford at Cambridge, who had achieved the total nullification of gravity.

The vessel continued to rotate and neither the station nor the Earth now appeared in the portholes. But other vessels came into view. There were small ships, similar to the shuttle, driven by engines which utilised Newton's Third Law—they fired out streams of steam to propel themselves.

These small ships plied the Void between the station and the true Voidships. In the distance she saw a squadron of three Royal Navy vessels, iron-hulled and mounted with batteries of artillery, with huge ether-propellers in their sterns to drive them across the vast expanses between planets. Another invention of Tesla and Rutherford, though one known to all and utilised by all Void-faring nations. Except one.

The thought caught in her mind and stuck. She had always thought of Timmons as owning a fleet of slaving vessels and carrying people away to work on Venus and Mars—perhaps other places. But how did their behaviour differ from that of the early colonists of, say, the Americas? People who had nothing to lose journeying across the sea to make a new life? Was that truly different from what Timmons was doing with the South African farmers and who knew what other people?

What did that mean? How many thousands of people had Timmons taken?

The shuttle juddered as its main engines fired, and she was pressed back into the seat. Lilith woke suddenly and cried out. Maliha held her close and reached out her hand to Izak, who clung to it.

What if Timmons' empire was exactly that? An empire?

A metallic clang reverberated through the ship and the portholes went dark.

They had arrived.

vii

Propriety suffered at the whim of nature. The vessel continued virtually weightless, since the rotation in the central hub of the station was not significant, but all the passengers were required to disembark.

Handholds on the chairs and in the ceiling were designed to assist the process, but most people found it impossible to maintain themselves in even the semblance of an upright position. For the ladies this meant their skirts floated around in a most indecorous manner, revealing ankles, calves and, in some cases, even knees.

There were many red faces, but this was one of the adventures of travel in the Void.

Maliha noted that some dresses did not fly up; there had been reference to attachments that were the opposite of skirt-lifters, designed to keep skirts around the ankles at all times. Maliha thought that donning male attire or even opting for bloomers would have been more sensible.

The white passengers assumed that she and the children would wait, since they lacked the authority accorded to those of paler colouring. This suited Maliha.

As the last of the other passengers made their way out, she let Izak make his own way towards the door. She looked at Lilith's glum face. "Sellie promised you the chance to fly, didn't she?"

Lilith took a moment to remember who Maliha was referring to, then nodded.

Maliha smiled, took her by one hand and lifted her into the air. This had the advantage of pressing Maliha into the deck. She took a step forward and grabbed one of the handholds. She pulled herself forwards, dragging Lilith through the air like a balloon on a stick.

Lilith squealed and then realised she wasn't falling.

Keeping a firm grip of her charge, Maliha made her way towards the exit. The steward smiled. "Take care, Miss Ganapathy, you don't want to lose her."

Maliha frowned. That seemed a strange comment, but perhaps he had just meant it would be dangerous to have the child floating about in the open spaces of the station.

They made their way out. They were not greeted by wide spaces filled with people flying hither and thither; instead it was a tight corridor with more rails and handholds and no obvious sense of which way was up. There was no carpeted floor, and electric lights were placed behind protective metal grids in no apparent pattern.

At the far end stood a hatchway capable of sealing against the vacuum of the Void, but it stood open. They emerged into a larger room, still not a large space but a reception area. Signs indicated the way to different parts of the station. The bulk of the passengers were following a sign towards the outer rings.

A large man stood holding onto a pole that ran between what might be assumed to be the floor and the ceiling—the signage provided some orientation of up and down. He held a neatly lettered sign: "Miss Ganapathy and party".

His suit was tight around his upper arms, thighs and chest, all of which appeared surprisingly wide. He did not strike her as someone of great intellect, while his distorted nose and one damaged ear suggested violence as his primary means of argument.

She had not arranged to meet anyone, but she could not ignore him and he was looking directly at her with a smile that did not appear to extend any further than his lips—as if he had been told at some time what a smile looked like and that it had a disarming effect on others. Mounted on his damaged face it had quite the opposite effect. Lilith gripped Maliha's wrist with both hands, while Izak put his arm about her waist.

Their presence emphasised Maliha's vulnerability. She knew why she had brought them, but it had always been a questionable choice.

"I am Alice Ganapathy."

"I have to show you to your room and then Mr Scott will have you for dinner."

"I see," said Maliha, translating his badly constructed sentence into something that meant the man had invited them to dinner. At least, that was what she hoped it meant. "And who is Mr Scott?"

His face reflected the difficulty he was having with being questioned when he had expected blind obedience.

"Never mind," said Maliha. "You do what you've been told, Mr—?"

"Brennan."

Maliha's documents indicated that they were staying in Ring B. At least Brennan knew his way around, like a rat knows its sewer.

They spent ten minutes moving lightly along more enclosed passages with no view of the outside, until they reached what looked like an elevator with a solid door instead of a concertina gate. The sign indicated it would take them to Ring B. They crowded inside. There was enough room for four adults, but Brennan took up enough space for two.

As the pod moved—presumably out along one of the spokes— their weight increased and the floor really became a floor, which their feet pressed against. Maliha heaved a sigh of relief. The constant weightless condition was quite exhausting.

"You got an hour," said Brennan when they arrived at the room, having acquired keys at a concierge desk by the elevator.

"That will be entirely satisfactory."

She unlocked the door and ushered the children inside. With another glance at Brennan, who had taken up station opposite and looked as if the end of the world would not shift him, she went in and locked the door behind her.

The gravity effect produced by the rotation of the ring was similar to that of a normal Faraday device so, while it allowed one to behave relatively normally, it did not provide a tremendous pull. Lilith bounced from floor to ceiling and jumped on the bed. Maliha let her release her pent-up energy.

There was a window on one side from which Maliha could see the unfinished Ring A and the stars in the Void. As they rotated, the three warships came into view, as well as many other large vessels—cargo ships for the most part—poised around the station, with smaller ships moving back and forth between them. She had not realised it was so busy.

Their luggage was in the room. Maliha fetched a change of clothes for them all. There was no bath but a small sealable compartment that fired water under pressure. Water was a scarce commodity here as it needed to be brought in, but travellers must be able to wash. It was a compromise.

Maliha cleaned herself and towelled herself dry. She dressed in the bathroom. Izak might still be young, but she was not about to show off her body to him. The thought gave her pause, considering all the things she had done, but no, everything she had done had been for good reason and with other adults. She was not being hypocritical.

She checked her watch. By the time she had finished tidying her hair as best she could, the hour was almost up.

"You two need to stay here," she said. "I don't know how long I'll be."

"What if you don't come back?" said Izak. Maliha wondered how many people had left him and never come back.

"I'll come back," she said with complete certainty, though he seemed unconvinced. "If I don't come back you find a crusher and tell them what happened."

"Don't trust crushers."

"You have to here," she said.

She kissed him on the cheek and hugged Lilith.

"I won't be long."

viii

Brennan was still outside when she emerged. She locked the door behind her and he set off without a word. They reached a crossing point with a tube that linked the rings. There was an airtight hatch at each end. No matter how luxurious they made the station, there was never any doubt that death lurked just beyond the hull.

They passed from Ring B to C and then directly across to D. While the passages could not be described as being thronged with people, there was seldom a moment when they were alone, for which Maliha was grateful.

They travelled around Ring D, passing through the residential section then a retail area, which gave onto a row of restaurants. Most duplicated the names of famous hotels, such as the Astoria, Hilton and Claridge's. They entered a small, sombre-looking establishment.

There was a list of expected guests on a lectern at the entrance, next to the *maître d'*. She glanced at it as she passed. The handwriting was perfectly clear. The man glanced at Brennan and then at her but did not stop them. She read the list from memory and saw Scott's name.

She brushed past Brennan and strode through the carefully arranged tables towards the only man seated on his own. There were other diners; the quality of their clothes indicated their available income, while the way they wore them indicated their breeding. The ones who were most relaxed were in plentiful possession of both.

Scott, however, had neither. While his clothing was of the very best quality, he looked uncomfortable, and she knew him for precisely what he was: a hired hand, just as much as Brennan. His only qualification was the cunning in his eyes.

He did not rise when Maliha approached. She sat without being asked.

The rectangular table was next to the wall and had been set for him alone, implying she would not be staying long. She placed herself diagonally opposite.

"Miss Anderson." His voice was higher pitched than she expected, and held a slight whine that she was sure would become irritating within a very short space of time. The fact he knew exactly who she was did not surprise her. If they had been awaiting her arrival, they would know.

He looked expectantly at her, as if he thought she would ask him what he wanted or perhaps protest that they had the wrong person, or some such. She saw no reason to make it easy for him. He might have the upper hand, but the more she kept silent the more he would talk.

She simply looked at him, studying his face. He had a scar on his forehead. Not a large one; most people would not even notice. She guessed his age to be about forty-five. His right hand was on the table and his left in his lap.

"What are you doing?" he said.

She paused in her appraisal of him and looked up into his eyes. They were brown. He had dark marks below his eyes, as if he had not been sleeping well.

"I'm sorry? Doing? In what respect?"

"You're looking at me."

"Not precisely, sir," she said. "I am *studying* you."

"Well, stop it."

His left hand came up defensively and his fingers intertwined. His eyes flicked towards Brennan and back to her. Her demure clothing reduced any womanliness she possessed to gentle curves with no flesh to examine. He still looked at her breasts—it was something she noticed was common to all men. She had concluded it meant little and was most likely a redundant evolutionary habit.

She did not give him the chance to take the initiative. She sat up straighter in her chair and leaned forward, a move that made him withdraw his hands and look over at Brennan again. It seemed he was unsure of her. "I don't have all night, Scott. What is it that Mr Timmons wants to say to me?"

He opened his mouth to answer and hesitated. With a visible effort he changed his response. "Think you're clever, do you?"

"Yes, Scott, I do. Considerably more so than you." She allowed biting sarcasm to infect her words. "You are merely an errand boy, lacking the manners even Brennan here could manage. You thought you would intimidate me, but it takes a great deal more than someone like you to do that.

"Now, if you would be so good as to pass on the message, I will be on my way."

She did not raise her voice, but she could see that it had worked by the way he pushed back into the chair as if trying to escape her.

"You don't seem to understand what you're dealing with, *Miss* Anderson," he hissed. "I could have Brennan snuff out your life with his hands around your pretty little neck."

The man was so lacking in skills he spoke in clichés. The dress she wore had a high collar—he had no idea whether her neck was pretty or not.

"Of course you can't, because then Mr Timmons would have Brennan here end yours with equal finality. You cannot touch me, Scott." She took a breath and sat back. "Now if you can stop playing childish games, you can give me the message from Timmons."

She watched Scott fighting with his natural inclination to put women in their place. "Mr Timmons says that if you turn around and get back on the shuttle to Earth he will leave you and yours alone."

"How generous of him."

Scott leaned forward. "It's *very* generous, and if you're as clever as you think you are you'll take his offer."

"I take it Mr Timmons has never, to your knowledge, made this sort of offer before."

He sat back with a grin and crossed his arms. "Never."

"He deals with his enemies by having them killed."

"Always."

"And what are your orders if I don't agree?"

"What do you mean?"

Maliha stood up. "Thank you for this little chat, Mr Scott. It really has been very enlightening."

Brennan moved out from the shadows and loomed over her. "It's all right, Mr Brennan, I can find my own way back. I won't be needing an escort."

"What's your answer?" said Scott.

"I will give Mr Timmons' offer serious consideration," she said. "But if you have nothing further to say I will be going."

Scott stood up. He barely even reached her height and he was bow-legged, probably the result of polio.

"Mr Timmons said you might try to be clever," said Scott, "so there was one other thing: your accomplice on the other ship, the one that tried to help you: he was executed."

Cold ran through her body. She opened her mouth to speak but found she had nothing to say.

Scott grinned lopsidedly. "Yeah, dead as a doornail. They threw him out the ship, just like you, only they were halfway into the Void at the time."

Maliha found she was breathing heavily. She controlled herself and felt suddenly very aware of Valentine's ring on her finger. The cold of fear was replaced by cold a thousand times cooler, a rage that burned through her veins like ice. She turned her eyes to Scott and he stepped back.

"Do you know what the Durga Maa is?" she said in a low hiss.

He was back to wringing his hands. He simply shook his head.

"The Durga Maa is the Goddess of Vengeance," she said.

She moved forward and placed her hands on the table. Brennan moved in. She snapped her head in his direction and he stopped. She returned her attention to the ferret Scott.

"You're not looking well, Mr Scott," she said. "You have a touch of jaundice, have you noticed?"

He shook his head.

"Your skin is a little yellow, and the whites of your eyes."

His hands rose to his face, he touched his cheeks and rubbed his eyes.

"You'll notice the itching next," she said. "First just a little, but it grows and you mustn't scratch it. If you scratch it, it just gets worse."

Without even realising, he rubbed his forearm.

"And then the pains start until finally you die in agony."

She stood up and stepped back. "I won't say *au revoir*, Mr Scott, because we won't meet again this side of the pearly gates."

She turned on her heel and stalked from the restaurant. Some of the diners watched her go. She took no notice.

CHAPTER 4

i

Two days later they took up their berth on the *Atacama Sea,* bound for Williams Port in orbit around Venus, from which they would descend to the city of Regina.

She had done with crying for Valentine. She could not change anything; she must learn to live with it. If anything it gave her even more purpose, though she now wished she had not taken such careful precautions against pregnancy.

But that would not have helped.

They were in second class again, using the false name even if it was redundant. The cabin was a reasonable size and all three could sleep in it without difficulty. Once more she and Lilith took to the bed, while Izak had a sofa that transformed into a bed for the night.

In order to provide some semblance of gravity, the vessel was designed around the ether propeller. This was located at the base of the ship, and the decks were constructed upwards along its axis. So, where a Sky-Liner is built in a similar fashion to sea-going ships, a passenger Voidship is more like a building.

The constant push from the propeller provided light gravity, which at least meant there was a genuine sense of up and down, even if movement was more like a ballet. During the period of adaptation she had to be sympathetic to both children, when they misjudged the required effort for any movement and crashed into a wall or ceiling.

She had told them Valentine had been killed, but death was such a commonplace to them it seemed as if they barely cared. Though, of course, they had hardly known him.

The vessel was underway and the bell had been rung for the evening meal. The children had terrible table manners, unsurprisingly, and she thought she might as well educate them even if they drew looks from other passengers.

Their cabin was located on Deck 10, which was two levels above the engineering decks. The refectory and various lounges were on Deck 5, while Deck 4 had more lounges, the library and some courts for sports. Above those were administrative cabins, crew quarters and the bridge.

Movement between the levels involved using one of two shafts located opposite one another. One was for ascending, the other for descending. The shafts allowed passengers to fly between the levels. Straps, handholds and poles were provided to allow one to pull oneself along. Maliha suspected there were other shafts for crew use only.

Passengers were allowed up to Deck 4 if they needed the Bursar but no further, the sole exception being a viewing lounge right at the top of the vessel, which was accessible by a special shaft with exits only at the bottom and the top.

While they waited, Maliha wondered idly what would become of Mr Scott. She had never had occasion to attempt mesmerism before; she did not consider it ethical and it had certainly been utilised for quite improper purposes in the hands of dishonest people. But she could not fault its effectiveness. Of course, Scott was easily susceptible—the less educated a person the easier it was to impose one's will upon them.

She wished she could follow it up, to see how far her suggestion that he had jaundice would take him. She had chosen jaundice because there was a very slight pallor to his skin that might have been the disease. Could the mind impose itself so thoroughly on the body? There was no doubt that certain illnesses were derived from the mind.

She was not fool enough to deny that the supposedly miraculous cure of her leg, after the Guru had manipulated it, was more to do with the change in her state of mind than any form of magic.

She sighed and corrected the way Izak was holding his fork. The severe lack of gravity made eating a trial anyway. Food could fly from the plate and across the room if struck too hard. Izak and Lilith had suffered from this at first and Maliha was forced to relocate them as far as possible from the other diners. The meal they were given was mashed potatoes and meat, followed by a gloopy dessert, which had less of a tendency to fly away.

The menu was fixed regardless of one's station. Carrying a little over two hundred passengers millions of miles across the Void required some compromises. Choice of menu was one of them and when the meals were eaten was another. There were three sittings for each, though there were usually some spare tables. Maliha's party was in the first sitting.

The serving staff cleared away the dessert dishes barely forty-five minutes after Maliha and the children had taken their seats. Clearly it was time to move on.

She took the children back to the room.

"I'm going up to the observation deck," she said. "Will you be all right here?"

"Can we come?" asked Lilith, using the same plaintive tone Maliha remembered using when she was young. In truth, she desired to be alone—she wanted to think about Valentine, and perhaps let her grief escape the prison in which she held it. But she remembered her mother.

"Can I come, Momma?"

"I am going to the temple, Maliha." She was dressed in her finest clothing, the pallu *of her deep blue sari cast over her left shoulder, her eyes and lips emphasised by heavy make-up. She looked as beautiful as a doll.*

"I can go to the temple with you."

"You must stay here, little one," said her mother, leaning over her and smiling. "You must study and learn your words."

"I know all the words, Momma."

"You know many things, but knowledge is not wisdom."

Maliha looked at Lilith. "If you want to, little one." She turned to Izak, but he shook his head. "I'm going to look at the stars," she said, as if trying to persuade him.

"You have to come," said Lilith to Izak. "You *know* why."

"Why?" said Maliha.

"Mama Kosi said," said Lilith.

They travelled up the shaft. Lilith held tight to Maliha's skirt instead of climbing up herself. They reached Deck 4 and followed the signs, past the Bursar's office and the Infirmary, to the observatory shaft. There was only one of these shafts, with one side designated as up and the other down.

The observatory was a domed area with a number of large potted plants from Earth, along with comfortable-looking sofas and armchairs. Around the edges of the circular area were benches and other sofas that all faced out towards the Void. Lights hung from the ceiling, but at present they were not lit, as the Sun was burning in on them.

The dome itself comprised at least two layers of glass braced with steel. Beyond it, in spite of the Sun's brightness, were the stars. The Earth and Moon were not in view, being behind the vessel.

It was the quiet that struck Maliha. Deep in the ship there were constant small noises—some repeating, others at random moments—and sometimes the distant murmur of voices. But always there was the sound of humanity. There were voices here too, but beyond that was a deeper silence than she had ever experienced. It was unnerving.

Maliha glanced around; there were a few people here. A group of three men was seated off to one side, the voices that hung above the precipice of silence. There were the sun-haloed heads of several others scattered around the rim. She located the seat that had the fewest people nearby and headed for it.

Lilith clung to her hand and she could feel Izak's presence beside her on the other side. She wondered briefly about their secret.

They sat on the bench. There were straps in each seating position. Maliha wondered about them but did not use them on the children or herself.

Maliha stared at the stars and attempted to orient herself. The constellations were there, but the dark gaps in between were filled with the glowing dust of a myriad stars unseen on Earth. It made the ancient patterns harder to spot.

Then she saw Orion. Then Gemini and, following from there, Ursa Major and Minor. She found the Pole Star. The Sun was located in Pisces, and off from it, in Aries, was the bright white half-disk of Venus. She was unsure of the location of Mars and could not see its rust-red glow. It might be behind them.

Quietly, so as not to disturb the other occupants, she described the constellations and the planet to the children. She pointed them out but did not know if the children were really seeing or understanding. Their lives had been empty of academic education; the only thing of value to them had been the barren facts of how to survive.

She could have spent hours here contemplating the stars but the children could not. Maliha stood carefully to avoid flying up to bump against the dome.

With Izak and Lilith in tow she headed back towards the shaft, but her attention was caught by two people she had not noticed before, slumped on a settee. The woman was leaning in towards the man, but he had slid from his chair and was poised half on and half off it. As she watched he slipped a little more.

It was not that there were two dead people here that shocked her. It was the fact she recognised them.

They were Valerie and Maxwell Spencer.

ii

"She's been stabbed," said Dr Leeming, noting the blood that had oozed from Valerie's middle section and soaked into her dress. "And he's been shot in the head. He still has the gun, so it's probably suicide."

"I think most people would have been able to work that out," said the captain. "How long have they been here?"

Maliha stood nearby. A steward had been fetched to take the children to the room and stay with them. They had protested considerably more than Maliha would have expected. They only agreed to go quietly when they had extracted a promise, from Captain Beauchamp himself no less, that he would be personally responsible for Maliha's safety.

She stared at the two of them.

"What was she stabbed with?" asked Maliha. She already knew the answer without seeing the nature of the wound. Her blood was running cold in her veins. This was a warning. Or perhaps a game played by someone with a very sick mind.

"I couldn't say," said the doctor, examining Valerie's midriff.

"Did you know the Spencers, Miss Ganapathy?"

She stared at him. Why would these two be using the same name, and pretending to be married, as they had on the *RMS Macedonia*? If she had thought this was a coincidence before, she now knew as a certainty that it had been planned and aimed directly at her.

This must be a message from Timmons. A message for her, planned in the event that she came aboard after the warning from

Scott. She had ignored it and now two people were dead. She had no idea what to do.

"Miss Ganapathy?"

Her thigh hurt. It had no reason to do that. It was not under any strain or pressure.

She stared at the bodies. She could not reveal herself; she must stay hidden.

But she was not hidden—Timmons knew who she was and his men knew. She should not have brought the children. But she needed to have Lilith with her; it was important.

"I don't know what to do," she said, barely above a whisper. "I am tangled in my own web."

"Perhaps you should sit down," said the doctor, coming towards her with a sympathetic smile on his face.

Maliha jerked her head up. Anyone could have done it. Passenger, crew, it could even be the captain or the doctor. The *Atacama Sea* was one of Timmons' official fleet. Everyone aboard was in his pay, quite literally.

"Don't touch me," she hissed and held up her hand to fend him off. "Stay away."

He stopped and glanced at the captain, who gave a slight shake of his head. The doctor returned to the bodies and proceeded to check Maxwell Spencer.

"Perhaps you should go back to your room, Miss," said the captain. "This must have been a terrible shock for you. I will need your statement about these two, but there's no hurry."

"Ah, found it," the doctor said triumphantly. He stepped back and showed the captain something metallic that glinted with reflected red.

Maliha stared at the scissors in the doctor's hand. She felt the strength go from her right thigh and collapsed slowly under the weak gravity. She felt lightheaded. The dome and stars swam as she passed from sunlight into the black.

* * *

"Don't touch me!" she screamed and shook off the hand that crept along her left arm.

"Goddess?" came Lilith's voice, from the right.

Maliha turned her head in that direction and opened her eyes. Lilith stood beside the bed, barely tall enough to see over it. Izak stood behind her with a hand on her shoulder. They both looked scared.

The antiseptic smell invaded Maliha's nose and mouth as she took in a deep breath. There was something wrapped around her arm, getting tighter.

"Don't touch me," she said again.

"I am taking your blood pressure, Alice."

Maliha shivered. Every girl who ended up in the school infirmary suffered Dr Jenkins' extensive and unwarranted examination. And no one would believe them. With her leg in a cast from ankle almost to hip, she could not defend herself. *Just giving you a proper examination, dear child.*

She blinked. There was a black strap around her arm just above the elbow. It was not Jenkins. It was Leeming, with a stethoscope in his ears and holding a rubber bladder in the other. She recognised the modern sphygmomanometer.

"I'm sorry," she said and lay back. The cold metal of the stethoscope was pressed against the inner part of her elbow joint. The bladder puffed as he pressed it. The cuff around her arm tightened, cutting off the blood flow. Then it hissed as he let out the pressure.

He made notes in a small book.

- 118 -

She turned towards the children and forced a smile onto her face. "It's all right," she said. "He's making sure I'm not ill." They did not look reassured; modern medicine was not within the realms of their experience.

I can't be ill, she thought, *there's no time for illness.*

The doctor went through the procedure again and then loosened the cuff so that it could be removed.

"Blood pressure is a little high, Miss Ganapathy," he said.

She turned to him. "Really?"

He shrugged. "Not entirely unusual when one has not travelled in the Void before. It can be a particular problem for the fairer sex."

He smiled with sickly sweet condescension. If anything was likely to increase her blood pressure, she thought, it would be that. But he hadn't finished. "And finding those people just put the cherry on the cake, as it were."

He went to a cabinet and, using a key from his pocket to unlock it, took out a small pill bottle. She sat up on the brown leather examination couch and put her legs over the side. She rubbed her thigh; it seemed to be back to normal. He counted out several tablets into a pillbox and came back.

"These should calm you," he said. "A cocaine preparation of my own. Very good for the nerves. Just take one with water before you go to sleep." He held out the small tin box.

"Thank you, Doctor," she said, taking it. "Can I return to my room now?"

He beamed with *bonhomie*. "Be my guest," he said. "If you have any other problems, don't hesitate to drop by."

Maliha nodded her thanks. With a slight push from her hand she moved up off the couch and gently came down to the floor. Her shoes had been removed.

"Will you carry my shoes, Lilith?"

The girl moved round the bed, using it as an anchor, and collected them.

"Thank you again, Doctor," she said and left the room.

iii

Back in the room, Maliha stowed the pillbox in her luggage. She would not be taking the pills, but she might require them.

It was possible her faint had been the result of the low gravity and the over-excitement. The helplessness she had felt was a very new experience and one she was not comfortable with. She needed a plan.

She looked at her watch; it was late evening. The children went to bed. It had not been easy for them to become accustomed to doing as an adult instructed, or being forced to keep regular hours when they normally did as they pleased. They tried not to sleep even though they obeyed like any child. And, like any child, they eventually slept.

Maliha stood at the porthole, which was more of a window.

Apart from its constant yet low acceleration, the ship also rotated, again very slowly so there was barely a hint of any force moving things towards the hull. It meant that the view changed, though it was always stars. And from time to time the Sun slanted in.

There was nothing to be done.

She could not investigate the deaths of the Spencers—the Rileys, in fact: Margaret and Clement Riley, brother and sister fraudsters and thieves. Idly she wondered whether, after all these years of travelling as man and wife, they had enjoyed carnal relations. Irrelevant. She did not need to investigate their murders because she knew who had ordered their deaths.

But to go to this much trouble?

The Rileys must have been employed to join the ship she was on—once that was known—without the knowledge they would be killed. The murderer had gone to the trouble of staging it as a murder–suicide, exactly the way Lochana Modi and the General had died.

She needed to get away from the idea that everyone on the ship was her enemy; that was simply paranoia. Probably the result of her temporary condition. She would not be caught out that way again.

But why go to this much trouble? The question kept going round in her mind.

It was a demonstration of power. Timmons was showing her what he was capable of, how he was the one who held the power of life and death over her.

Lilith whined in her sleep. Maliha went over to her and stroked her hair, humming an Indian lullaby her mother had sung to her. The child quieted.

Then something further occurred to her: The Rileys had been in prison. She was very sure their period of detention was more than eighteen months. That meant Timmons had the power to have them released as well. He was able to manipulate the justice system, assuming they had not simply been broken out—though she would have noticed that in the newspapers.

Very well, she thought as she wiped a bead of sweat from Lilith's brow. *Let us say that it was a warning, what am I expected to do to show that I understand? Or is it too late for that?*

Perhaps if she were to book passage back to Earth immediately? She could do this with the Bursar. She did not imagine she would be the first person to take fright at their situation and want to go home as soon as possible.

She turned away from the stars. When they were always visible they lost their allure. They were merely burning balls of gas, like humanity's own sun. She leaned back against the wall and pressed the back of her head against the glass.

In the world of trade, Timmons was a man with considerable influence. He clearly possessed far more of it in the shadow world of his illicit dealings. A man who was used to getting his own way, to doing exactly as he desired with no one to gainsay it.

He was also in his late fifties, which made him a product of the best period of the British Empire's industrial growth, and the worst in terms of its social attitudes.

And here was she. A woman—worse, an Indian woman—who had thwarted him twice. She had removed the Guru, whom he had used to gain stock market knowledge, and she had exposed his scientists for killing children.

She had made him look weak.

And now he was getting his revenge, a concept she understood. He did not want to recruit her, nor did he want to send her running. She was precisely where he desired her to be, trapped aboard one of his own vessels and powerless.

He was wreaking a prolonged revenge upon her. He had killed Valentine and ensured that she knew about it. The purpose of the interview with Scott was not to warn her off, it was to bring her in, to ensure she boarded the vessel.

Once she was within their power he began his true revenge: killing the Rileys the way Lochana and the General had died. Making it look as if Clement had killed Margaret and then committed suicide was clever.

There were two conclusions that could be made from that. The first was a comfort: the need to hide the existence of the murderer from the crew suggested that they were not part of the conspiracy against her.

The second conclusion was more worrying and sinister. If he was wreaking his revenge on her, there would be more murders. No doubt in the style of her other 'cases'.

She took a bottle of water from the cabinet. All the drinks had drinking straws; in the extreme lack of gravity, liquids would not pour at all, preferring to cling to their containers with their surface tension. Sucking through straws was the only practicable solution.

She sat on the edge of the bed beside Lilith, who was now quiet.

There was a decision to be made. She could either ignore the murders to come or investigate and attempt to prevent them.

She was now engaged in a game with Timmons. She could simply choose not to play, but it was a little late for that. She had committed herself by coming aboard. It was her error for not realising what Timmons' might be capable of. If she had not come aboard, the Rileys would still be alive.

And there were the people who would now die—innocent people. It was not possible for her to stand idly by and become an accomplice to their deaths. She was responsible for them even if they were unaware of it.

Besides, any opportunity to thwart Timmons' murderer would add to the indignity suffered by the man. What better way to push his face deeper into failure than for the ship to arrive with those destined to die still alive and the murderer found…

She paused in her train of thought.

Not 'found', she thought. *Dead.*

iv

"Thank you for seeing me, Captain," said Maliha. He stood politely behind his desk. She had noted how Voidshipmen tended to be clean-shaven, unlike the traditional seafarers. Perhaps it was because those who flew between planets were not subject to weather.

She had brought Izak and Lilith. She did not fear for their safety, at least not yet; there were other deaths that would have to occur before they became at risk. She sat them on seats by the wall and asked them to be quiet, then took the seat on the other side of the desk to the captain.

"Well, I do need to have your statement of events, Miss Ganapathy."

Maliha opened her reticule and extracted a sheet of paper. Pens did not work very well in extremely low gravity, so she had written in pencil.

"This is my statement as Alice Ganapathy," she said.

He took it from her and glanced at it, then placed it under a glass paperweight which contained the flower of a Martian Iron Lotus in its centre.

"'As' Alice Ganapathy?"

"Quite so. That is a name I can use, but it is not the name I generally go by," she said. "Do you know the name Maliha Anderson, Captain?"

He shook his head. "I can't say I do."

"She's the goddess," said Lilith in the pause Maliha had left.

The captain frowned.

"I do apologise, Captain," said Maliha. "I am escorting these children to Venus. They have very poor manners and have not learnt much discipline as yet."

"Spare the rod," he said.

"Yes, of course," said Maliha. "However, if we can get back to the point?"

"I do not know what the point is, Miss—what should I call you?"

"Ganapathy would probably be best," she said. "If you do not know my name—although it has been in the papers once or twice—I will have to explain."

"I would be grateful if you would."

"Captain, I am, for want of a better word, a detective."

He burst out laughing. Maliha sighed.

"Have you received a report from Dr Leeming yet?" she asked.

"I'm not sure what business that is of yours?" He frowned and his eyes darkened as the humour went from him.

"Sir, you clearly do not take me seriously and I am about to demonstrate that you should," she said. "And from your reaction I deduce that you have received the report."

"What of it?"

"Maxwell Spencer had a severe blow to the head, did he not?"

"How could you possibly know that?"

"Because Valerie and Maxwell Spencer were murdered by a third party, and the event was staged to appear as if he stabbed her with scissors and then killed himself."

"The blow to the head is not conclusive of that."

"Of course not, but when you take into consideration the other facts, it is inescapable," she said.

"What facts?"

"Why would he go to the trouble of using scissors, which would be extremely difficult, when he could just shoot her?"

He looked troubled and pulled a folder from under a rock on his desk.

"I did wonder," he said.

"The last thing you want on your ship is a murderer on the loose."

He nodded, looking quite unhappy. Not an unusual expression for the people she dealt with.

She proceeded to explain that the Spencers were really the Rileys, had recently been in prison, and that she had known them from an earlier case. She did not go into detail on that; it would be inconvenient if he thought she was at the centre of it all. As indeed she was.

"Can you find the murderer?" he asked.

"I can try," she said. "I will need your cooperation, but I stand the best chance if no one knows I am investigating."

He nodded. "Do you have any suspicions?"

"Not yet."

She got to her feet by the simple expedient of applying pressure to the arms of the chair with her hands. He rose as well.

"I would like to be kept up to date on your progress," he said.

"I cannot keep coming to your office," said Maliha. "Perhaps we could allow the doctor in on the secret? It would not be unusual for me to visit him regularly, after my faint. He can carry messages between us?"

The captain nodded. "Yes, I will speak to him."

With that, she gathered up the children and prepared to leave. "One more thing, Captain. I require a complete list of all crew and passengers."

"Oh," he said. "Is that entirely necessary?"

"Entirely," she said. "If you can arrange for the doctor to bring it to me as soon as possible, please."

"Very well."

Maliha took her leave of him and made her way back down to Deck 4 and took the shaft up to the dome. She headed to the bench where the Rileys had died. She did not expect to find anything, but she had to look.

"Are you going to kill the murderer, Goddess?" asked Lilith as Maliha examined the bench itself, then looked under it.

"I would prefer not to," she said, scanning the ground. It had been swept recently and there was nothing to see. *Though I will not hesitate if I must.*

"Why not?"

Maliha stood up and looked around. There was a stand of tall plants in pots five paces behind the seat. She went over to it. There was very little ambient light, as the Sun's rays did not penetrate miles of atmosphere. The shadows were sharp and deep.

She searched carefully as she spoke. "Because it would be much more satisfying to stop him without killing him, and then deliver him to his master to demonstrate just how powerless he really is," she said with a smile. "That, Lilith, would be the true essence of vengeance."

The first pot was empty. Maliha went to the next one. Nothing.

"And then you'll kill the master?" asked Izak.

"He killed your Valentine," said Lilith.

Maliha lost her smile. "Yes, children, I think killing the master at that point, when he knows he has failed, would be the perfect moment."

"But you have to find the murderer first?" said Izak.

Maliha nodded. "Yes, but in truth I do not think I will be able to until after the next death."

"Why?"

Maliha sat on the bench and glanced at the stars rotating beyond the dome.

"The deaths of these two were carefully planned. There is no evidence to find."

Clement Riley/Maxwell Spencer had had a severe blow to the head. No direct evidence, but there were hints and suggestions.

"Children, would you mind sitting here and pretending to be the poor people who were killed?"

She placed them next to each other. "I'm going to pretend to be the murderer. When I say 'go' you pretend to be grown-ups talking while I creep up on you."

She went to the plants and stood out of view. "Go."

"Sit up straight and use your fork," said Lilith sternly. Maliha smiled and then came out of hiding and moved across the gap.

"I saw you," said Izak as she approached.

"Which means they probably knew the person or weren't concerned about him," she said. "Now I just want to try something."

She took off her shoe. It wasn't very heavy, but it would serve. Standing back slightly, she swung her arm as hard as possible, as if she were coshing Izak over the head.

She flew upwards. Lilith and Izak both laughed.

When she finally fell back to the deck she came up to the seat and had Izak move out of the way. She repeated the blow, but this time she held on to the back of the bench. The blow would have landed successfully.

"Well, that answers that question," she said. "The person who did it was either a regular passenger with experience of the environment, or one of the crew. Anyone else would have made a complete mess of it."

v

The ladies' room was buzzing with the news of the murders. Maliha had decided to brave that den of prejudice and spite to see if there was anything she could discover.

The room bore some similarity to the reading room on board the *Macedonia*. There were racks of newspapers and magazines, shelves of books, and various groups of settees and comfortable chairs. A major difference was that every piece of furniture was firmly bolted to the deck and had belts to assist a lady to remain demurely in place.

There was no possibility of crossing the room with any decorum, but at least it was the same for everyone. Void-travel held no prejudice; it made everyone suffer.

Even so, there was a slight diminution in the volume when she entered. She had returned to standard Edwardian dress in order to reduce her conspicuousness. Unfortunately her darker skin tone, with her father's European bone structure, was all the women needed to categorise her as someone to gossip about but not to speak to.

"Maliha! Hey, Maliha!"

She jerked her head up at the American accent, and a white arm was thrust above the sea of heads and bonnets. A wave of disapproval and tutting circulated around the room. It was almost impossible to increase her pace without risking collision with some piece of furniture or, worse, one of the ladies, so Maliha resigned herself to following the path between them with care, and suffering the glares of those who felt they had been violated.

"Excuse me if I don't get up," said Constance Mayberry, indicating the belt she had buckled about her midriff. There was a book on the table beside her, held in place by a spring-clip. She looked expectantly at Maliha with her hand held out; it took a few moments for her to realise the woman expected a kiss.

Maliha took her hand and allowed herself to been drawn down, and they touched cheeks. Maliha took the opportunity to whisper in her ear, "Call me Alice only."

There was a conspiratorial smile on Constance's face as Maliha drew back and settled herself into the chair beside her.

"I am so happy to see a friendly face, *Alice*," said Constance with more volume than was required. "Someone I can talk to."

Maliha, however, was less than happy. She wondered what pretext had brought Constance on board. It was not that she thought Constance's life was at immediate risk—if the murderer followed the rules Maliha was expecting, then it would be someone close to Constance who would die so she could be accused and convicted. But that was not a certainty.

"We need to catch up," said Constance. "Let's go for a walk, shall we?"

So Maliha was forced to run the gauntlet of stares once again.

"What a place," said Constance with a grin—and before she had shut the door, so her words certainly penetrated some distance back into the room.

"Are you with your husband?" asked Maliha without a pause.

"My husband is on Venus," said Constance in a tone of disgust. "And he has demanded my presence." Constance tucked her arm into Maliha's. "Enough about him. Let's go up to the dome and you can show me where those two were murdered."

Maliha had no choice but to match her pace as she set off in the direction of the shaft to Deck 4.

"I don't know anything about it."

"You, Ma—Alice, are a terrible liar," said Constance. "And since you are here using a false name—"

"It is my name."

"—using a different name to the usual," said Constance without hesitation, "I know you know all about it."

Maliha said nothing.

"And you're here all by yourself—"

"I'm not by myself."

"Every detective needs a sidekick to ask the stupid questions."

They reached the shaft. Constance plunged into empty space and caught hold of one of the rails, bringing herself to a stop. Maliha swung out over nothing and grabbed another handhold with her free arm.

"Up we go," said Constance and pulled.

By the time they reached the dome, Maliha had resigned herself. It was a small vessel and it was far easier to let Constance think she was helping than to stop her. Besides, it would be easier to keep her safe if she was close.

"So this is the place of the grisly murder–suicide." She almost seemed to be drooling. Americans were so unlike the British it was hard to imagine they came from the same stock, even though

Constance was from one of the oldest states and was probably as close to being British as anyone from that huge continent. "Can I sit where she was sitting?"

Maliha grimaced and then pointed at the place. Constance took hold of the back of the bench and pulled herself into position, then flung out her arms and legs and played dead.

She held the pose for a few moments as she rose into the air and dropped down again.

Maliha glanced around. There were a few other passengers on the far side of the dome but no one close enough to overhear.

"How are you nowadays, Constance?"

"I'm fine, Alice," she said. "Couldn't be better."

"You're not—" Maliha hesitated over the best wording for her question, "missing the Guru?"

Constance stopped pretending to be dead. She brought in her limbs to appropriate positions and sat up. "Oh, you mean *that*."

"I wouldn't want you to be…"

"Locked up with hysteria?" Constance said. "You should have thought of that before you had your boyfriend kill him—or is he your fiancé now?" She eyed the ring on Maliha's finger.

Maliha felt the tears before they blurred her vision. She wiped them away and, in that moment of not being able to see, she felt the impact of Constance, her arms wrapping around her, holding her very tight.

Maliha sobbed. Her grief had welled up out of nowhere, shattering the wall she had erected. She wanted to cry and scream, but that would not be British. And there were people listening. So instead her pain leaked out little by little as each sob shook her. But there was no catharsis.

"It's all right, honey," said Constance and patted her back. "You cry it out."

Maliha sat with Constance on one of the benches facing out into the Void. The tears had dried up and, with Constance's help, she had repaired the damage to her minimal make-up. She looked out on the stars. She could reach out and touch the glass if she wanted to. But she did not.

"Do you want to talk about it?" said Constance. "Did you part on bad terms?"

Maliha shook her head. "No, nothing like that. We had different paths to follow." She felt the tears welling up again. Her voice croaked. "I think he's dead."

Constance put her arm around Maliha's shoulder and gave her a firm squeeze. "Bill, dead? No."

"I had a message saying he was dead."

"I can't believe it."

"It's the same person who had that man and woman killed."

"Oh," said Constance. "Someone who plays for keeps, then. You sure must have got under his skin."

"Terence Timmons."

"Terry Timmons, the magnate?"

Maliha looked up. "You know him?"

"Not exactly *know* him, I guess," she said. "He's failed to turn up at any number of galas I've put on, or those of any of the other wives."

"Your husband knows him? Does business with him?"

"Everyone does business with Terry Timmons," she said. "He's got his fingers deep into every pie crust. He's richer than Croesus and, if the stories are true, he's the cleverest businessman this side of Hudson Bay." She thought for a moment. "Never thought he was crooked, though I guess that doesn't surprise me."

"Have you ever met him?"

"Once. He's got the manners of a prince." She absently rubbed her fingers across the back of her right hand where the man would have kissed her. "And a smile like a snake. When he looks you in the eye it's as if he's going to eat you whole and spit out the bones."

Maliha's tears were dry now. "Well, I'm going to kill him," she said.

If she thought her words would disturb the other woman, she was mistaken. Constance put her hand over Maliha's and squeezed. "If I can help, just say the word."

Maliha stared out at the stars. "Did your husband say why he wanted you on Venus?"

"Not really. He implied there were events to be organised, and that's my job, of course. So I have to be dragged across the Void to do it for him."

More machinations by Timmons? Maliha did not know whether she should tell Constance. Would it scare her? Would she even believe the story? It would be unfair not to mention it; she could be on her guard.

"Do you think it unusual your husband should demand your presence?" she said at last.

"We had spent a lot of time arguing about it before he left," said Constance. "I had no desire to go and for him the trip was just business. I was expecting his return. Instead I got a message. I mean, Venus is the devil's backside, if you know what I mean. Well, I've seen Buffalo Bill's show and that's the closest I want to get to any incarnation of the Wild West."

"Timmons is trying to hurt me, Constance."

Constance squeezed her hand again. "Trying? I think he's succeeded whether it's truth or lies."

"No, I mean he's playing games," Maliha said. "The two people who died here, I knew them. I mean, I'd met them. They were involved in the case with the General and his nurse."

Constance looked suitably shocked. "She was stabbed and he committed suicide, I remember."

Of course she did. On their first meeting, Constance and her friends had been all over Maliha because she was the only thing interesting in their lives—except for the Guru. They read the newspapers avidly and gossiped about everything.

Maliha nodded.

"I'm worried Timmons has someone on the vessel committing crimes that mirror my cases," she said. "He's taunting me and challenging me."

Constance was quiet for a few moments. "You think I was brought on board on a pretext."

"Yes."

"You think I'm in danger?" Her voice had become taut and her grip on Maliha's hand tightened.

"Or someone close to you."

"Your second case was the murdered teacher?"

"She was someone I knew from school," said Maliha. "Not a friend, but I knew her vaguely. She was older by a couple of years."

"You think he might use me to represent the friend?"

Maliha nodded. "Yes, or perhaps save you to be accused of murder later."

Constance sat back and sighed. "Don't that just take the biscuit," she said. "I could be a victim or a patsy. I always did enjoy following your adventures, Maliha, but I never wanted to be on the bad end of one of them."

"Alice."

"Sorry."

"So am I, for getting you into this trouble."

"It ain't your fault, honey," said Constance. "I know how to cut blame so it fits."

They were quiet for a time. Maliha's thoughts began to turn to the children—they were with a maid, but she couldn't leave them too long. Especially not Lilith.

"I have to go, Constance."

"Oh," she said. "I thought we might stick together. You know, best pals, and we'll be safer in numbers."

"I'm with someone."

"And they're more important than me?" Constance exploded and grabbed Maliha's arm, digging her fingers in painfully. Maliha looked into her friend's eyes and saw terror. She put her hand on her knee.

"I shouldn't have told you," said Maliha. "I'm sorry."

Constance's face dissolved into tears. "No, you're right. I'm being selfish."

"Come with me."

"No, you should go to whoever needs you."

Maliha did not think the overt emotional blackmail in Constance's words had been intentional. She was trying, despite her fears, to acknowledge Maliha's right to her own life. But that did not mean she wasn't moved.

"No, come with me," repeated Maliha. "It's all right, really. They're children. I can't leave them too long. One of them is not well."

"Oh," said Constance and visibly changed her thinking. "Sure."

They stood and made their way back down through the vessel.

"Where did you pick up a couple of kids?"

"In South Africa."

"Never been," said Constance. "What are their names?"

"The boy's name is Izak and the girl is Lilith."

Constance floated to a stop. "They're not Jews, are they?"

Maliha put out her hand and dragged herself to a stop, turning at the same time. The fire in her belly burned again. She had found it so easy to get angry since Johannesburg.

"What if they are?"

Constance caved in on herself. "Nothing."

"I'm half-Indian, Constance."

"I know."

"My maid was a man who wanted to be a woman."

Constance's face paled as what that meant seeped through her mind.

Maliha glanced round to ensure they were alone. "You allowed a man to relieve your *frustrations*." She spoke in forceful but low tones. She hesitated, but the anger burned too strong. "And I have bedded a woman."

Constance's expression was turning to one of fear again, but this time the cause was Maliha, who did not stop. "I, too, let the Guru have his way with me, in order to make him confess his crimes. I have witnessed men loving one another tenderly and I have seen children who have been abused for another's pleasure." She paused for a breath. "Do not presume to judge others, Constance Mayberry. Not if you want my protection." *Assuming I can provide it.*

Constance nodded and they continued in silence.

vii

Lilith shot across the room like a cork from a champagne bottle as Maliha entered. The girl ricocheted neatly off the ceiling, hit Maliha around her middle and clung. "Goddess!"

So much for being ill. Maliha sighed inwardly. The girl was young; she could never remember not to call her that in the presence of strangers.

Maliha introduced the very quiet and severely chastised Constance to Lilith and then a sulky Izak. She deposited Lilith on the floor and went to the door with the maid—Indian, like herself, perhaps in her late twenties, low caste by her skin and unmarried by her hair.

"How were they?"

"They are children, Miss," she said.

"How was the girl?" Maliha did not like asking leading questions, but she was unlikely to get anything volunteered.

The woman's eyes flicked in Lilith's direction and she hesitated.

"The truth," said Maliha. "Not what you think I want to hear."

"Yes, *sahiba*," she said. "She scratches sometimes as if she has lice, but there are no lice to see."

Maliha nodded; she had noticed the scratching.

"You are Durga Maa?"

Maliha weighed answers in her mind. "There are those who say so."

The woman fell to her knees, though in the low gravity it was a gentle descent, and touched Maliha's feet. Without even thinking, Maliha touched her head in blessing. She knew it was pointless to hope Constance had not seen it.

"Get up," she said, not unkindly. "Your first service is to the ship."

The woman did so with practised ease and did not fly up towards the ceiling. "The man and woman who died, was that your vengeance, Goddess?"

"My vengeance will be on the one who killed them," said Maliha. There was little point in telling the woman not to talk about her; it would only make her fear the wrath of the goddess when she let it slip. "Go along now."

The woman half-bowed and pressed her palms together at her forehead, then left. Maliha locked the door behind her.

"What was that about?" asked Constance.

"Doesn't matter," said Maliha.

"You talk funny," said Lilith to Constance.

"That's because I'm an American. You know where that is?"

Lilith shook her head.

"I do," said Izak. "It's on the other side of the world."

"Sure," said Constance. "But for me *your* country is on the other side of the world."

Maliha sat in the armchair. Movement on the ship was exhausting despite the low gravity. Sir Isaac Newton's inertia was still in full swing. One had to expend the same amount of energy to make the body move, but now one had to exert the same force to stop it again. Back on Earth one automatically relied on friction and gravity to do much of the 'stopping' for you.

There was also something comforting about being in the seated position.

She closed her eyes.

* * *

"They're asleep."

Maliha jumped and opened her eyes. The main lights in the room had been switched off and just the side light on the dressing table left on. Constance was crouching at her side. The forms of Izak and Lilith were lying in the bed.

"I sleep in the bed with Lilith," said Maliha.

Constance shrugged. In an easy movement, keeping hold of the side of Maliha's chair, she stood up. "Having all the furniture screwed to the floor makes things a mite inconvenient," she said.

"What sort of things?"

"Mind if I squeeze in beside you?"

Maliha shuffled over. The seat was wide enough to take both of them, though they were pressed together. Maliha could smell a lemon scent from Constance's dark hair, and her arm was only comfortable wrapped around the other woman's waist.

"I never bedded a woman," said Constance. "What's it like?"

"How have you been dealing with your hysteria?" asked Maliha. She did not put it past the American to want to use Maliha for her personal relief.

"Oh, I got one of those devices," she said. "The ones that vibrate?"

Maliha nodded; she had seen the adverts. "Does it work?"

"Oh yes, quite satisfactory. Though", said Constance, smiling, "not as rewarding as the personal touch."

"You miss the Guru?"

"Of course I do."

"I'm sorry."

"I don't miss the man, just what he could do."

Maliha suppressed the words of agreement she had been about to utter. She could feel them coming out with far too much enthusiasm. The man had been very knowledgeable and experienced. Instead she reached around Constance's waist with her other arm and held her tighter in silent acknowledgement.

"You avoided my question, Miss Anderson."

Maliha sighed. "It is different but equally pleasant."

There was a long silence.

"Could we…?" said Constance. Her voice was almost pleading and Maliha wondered whether her mechanical stimulator was as effective as she claimed.

"No."

"Why not?"

"I did it because I was angry with myself for driving Valentine away," said Maliha. "It was like a justification."

"That doesn't make any sense."

"No." *And it means I'm as human as everyone else.*

There was another silence. The throbbing of the ship's engine filtered through the walls and floor. It permeated the ship, but only when there was complete quiet was it noticeable.

"Am I going to die, Goddess?" said Constance.

"Don't call me that."

"Your Lilith calls you that, and so did the maid."

"For a start, Mrs Constance Mayberry, you are an American and no doubt ostensibly a Christian, if you believe in anything at all. And that means you're just being hypocritical."

"I won't deny it. I perform the required actions, but my soul is not in it."

Maliha laughed quietly at the joke.

"But," Constance paused, as if trying to force her thoughts into words, "perhaps I just need something to believe in."

"I don't think I'm a safe bet."

"At least you're real. I can touch you. Maybe that's what people really want from their deities."

"That's very philosophical."

"I think you get a right to be philosophical when you're under a sentence of death."

They both looked up as a knock came at the door.

viii

"Miss Ganapathy," said the doctor at the door. "You did not make your appointment. I was concerned for you." He glanced through and saw her guest. "And Mrs Mayberry, good evening."

"Doctor."

Maliha frowned. She had been so distracted by Constance she had entirely forgotten her scheduled meeting with the doctor. She was not concerned that she had failed to turn up for her appointment, but forgetting was entirely unlike her. She did not forget *anything*.

He stood at the door, clutching a blue pillbox and his bag. "Perhaps I should return another time?"

"No, Doctor, please come in."

He entered the dimly lit room and took in the forms of the sleeping children.

"I'll be brief, of course," he said. "Your sleeping pills." He handed over the box, which rattled. He hesitated and glanced at Constance. "Perhaps if you could come by the surgery in the morning?" he said. "For the other matter we discussed…?"

"It's all right, Doctor," said Maliha. "Mrs Mayberry is an old friend and is aware of the matter. You have some documents for me?"

He glanced at Constance again and then fiddled with the clasps on his bag. Once open, he removed several sheets of paper and handed them over.

He frowned. "Are you sure the deaths were committed by a third person?"

"I am afraid so."

"The first murders in the Void."

Maliha thought of Valentine but chose not to disagree with Leeming.

"Well, I'll be moving on then," he said as Maliha studied the sheets. She flipped from one to the next, scanning across the double columns of names, addresses, nationalities and cabin numbers.

"Please take these with you," said Maliha as she finished the final page and thrust the sheets at him.

"But I thought you needed them."

"I have a total memory, Doctor," she said. "I only have to see the list once and I can recall every detail."

He looked at her as if he didn't believe her.

"On the third sheet, second column, fourth name down." She waited while he wrestled with his bag and the sheets. "You'll find Francis Gray, British, country of birth, France."

She stopped. Francis Gray?

"That is quite amazing."

He continued to speak, but Maliha wasn't listening. Why had that name stuck out? She did not know a Francis Gray but it sounded a little like …

"Françoise!"

Animated into sudden motion, Maliha pushed past the doctor and used the impetus to drive herself towards the door, throwing him backwards and off-balance. She pressed her left hand against the wall, arresting her motion, and yanked open the door with her right.

She pulled herself forward into the doorway, then lifted her feet and thrust against the frame as if jumping sideways. She flew along the corridor like an avenging angel, heading for the nearest shaft between floors.

Her destination was two decks up. This shaft was the down one, but she had no time to waste.

She barely touched the floor as she cannoned through the corridors, twisting and bouncing at the corners. She caught hold of the central cable of the shaft and brought herself to a halt. She was breathing hard with the exertion and her corset pinched.

She glanced up as she pulled hard, launching herself upwards. She careened past a man in a brown suit, who uttered an indignant epithet at her.

On the correct level she stopped for a moment to take stock. The rooms were similarly numbered to her own deck and the one she wanted was nearby to the right, but the concierge's desk was in the other direction.

There was no point going to the room if she could not get in.

She controlled her breathing and was grateful that her complexion would hide the flush from her exertions. She pulled herself to the left briskly but not too fast.

The man at the desk smiled as she approached.

"Lost, Miss?"

"Francis Gray in room 34."

"Yes?"

"I believe she may be ill—"

"*Mr* Francis Gray?"

Maliha's head span. It *had* said 'Francis' in the document, the man's spelling of the name. She had been so certain. It made such perfect sense. It fitted.

But a man and not a woman.

The giddiness had not left her. The concierge and his desk seemed to turn upside down as she stretched out her arm to prevent the impact with the floor that was slowly approaching her.

* * *

"Miss Ganapathy?"

Maliha opened her eyes. It was the doctor. She was in a small cabin with administrative notices on the walls and a pile of linen on a desk. The concierge's backroom, then. There was a clock on the wall; less than five minutes had passed.

"How did you know where I was?"

"Can you sit up?"

There was some residual dizziness eddying through her head, but she nodded and allowed the doctor to assist her onto a chair.

"This is the second time you've had a fainting spell," he said and took her wrist in his fingers to take her pulse. He pulled out his watch and counted for ten seconds. "A little high but not too much. As I said before, you should be resting."

"I am not ill," she said. *I cannot be ill.*

"Weightlessness can affect people in different ways," said the doctor. "Some never take to it at all. I insist you rest for at least an hour after meals. Your friend, Mrs Mayberry, says she will ensure your cooperation in this matter."

If it means Constance stays close by, that would be helpful, thought Maliha, then she said, "You still haven't said how you found me so quickly."

"One did not need to be a detective," he winked. "Obviously you were intending to visit the cabin of this Francis Gray. I was intercepted by a crewman who had been sent in search of me."

"I see."

"Mrs Mayberry is waiting outside," said the doctor. "She'll see you back to your room."

Maliha stood up and gripped the bolted-down chair to ensure she remained steady. "Thank you, Doctor."

CHAPTER 5

i

The following days passed without event. Maliha remained in her cabin with the children between meals. Constance stayed with her most of the time.

The minimal gravity lessened as they progressed. This was a problem with the ether-propellers. For a given propeller there was a limit to how much force it could exert through the ether itself. This translated into a maximum velocity for any vessel. It took *Atacama Sea* seven days to accelerate to its maximum and the same to reduce back to nothing. The middle section of any voyage was, therefore, spent in complete weightlessness and, for this trip, that period was eight days.

As they approached the vessel's maximum velocity, what little gravity there was became less.

In very low and zero gravity the passengers were encouraged to remain in their cabins, strapped down whenever possible. The majority complied, since the experience was quite unsettling. Food was supplied directly to cabins by the stewards and consisted of paste in flexible containers.

Izak was difficult to manage; he fretted at the confinement. Constance took him under her wing and found reading books in the library. She attempted to instruct him in his letters, but writing was difficult in this environment. However, she managed to get some of the fundamentals of reading into him.

It was Lilith who gave Maliha most concern. After her initial exuberance and joy at the weightlessness, she tended to sulk more and became listless. Keeping her in her bed was not the trial that Maliha believed it should be for one so young.

"Why don't you let the doctor examine her?" said Constance on the second day of their confinement. It was late evening by the ship's clock and the children were in bed.

Maliha shook her head. "I know as much of disease pathology as he does."

"But you do not have his experience."

"He will not know what this is." Maliha felt the tears welling up in her eyes. She wiped them away with her sleeve. They would not roll down her cheeks but simply hung on her eyelashes.

"She is going to die, Constance," said Maliha. "And there is nothing anyone here can do about it." She paused. "Nothing that I can do about it."

"What are you talking about?"

"Are you aware of the introduction of the eastern grey squirrel into England?"

Constance shook her head. "What's this got to do—"

"Evidence is mounting that the grey squirrel is displacing the native red squirrel."

"But I don't see—"

"The rhododendron was introduced as a decorative plant into the gardens of England, but it escaped captivity and is now growing across the landscape."

"So everyone can enjoy it, not just the privileged few."

"It has no predators," said Maliha patiently. "What's to stop its spread?"

"It's just a plant."

"The grey squirrel is bigger and more powerful than the red; it can survive the winters better. What's to stop it?"

Constance looked blank. Maliha continued. "Kew Gardens closed an exhibit of Martian plants last winter when some moisture crept into the display of red weed."

The other woman brightened up at that. "Oh yes, I read about that in the paper."

"What if it had been raining?"

"But it wasn't."

Maliha sighed. The arrogance of humanity sometimes made her despair.

"Look, Alice," said Constance, carefully remembering the correct name. "I just don't get your point at all."

"Our scientists, hunters, botanists, zoologists and just plain tourists bring creatures into environments in which they have no predators, nothing natural to control them, and then those things escape."

"You're saying something has been brought in?"

"What about the diseases that Westerners brought to indigenous races? Ones *we* knew how to handle but their bodies did not?"

Constance glanced at Lilith on the bed. A wide strap held her gently but firmly in position.

"She's got a disease?" Constance looked scared. "You have me in here when she's got a disease?"

"It's all right," said Maliha. "She does not have a disease, but she has been infected with something and she is not contagious." *At least, not yet.*

"She should be in the Infirmary," said Constance and began to fiddle with her buckle.

"She cannot go to the Infirmary, Constance," Maliha said calmly. "I know how to deal with it."

Constance glanced again at the child, as if she were a monster poised to pounce.

"You should have told me."

"I just did."

"How bad will it be?"

"I do not know the details." Maliha remembered the dying child in the crib in the deserted diamond mine. Eyeless and whimpering but vicious, like a cornered rat. Her eyes burned once more as she thought of Lilith that way.

Constance turned back to Maliha just as she wiped more tears from her eyes. She looked almost surprised to see them there. *Most people think I am no more than an automaton*, thought Maliha. *Why?*

"Can we talk about something else?" said Constance. "Something more cheerful?"

"Such as?"

Constance looked away and her cheeks turned pink.

Maliha sighed. "You want me to tell you about my lovers."

"I am so frustrated … Alice, you have no idea."

Maliha wondered why it should be assumed that she had no idea what it was like to be frustrated in one's physical desires. Valentine was kind and gentle, but he lacked skill. After the Guru and Françoise, that was frustrating.

"Not here," said Maliha, and Constance looked relieved, as if she would be glad to escape the room that contained the dying child. "Let's go up to the dome."

Constance smiled. "Are you drawing out the anticipation to increase the enjoyment?"

Maliha merely frowned and shook her head slightly. It was simply the best place to have a private discussion, since almost everyone would be confined to their rooms.

She drifted across to the bed and checked the children to ensure their straps were properly fastened. Although the doctor had not ordered it, she had abandoned her support underwear and felt more relaxed.

It was terrible to think that beneath Lilith's dark-skinned exterior the fungus was growing and entangling itself around her nerves, as well as through her brain. The tears threatened to seep from her eyes again, but she had to school herself against it. She must observe everything she could; they could do nothing about the infection now, but perhaps in the future there would be a defence against it.

She feared that was wishful thinking. It was a certainty the fungi of Venus had their own predators, but what damage would those do if they were introduced into our environment to deal with the first invasion?

There were too many imponderables. She doubted it could be calculated even if they had a Babbage machine the size of St Paul's Cathedral.

"Come on, Alice."

Maliha went.

ii

They did not hurry as they floated in complete weightlessness along the companionways and up the shaft. They transferred to the second vertical passage to take them to the dome.

The terms 'horizontal' and 'vertical', 'up' and 'down', had no real meaning any more, but humans had built their vessels with those concepts in mind, so if one saw a bench and table above one's head and the stars at one's feet, one would feel instinctively that one was inverted even without the sensation of gravity to enforce it.

Maliha righted herself by grabbing the back of the bench and applying turning pressure. She and Constance did not sit on the bench but hung in the air. Maliha was not sure why she was acquiescing to the prurient curiosity of her friend. Was it because she had never been party to this sort of conversation when she had been at school?

It seemed as if boarding school was a lifetime away, and yet it was barely two years since she had finished the examinations and taken leave of the terrible place. In that time she had done things she would have thought quite inconceivable. And gained the love of a good man.

And lost him.

Tears again. It was not that she was incapable of crying—she had done enough of it at school when there was no one to hear or see—but she seemed to be doing so much more of it. Perhaps she should not be surprised.

She pushed against the bench with her foot and drifted towards the glass dome. If she squinted she could imagine there was nothing between her and the black, and she would drift out beyond the ship to travel on forever completely alone. There was something about the fancy that appealed to her.

She cancelled her motion with a simple touch of her hand against the glass. Constance came up behind her. They were in near darkness, as the ship had already rotated and the Sun was now behind them. She searched for the Earth among the stars and found its pearl-white brilliance glowing in the Sun's reflected glory.

"Did you let the Guru touch you?" asked Constance.

Maliha thought it was strange: the Guru had had so many women in his power and he had 'touched' them all. She and Constance had shared a man.

"Yes." Then Valentine had crashed in and killed him.

"Did you enjoy it?"

"I was there to force a confession from him, which I did."

"But did you enjoy it?"

Yes. "He gave me physical pleasure, just the way he did for every woman he touched," said Maliha. "So that he could gain information about your husband's business from you."

Constance was silent for only a moment. "Why do you make it sound as if I'm being punished?"

"I'm just stating the truth, Constance."

Maliha turned away and propelled herself along the dome, with the floor eight feet 'below' her. This was flying.

The vessel was still rotating and the constellation of Orion floated into view. It was so much more vivid here than from Earth: Rigel, Betelgeuse, Bellatrix and Saiph at the shoulders and feet, all a hard blue colour, save for the red of Betelgeuse; Alnitak, Alnilam and Mintaka, the stars in the belt, and in the scabbard, the smudge of cloud that comprised the Nebula of Orion. So distant yet visible, and therefore bigger than the human mind could comprehend.

"Who next? Valentine or your woman?" said Constance, catching up with her.

"I drove Valentine away for killing the Guru," said Maliha.

"So this woman seduced you because you were lonely and in need?"

"No, I kissed her first."

"You did?" Constance sounded both astonished and impressed. Maliha did not understand why. It had made perfect sense at the time. She did not regret it; she had learnt a lot. "And she didn't object?"

Maliha smiled. "Well, she was surprised, but that was only because she had been trying to find the right time to do it to me. She prefers women to men."

"And you took her to your bed?"

"I was overwrought. I went to her and we comforted one another."

"Comforted? If you want to call it that," said Constance. "What's it like with a woman?"

Maliha pushed off and glided smoothly up towards the apex of the dome, nearly thirty feet from the deck, though it did not feel that way. The electric lights were on and cast pools of brightness among the shadows. They were alone.

"What's it like?" demanded Constance.

"Some of it was tender, but she was quite domineering, forceful like a man. Almost as if she had been born into the wrong body."

"But she felt like a woman?"

Maliha turned and frowned. "Of course."

Constance whispered. "Did you achieve paroxysm?"

"We both did several times that night." Maliha smiled at the memory. For a little while Françoise had made her forget and that was the reason she had gone to bed with her, to achieve oblivion.

"Several times," repeated Constance, with a sad longing in her voice. Maliha wondered whether pandering to her friend's curiosity was perhaps not a good idea after all.

Constance's next words were so quiet Maliha could barely hear them, and yet they were so predictable she almost did not have to.

"Would you spend the night with me, Maliha?"

Maliha looked out into the black onto which a myriad diamonds, sapphires and rubies had been sprinkled.

"I cannot."

"I need you, Maliha, please." Her voice cracked as she uttered the words.

"I'm sorry."

"Aren't I good enough?" she said, her voice rising in volume. "You'll bed some French bitch but not me?"

"It's not the same," said Maliha. "I'm not the same."

"Please, Maliha, I'm going quietly crazy here," she said. "This is why I went to the Guru in the first place. You just don't get it."

"Can you not do it for yourself?"

"It's not enough."

"Do you not have your device?"

"That is not enough."

"What about one of the stewards?"

"You expect me to fuck just anyone?"

Maliha hid her surprise at the language, but they were discussing taboo matters that no one discussed so why should one not use forbidden words as well? "No, but..." *But what?* "What did you do before?"

"I went mad with frustrated desire," hissed Constance.

"And you're telling me that you did not indulge your sexual appetite?"

Constance went silent for a few moments, looking deep inside. "You think I haven't tried?" she said. "Yes, all right, I have been with men, lots of men, more men than I can even remember. Does that shock you?"

Maliha would have shaken her head at the question but thought better of it.

"But you know what men are like, they can't think past their own needs, beyond their own pleasure." Her words were pouring out in sobs that drifted out into the dome and disappeared into the dark. "You're lucky if you achieve any pleasure in their hands."

It was something Maliha could not deny.

Constance pointed accusingly at Maliha. "The only one who knew what to do was the Guru and you killed him."

"He was taking advantage of you."

"*Do you think I cared?*" Constance screamed and broke down in tears, her chest heaving with sobs. "He ... made ... it ... stop."

Using a steel girder for leverage, Maliha pushed herself in her friend's direction and, as they bumped gently, she put her arms around her. She thrust against the glass dome with her foot, pushing them towards the exit.

"I can't stand it," sobbed Constance. "You just don't know what it's like. My every thought is how to reach that point. My body aches for it. I would do anything. You're the goddess, Maliha. Please make it stop."

iii

Maliha had taken Constance back to her own room, but took care not to cross the threshold. She had the fear in the back of her mind that Constance's desperation might cause her to force herself on Maliha. Her repeated attempts at inviting her in only confirmed that fear.

Constance had given up finally, her eyes swollen with tears and holding a kerchief to her nose. Noses did not run; their contents oozed out. It was not pretty, but a crying woman never looks her best.

Maliha returned along the passageways with her thoughts turning and twisting almost at random through her mind.

The name Francis Gray kept returning to her. She had managed to hold it at bay for several days, but nothing further had happened on board the vessel. It was almost as if the deaths had really been a murder–suicide and nothing else would occur, as if everything she had thought was just her imagination.

But it could not be. The Rileys had been aboard, released prematurely from prison. Constance was here too. If it had been just one of them, she might have accepted a coincidence, but both? No, she was not wrong.

Which brought her to Francis Gray. Was it too much of a stretch to link the name with Françoise Greaux?

Maliha's second case after leaving England had involved the torture and death of an old school acquaintance. But Francis Gray was a man, the concierge had confirmed it.

Maliha looked at her watch; it was 10:30pm ship's time and they were still a few days from the beginning of the deceleration procedure. She had not confirmed the truth of the concierge's statement. He might have been bribed, or Françoise might be dressing as a man. Given her sexual preferences, that was not entirely unlikely.

Maliha needed Izak.

With a purpose in mind at last, Maliha accelerated her motion and flew along the companionways and shafts until she reached the concierge's station on her own deck.

"How can I help, Miss Ganapathy?"

"I need someone to sit with my charge, the girl, for an hour or two," she said. "Can you arrange that?"

He could. And it was a few minutes later that one of the female staff arrived, looking tired and a little out of sorts. It could not be helped. Maliha would ease her disgruntlement with a generous tip.

She woke Izak, or, more accurately, discovered he was awake. "I stay awake when you leave, mother," he said. "For my sister."

She had him dress, then, out of earshot of the servant, she said, "I may need you to open a locked door."

He looked her in the eye and nodded with a serious face. "Is it the same as this one?"

"A passenger cabin, yes," she said. "What will you need?"

"Hair pins."

Maliha collected them and placed them in her reticule, then added a couple of metal clips and a measuring tape—just in case they might come in useful.

Leaving Lilith and the maid, they made their way back through the ship. It was now past eleven and the electric lights had been switched to night. Only every third one was lit and that had reduced brightness, so they floated like ghosts along shadowy corridors.

They used the correct shaft to move up two decks because it was farthest from the concierge, then they went around the deserted companionways so as not to pass his station.

At the door of Francis Gray, Maliha hesitated. She could not decide whether to knock first. If she was wrong then Francis Gray would be inside, either awake or perhaps asleep. If she knocked she could pass off her error as simply being on the wrong deck.

If she was right the perpetrator might be inside. She shivered at the thought of what she would find.

She pressed her ear to the door but could hear nothing. She examined the frame—even turning upside down completely to look at the gap at the door's base—in an attempt to determine whether there was any light in the interior. She thought not. In the end she decided against knocking and indicated for Izak to break in.

She moved away to give him space and kept her attention on the approaches from each direction. Sounds of two people talking filtered from somewhere. A man and woman arguing. Izak was hunched around the lock with his legs floating up behind him as he worked.

He had looped the measuring tape around his wrist and then the door handle to stop himself from floating away as he applied pressure to his tools. The clunk of the door unlocking was ominously loud. Before Maliha could stop him, Izak took hold of the grip beside the door and opened it.

Maliha pushed off from the wall and entered the room, flying over Izak's head. The room was illuminated by a bedside lamp that cast a light as dim as the one in the corridors. The layout of the room was similar to her own, with identical furnishings, except it lacked a sofa. The bed lay to the left and the bottom end came into view first.

There was a figure lying in the bed. No, not lying on it but floating above it: naked and tied spread-eagled.

"Izak, get help," she ordered quietly. "Find the doctor, don't tell anyone else." Her trajectory took her to the far side of the room and she impacted the wall almost directly above the figure. She turned. Izak was staring, his eyes wide in horror. "Go, now. And shut the door."

He focused on her and nodded. With a final glance at the body, he pulled himself from the room and closed the door. Maliha scanned the room more thoroughly and allowed herself to breathe a little more easily. She had not trapped herself in the room with the perpetrator.

She drifted up to the ceiling and used it to push herself down beside the bed.

Although the head was covered in a sack, the body of the woman in the bed was known to Maliha.

Françoise.

Her beautiful skin had been mutilated with bruises, cuts, cigarette burns and parallel lines sliced across her abdomen. Darkened marks between her legs suggested she had been raped violently. Maliha untied the sack and pulled it from Françoise's face. Her hair was cropped short like a man's and her face was barely recognisable beneath the bruising.

Her skin was pale and cool to the touch.

Grief overtook Maliha and she wept. She brought herself closer and reached out to touch the cheeks with her tear-dampened fingers. She ran the tips across the woman's swollen lips.

At her touch the lower lip moved. Maliha froze. She rubbed her eyes to see more clearly then brought the salty tears to Françoise's mouth. At the touch of the liquid they moved again.

Like sandpaper across metal, a word crawled from her throat. "Please."

Françoise's chest moved in a sudden intake of breath.

For a second all conscious thought was lost to Maliha—she had been so sure Françoise was dead—then she became action and threw herself across to the basin. She pumped out a globule of water and, carrying it in her hand, brought it back.

She dipped her finger into the twisting bubble of water and brought it out with drops of liquid attached. These she applied to the girl's lips; Françoise sucked them into her mouth like a baby, and Maliha saw her neck convulse in swallowing motions.

Maliha repeated the manoeuvre again and again. When all the water was gone she applied herself to the knots. It took an age to get them free, but eventually she succeeded and Françoise curled in on herself. Maliha found a dressing gown and wrapped it about her. Françoise floated like an unborn child wrapped in its amniotic membrane.

Maliha fetched more water and fed it to her.

One of Françoise's eyes was so bruised it could not even be seen, but the other was less damaged. It opened.

"He said you would not come," she whispered.

iv

"She needs to be moved," said Maliha.

"I agree. The Infirmary would be best." The doctor had spent the last hour assessing the damage and tending to Françoise's external injuries.

"No," said Maliha. "She needs to be reported as dead."

"I really don't think I can do that."

Françoise lay in the bed. She was covered by a sheet, which had been tied to the bedposts at the corners. It provided a gentle but firm restraint against her drifting off into space. She had lapsed into unconsciousness again.

Izak was no longer with them. After returning with the doctor, Maliha had sent him back to their cabin with orders to lock the door and not open it for anyone except her.

Maliha turned back to the doctor. "I understand you have your usual protocols, Doctor, but this is a highly unusual situation." *And it has everything to do with me.* "The person who committed this crime was the same one that killed the Spencers," she said. "And if he knows that he has not succeeded in killing her, he may attack another passenger."

"I don't see—"

"Doctor, you are aware that I am undercover and investigating these deaths?"

"So the captain said…"

"Exactly. Your captain." She stopped. She was fairly sure she had said enough now, and that he just needed a little time to absorb the new idea.

"But if not the Infirmary, then where?"

"The cabin of Mrs Mayberry," said Maliha. "She will be able to tend her." *Which will serve the double purpose of occupying her mind and keeping her out of harm's way.*

"Do you think she will agree?"

"Oh, I am certain of it. She is a very sensitive woman."

"I will arrange it in the morning."

"Now."

"Oh, come now, Miss Ganapathy," said the doctor. "You cannot expect me to be waking up staff to move her."

"I think you are missing the point completely," she said. "The person who did this could return at any moment" —the man's eyes flicked towards the door—"and she needs to be gone before he does."

He hesitated and she could almost perceive the machinery of his mind considering the possible consequences. "I see…"

"In addition, the fewer people who know the better. So that means your good self alone and not the captain."

"You don't expect me to lie to the captain?"

She said nothing.

"But surely you don't suspect *him*?"

Maliha crossed her arms.

"I see. If I am the only one to know then, if the murderer attacks her again in the new location, you will know the information came from me."

Maliha doubted he had noticed the smudges of blood on the walls. The man who had done this had been entirely happy to slam his victim into the walls and ceiling like an angry child venting its anger on a doll or teddy bear.

Was it rage or just work to him?

He sighed and looked at his patient. "As she has lasted this long it is unlikely she is haemorrhaging internally. We can move her."

She hoped it was the former—rage. Dealing with cold rationality was harder.

"Well then," said the doctor. "We must be about it, time is getting on."

If they were on Earth or even Mars, moving Françoise, particularly in secret, would have presented some difficult obstacles. But in weightlessness the problem was far less serious and was unlikely to cause their patient any more harm.

They released Françoise from the sheet and wrapped her in a yellow and black-spotted fur coat from the wardrobe. It made her appear dressed and kept her warm. It seemed almost callous to Maliha, the way they dressed her even though she remained unconscious. A scarf around her head hid the evidence of damage.

Together they gently guided the limp body through the passages and up the shaft to Constance's cabin. They encountered no one on the way. The dimly lit passenger corridors were completely deserted.

"You had best go make your report, Doctor," she said. "If you could leave my name out of it, that would be preferable."

The doctor nodded. "This is a worrying business, Miss Ganapathy," he said. "Do you think there will be any more attacks?"

With ten more days before landfall? thought Maliha. *It is almost a certainty unless I can do something about it.*

"I hope not," she said. "But we must be on our guard."

As the doctor disappeared around the corner, Maliha knocked on the door.

"Who is it?"

"Alice Ganapathy."

"Oh."

There was a long pause. Françoise's body tended to drift towards the wall. Maliha puzzled over this until she realised it was due to the gentle rotation of the vessel.

There was a click as the door unlocked and the flushed face of Constance appeared. She looked about to say something then saw the floating body. Not only was she unable to speak, she did not move. Maliha took the initiative and manoeuvred the body through the door, forcing Constance to back away.

Maliha followed, shut the door and turned the key.

She glanced around the cabin. One of the drawers of the dressing table was slightly open and Maliha could see part of a small device. Constance followed her gaze and pushed herself across to shut the drawer.

Maliha did not want to spend time in discussions, so she simply stripped the hat and coat from around Françoise and watched as the horror of her beaten body shook Constance.

"Is she dead?"

"No," said Maliha. "And Miss Greaux is keen to live."

Maliha brought the unconscious woman across the room, stripped back the bed's top sheet and gently turned her until she was lying in the bed. Maliha tucked her in as before.

"You're leaving her here?"

"Yes, this is the safest place." Maliha turned round and faced Constance, whose flush had dissipated, making her paler than usual. "The doctor is going to report that she was found dead."

"But that means the murderer will move onto the next stage of the plan."

"It does."

"Me."

Maliha shook her head. "No, Selina and her mother were implicated as murderers, they did not themselves die."

"So he will try to frame me for murder?"

"If you remain in here with Françoise, that will not happen."

"But—"

"Constance, you need to remain safe and Miss Greaux must be tended back to health. It is a perfect situation."

"But—"

"Please do not argue. I have enough to worry about. I need to know that I can rely on you." It was difficult to strike a stern pose in weightlessness; Maliha had to make do with a look.

"All right."

"Thank you," said Maliha. "When she wakes she will want water; she is quite badly dehydrated. She won't feel hunger for a while. The doctor says that, although the injuries look bad, they are, for the most part, superficial. He could find no broken bones." *Though several joints were dislocated. It is just as well she was unconscious when they were repositioned.*

"I understand."

Maliha pushed against the bed and floated over to where Constance stood, next to the dresser. Taking her hand, Maliha brought it up to chest height and clasped it tight. "I am counting on you, Constance."

She nodded.

Maliha kissed her on the cheek and felt the woman tremble.

The touch of Constance's cheek was like a promise Maliha knew she would never fulfil and she felt the guilt of it.

v

Despite the risk, Maliha returned to Françoise's cabin.

The ropes that had bound her were still attached to the bedposts in neat loops, with stains of blood on the ends she had untied. She searched the obvious locations but found no weapons.

Françoise's wardrobe contained men's off-the-peg suits. Their labels indicated that they were from the Army & Navy Stores, easy for a woman to walk into and pretend she was buying for her husband. There were also men's undergarments, socks and shoes, all from the same shop. Pondicherry, being a French territory, did not possess an Army & Navy store, but all major British ports did and they sold everything a person might need for an expedition or just a journey.

It seems she had fully equipped herself at the Fortress before boarding.

There were no ladies' accoutrements to be found at all, beyond a large cigar box containing cotton sanitary pads. Perhaps she had her usual clothes in her hold luggage. Or she had decided to dress as a man permanently. Still, that was not relevant.

If Françoise was on this vessel, it meant that she had been persuaded to come by an agent of Maliha's nemesis. Françoise seemed to have very little in the way of paperwork; there were her travel documents, in the name of Francis Gray, and a ticket. But no other correspondence. Then again, that was not unreasonable—who would have written to the newly created entity Francis Gray?

Maliha had been through every drawer and every cupboard; there was no further information about Françoise and nothing about the murderer. He was as careful as he had been with the Spencers. Perhaps he might have left fingerprints, but Maliha had no way of collecting them or comparing them to everybody's aboard the ship.

Well, that was one thing, she thought. The man was unquestionably on the vessel and there was no way off. They were both trapped.

Who was he?

Passenger or crew? If he was crew then he would probably have duties and shifts during which he could not be here torturing his victim. He had access to the necessary information about who to kill, but, as this vessel belonged to Timmons, that was not a signifier.

If he was crew he would also have access to more areas of the vessel and be able to use the crew passageways. A crew member would have better knowledge of the ship as a whole. Then there were the knots in the ropes that had been used to tie Françoise: they were neat bowlines, exactly the right knots to use in the circumstances, which again suggested someone in the crew. But it was not conclusive.

Maliha rubbed her eyes; she was tired. A glance at her watch told her it was now after midnight. It was hopeless. There was no way she could determine who it was from the meagre facts at her disposal.

But there was a way.

Maliha turned the lights off and returned the room to its original lighting.

She tied her hair back as tight and as close to her skull as she could. In the dim light it would probably look like no more than a shadow, at a distance.

As long as she was able to lure him into the room, she would be able to discover something about him. She opened a wardrobe door, removed her shoes and placed them inside.

She told herself that she was not a fool, but she acknowledged the pattern of behaviour she saw in herself. Each of her adventures reached the point at which she would sacrifice herself in order to achieve her goals.

Was it hubris or humility?

She disrobed, reaching behind herself for buttons as she turned slow somersaults in the air. If he were to come upon her now, she would be helpless. Wriggling from the cocoon of her dress, she placed them under a strap inside the wardrobe.

It had always worked before, allowing the murderer to imagine she was the victim. But always, before, she had had help nearby. This time she could not call for assistance. She glanced at the button that would summon the concierge. It might not save her life, but it would bring the man to justice.

The silk underwear was the last.

She shut the wardrobe door on her clothes and turned to the bed. She stretched and felt the scarred skin on her back pulling. Absently she rubbed the ridge on her thigh and then, for completeness, the one under her left breast. War wounds. She thought of Valentine.

There was the chance, of course, that the murderer would have heard that Françoise had been found and was dead. He would not return and this would be for nothing.

Maliha looked at the ropes. She could contrive to hold the ones that should be around her wrist, but what about the ones for her ankles? There was nothing she could do except make her own loop and slip her feet into them.

Floating above the bed, splayed out and naked, was the most vulnerable she had ever felt. It suited the importance of the situation.

When he opened the door the first thing he would see would be her feet, just as they had been the first thing she had seen of Françoise. Though her skin tone was a little darker than a European woman, it was white for an Indian, and in the half-light he would not notice.

Then he would come in and look further up her body. She was smaller and slimmer than Françoise, he would realise the difference quickly. She did not know what would happen then.

It was not long before the joints of her arms and legs ached from holding them in the same position for so long. It was similar to what she had experienced when she had demanded Valentine whip her, though at the time the pain from the lashing had been uppermost in her mind.

Valentine thought she had been punishing him and when she claimed she had done it for the experience she had thought she was telling the truth. But floating here she finally admitted the truth. She had explained to Françoise that being Indian was to feel shame. She had brought about the destruction of her own family what worse shame could there be? The scars she wore on her back were her shame.

She had kept her watch on; by the time he noticed that, he would know for certain she was not his expected victim. It was half-past one. There had been a chart on the captain's wall showing the various shift patterns for the crew. She brought it to mind and read it.

The next shift change was in half an hour. If the murderer was a crew member, he would probably turn up a little after that time, and the same went for a passenger—he would make sure he knew when the crew was most likely to be wandering about the companionways.

She sighed. She had to try to stay awake.

Maliha came awake from a doze at the sound of a key in the lock and someone humming tunelessly on the other side of the door. She went cold. The key rattled again with the action someone makes when they expect a key to turn but the door is already unlocked. The humming stopped.

He knew.

Would he enter anyway? Perhaps he would think he had forgotten to lock it. Would he run? She held her breath.

A patch of light grew across the ceiling above her as the door swung open.

"I'm coming in and I have a gun." The voice was that of a man, not young but not old either. Middle class and well-educated. A shadow moved into the path of light. "Oh goodness, you have nothing on. I'm going to shut the door and I won't look. Why don't you put a dressing gown on?"

Maliha had not known what precisely to expect, but everything she had considered involved some sort of aggression, whether physical or just verbal. She had not expected polite consideration. The light on the ceiling closed down again and she heard the latch click.

She lifted her head to see the dark form of a man. True to his word he was facing away from her, but he was holding out a gun so she could see it.

She unhooked her ankles from the loops and pushed herself across to the wardrobe, where she had seen a man's dressing gown. She pulled it out and wrapped it around herself.

"You're Miss Anderson?" he said without turning.

"Yes."

"Are you decent now?"

"I am."

He turned, keeping one hand on the door handle for leverage, and pointed the gun at her.

"He said you would find me."

"Who?"

"I am not permitted to say," he replied. "But he said it wouldn't be until we were approaching Venus. Perhaps you are cleverer than he thinks."

Maliha studied him. He was wearing the uniform of a steward, though he seemed a little old for the job, perhaps in his fifties. His skin was not as dark as one might expect a regular crewman's to be.

"You don't seem like a murderer," she said.

"No," he said. "Though I don't really know what a murderer is supposed to look like. Do you? It seems to me that anyone could be a murderer, with the correct leverage."

"It still requires the person to make the decision to do it."

He said nothing to that; his focus seemed less on her and more on himself.

"You don't look like a steward."

He shrugged.

"Are you going to shoot me—I don't know your name?"

"I'm not allowed to tell you that either," he said and glanced at the bed. "Is the woman dead?"

"Françoise?"

"Is that her real name? I thought it might be Frances."

"She's not dead."

"Oh, that's a relief," he said. "If you get the chance, could you apologise to her? I didn't mind killing the other two so much. They weren't very nice people. But torture is horrible and, while I don't know why she was dressed as a man, she didn't seem a bad sort, for a Frenchie."

Maliha frowned. "If I get the chance? Aren't you planning on shooting me?"

He looked up and his eyes glinted in the light like dark pools. Maliha reached over and switched on the main light near the bed. His skin was pale and unshaven. His eyes were solid black. Terror clutched her heart.

"He said you would know what this means."

She nodded.

"I don't want to die," he said. "But there's no hope for me now."

"Does it hurt?"

"Every muscle aches and sometimes I just lose an hour," he said. "It's been difficult keeping any sort of schedule. Or keeping food down. But the headaches are the worst and I really can't stand pain."

Without any further warning he lifted the gun to his temple and fired. His head jerked to the side and he went limp. The hand holding the gun reacted in the other direction and gun went sailing away. Maliha froze for the merest second as she watched the life go out of him. She did not know whether he had died too fast for the fungus inside him to react, but she could not take the chance.

She took the deepest breath she could and held it in. He was by the door. She dare not open it for fear of letting the fungus spores escape into the ship and infect others. But she could not hold her breath indefinitely. She pushed off, not for the door but after the gun. It struck the opposite wall with the clink of metal on metal.

She crashed into the wall and grabbed the weapon out of the air, then pushed off again towards the far side of the bed. Wedging herself under it, she tried to control her panic, then, holding the gun with both hands, she aimed it at the window.

The first shot almost ripped the gun from her grip and the bullet struck the metal above the window. It was a revolver and that meant only four bullets left. She had to get this right.

Her lungs throbbed with the desire to breathe. She fought the urge and took aim again. The second bullet hit the glass near one side and it cracked. The next hit on the right as her hands wavered. The pane shattered and shards flew off in all directions, but there was another layer beyond it. Her imagination filled the air with swarming spores as she took aim again and fired.

This time she managed to hit the middle. The outer pane cracked. She pulled the trigger again. It clicked. Click. Click. Empty. Spots formed in front of her eyes and Maliha desperately wanted to breathe in; there was lovely air all around her.

She heard the outer pane crack again and saw the striations extend through the pane. She flung the gun at it. It struck and the glass exploded outward. Wind whistled around her, escaping into the Void. The body of the murderer accelerated past her head and squeezed out through the empty window frame.

She could hear air screaming in around the door, but there was very little left in the room and she still could not breathe. Not until she was sure all the infected air was gone.

The gunshots would bring help but not fast enough for her.

The only thing big enough to cover the hole was the mattress, and that was attached to the bed frame. She let herself breathe out little by little as she felt along the mattress. There was a flap of cloth held by a button. She fumbled and undid it.

The sound of screaming air was reducing, but that meant there was very little air remaining to carry the sound. Cold seeped through her limbs and scalp.

She was sure the room would not be completely robbed of atmosphere as more would flow in around the door from the rest of the vessel. But the air pressure must now be the merest fraction of that on the highest mountain.

She found a second flap and unbuttoned it. The mattress flapped up and away from her, but it hinged on the other side where two more flaps no doubt held it in place.

The mattress had lain on a grid of interlocking metal springs. She clutched at them and pulled herself across the bed. Her naked legs lifted upwards as the flow of air pulled her towards the broken window. She clung tighter and walked herself across the bed.

Her eyes felt strange, as if they were pulling from her sockets. She slammed her eyelids shut and worked from memory. She found the first button and released it. Her lungs were empty of air as she found the final button. Her muscles were cold and she felt as if her entire body was freezing.

She desperately wanted to breathe in. Her head throbbed. But she only needed a little longer.

She forced her eyelids apart and looked up at the shard-edged window, into the deepest Void. She curled up to bring her legs under her and hooked them into the bed springs. Digging the fingers of her right hand into the mattress, she released the button with her left.

The mattress tried to pull away from her. She tightened her grip and dug her other hand into it. It stretched her out as it pulled towards the opening; only her toes held her in place. She took one last look to judge the angle, unhooked her toes and launched herself and the mattress at the window as she finally succumbed to the blackness.

vii

"Welcome back to the land of the living, Miss Ganapathy."

Maliha stared at the ceiling. Steel girders curved above her, painted pale blue. She felt stiff and there was a gentle pressure holding her on the bed. "How long have I been unconscious?"

The smiling face of the doctor came into view. "Four days."

"Four days!" she pushed back the sheet that covered her and found there was a restraining strap across the bed. She fumbled for the buckle.

The doctor placed his hand on her shoulder and pushed her back onto the pillow.

"There is no need for excitement," he said. "In fact, that is the last thing you should be experiencing."

"The children, Mrs Mayberry and her … responsibility."

"Naturally we took your charges under our wing and have a maid looking after them. They both insisted on coming to see you every day. They wanted to stay with you, so we have allowed two visits each day."

"Constance?"

"Mrs Mayberry also visited and sat with you."

"And Francis Gray?"

"Sadly Mr Gray has been reported as dead."

Maliha must have looked suddenly concerned.

"But Mrs Mayberry's young French companion is alive and well, if a little bruised."

Maliha tried to relax. She felt sick and various parts of her body ached.

"The captain asked to have a word with you as soon as you were awake."

She nodded. "Of course."

The doctor moved away and then turned back to her. "I can't decide whether you are tremendously brave or utterly foolhardy."

"You would not be the first person to ask that question, Dr Leeming."

Despite her desire to leave the bed and go in search of Izak and Lilith—especially Lilith—and determine the state of Françoise, Maliha forced herself to lie back.

She had no memory of what had happened after she had succeeded in sealing the window, or at least reducing the escape of atmosphere. She did not enjoy such high levels of physical activity; she would rather leave that to someone like Valentine.

The thought of him brought tears to her eyes once more. It seemed that her sojourn in the vacuum of space had not damaged her tear ducts.

* * *

"We are down one steward."

Maliha jumped; she realised she had drifted off to sleep. The captain stood a short distance away. He was not smiling.

"But on par with passengers," she replied. She wriggled to rise into a sitting position. The bedgown she had been given was of a thick material and loose enough to disguise the detail of her body. Only the broadest brushstrokes remained. Even so, she saw his eyes flick to her breasts.

"If you would care to explain?" he said.

"The steward was your murderer and I asked the doctor to declare Francis Gray dead from his injuries."

"You are quite presumptuous."

"You asked me to solve the murders," she said. "And I have done so."

"Except we have no murderer."

"He had the gun—it went off when I confronted him. The window was broken by gunfire and he was sucked out. I barely escaped with my life." She had not lied and it was a sufficient answer to satisfy him. He would fill in the parts she had omitted, incorrectly, just as she intended. "There was nothing I could do." *And if he had remained on board he might have infected everyone with his spores.*

Truthfully she was not entirely sure he would have done so. He was still in his right mind and perhaps that meant the fungus had not fully matured. But she had no idea and she certainly could not have taken the risk.

She could not be completely certain she was not infected, but she was fairly sure that, if she was, it was due to her previous exposure in Africa. It would take several weeks before she could declare herself in the clear, and they would be on Venus in a week at the most.

And then she would have a much more difficult task.

"And how am I supposed to deal with this additional passenger?"

"Why not say the documentation was filled in in error? Why not simply destroy it?"

"Francis Gray is not a man."

"No, but what's that to you?"

"A passenger travelling under false pretences."

"Like me."

"At least you have some claim to the name."

Maliha felt her constant simmering anger rising. "Honestly, Captain, I really don't care. This is not my problem. I have dealt with your murderer while attempting to protect your passengers. How you deal with the consequences is not my concern."

He looked for a moment as if he was going to respond in kind but then thought better of it. "I understand you must be tired, Miss Ganapathy. I am sorry to have disturbed you. Perhaps we can discuss this when you are feeling more yourself."

Maliha bit back a scathing retort to his condescending tone and simply nodded.

The captain withdrew, but the doctor came in as he exited. "I would say there is a little too much colour in your cheeks."

"Really?" she snapped. "How could you possibly tell?"

The doctor blinked once and retreated the way he had come. Maliha frowned and crossed her arms, but it felt awkward so she let them lie along her legs instead. She glanced around; there was a book on the bedside table. She picked it up and glanced at the spine: Milton's *Paradise Lost*. She tutted and put it back.

She forced herself to relax.

Could Valentine's death have so completely upset her equilibrium? She had never been so volatile before. Her time in the boarding school had taught her to suppress everything because any demonstration of emotion or interest would be used against her.

Perhaps she should use the powders the doctor had been giving her. But no, she needed to keep those for later.

She would have to apologise to the doctor. And the captain. She might need their help when they reached Venus.

After a quiet and boring hour, a steward brought a plate of food. She was very hungry and consumed every part of it. Once the tray had been cleared away Izak and Lilith were let in. He was very serious, while Lilith bounced around as usual. She made Maliha smile.

Maliha took Izak's hand. "What's wrong?"

"They said you died."

"I'm here."

"You're the goddess," put in Lilith. "You can die and come back."

"The doctor brought me back," said Maliha. "Because I had not completely gone."

"I did not really think you were a goddess before," said Izak.

Maliha paused with the words 'I'm not' on her lips, but she glanced at Lilith and did not say it. "There will always be those who believe and those who don't believe." *And those who do believe will be more useful than those who do not.* Maliha hoped that, if there really were a god, he wouldn't mind her pretence.

She shook herself mentally. She was not a goddess and, if there were a supreme being, it really wasn't going to care what she did.

CHAPTER 6

i

"We can't see it at all?" said Constance, staring out into the unchanging Void through the glass of the dome.

"We're decelerating," said Maliha, "so our ether propeller has to be towards the planet." She glanced up at Lilith, who clung to the girders twenty feet above her head. The child's continuing energy made Maliha think that she had been wrong about the infection, but in the last week the whites of her eyes had dulled, first to cream and now they were going grey.

Izak had acquired a small ball from somewhere and the children were tossing it to one another. He never laughed nowadays but tended to his sister. He knew she was ill and he was no fool. He had understood Maliha's reaction back at Mama Kosi's house in Johannesburg and the conversations that followed. He did not ask any questions.

"It is a shame." Françoise's French-accented voice was clear, although she still carried the marks of her torture. She was dressed as a man and carried it off very successfully. She continued to use Constance's cabin and had expressed no desire to move, particularly not back to her original cabin, even if it had been permitted.

"That's what I mean," said Constance and ran her fingers along the back of Françoise's hand. "It's a shame we can't see it."

Maliha noted Constance was far more settled than before and, seeing her intimacy with Françoise, she was satisfied the other part of her plan had worked.

"What will you do when we land?" Françoise's comment was directed at Maliha.

"I will find Terence Timmons and deal with him."

"Pah, you do not think, as ever," said Françoise. "You are so impulsive—are you sure you do not carry French blood in you?"

Maliha frowned at the insult.

"Of course," continued Françoise, "coming from that little French quarter of India I suppose it is not surprising."

"The part of my blood that is not Indian is Scottish."

"*Oui*, and what are *les Écossais* but barbarian French?"

Maliha sighed; it did not seem the right moment to give Françoise a history lesson. Besides, there *might* be French blood in her. Somewhere.

"I am not impulsive."

Françoise regarded her with her head on one side and a look that exuded French derision. She said nothing.

I am not impulsive, I make plans. "I make plans and carry them through to their conclusion."

"*Ma cherie*, you possess, without doubt, the most brilliant mind," said Françoise. "However, you adopt the plan that puts you in the most danger and disregard all else."

"She's right, Maliha … Alice," said Constance. "I mean, throwing yourself at the Guru. Jumping on that Voidship."

"How do you know about that?"

Constance glanced at the children. Maliha's frown deepened. This was why she did not like having friends and hangers-on: she could not have any secrets.

"Allowing yourself to be captured by the Dutch Ambassador."

Maliha sat upright and grabbed the bench just in time to prevent herself from shooting into the air. "How could you possibly—?"

Constance waved her hand. "Businessmen talk to their wives, wives talk to each other, especially when someone so heavily involved in trade turns up shot in his own residence."

"I think you did something like this with the murderess on the Sky-Liner from England, *non?*"

Maliha nodded.

"And you nearly died on this ship," concluded Constance.

"It's not being impulsive; it's doing what must be done."

"You see, *cherie?*" This time Françoise was addressing Constance and running her gloved hand down her cheek. Maliha watched as Constance seemed to melt at her touch. "I told you she would not listen. What have we mere mortals to say to a goddess?"

"That's enough," snapped Maliha. "For a start, if you two are going to make love in public, I'll take the children below. I am not a goddess, nor am I impulsive."

Françoise turned and smiled. "Make a plan then."

"I can't."

"Why not?"

"I don't know enough."

"How are you going to punish this man in his own castle?"

"I don't know."

"How will you even get there?"

"He'll invite me in."

"And you will think of something when you are there?"

"Yes."

"Impulsive. Unthinking. Barely a hint of a plan."

Maliha knew that Françoise was goading her. She knew she should just walk away. But she could not. Was Françoise right? Was she really impulsive? Did she create plans that had no ending? Did she really just make it up as she went along?

"Always…" she started and then hesitated. "It is the truth that matters." She stopped again. "Only the truth. Don't you see? I am not important, it does not matter whether I live or die, as long as I know the truth."

"But, *ma cherie*, you are important."

Maliha shook her head.

"*Bien sûr*. There are people who love you."

"Valentine is dead."

Françoise made a noise of derision. "You think he was the only one who loved you? Am I no-one? What of your Amita? *Madame* Makepeace-Flynn?"

"Me," added Constance then nodded at the children. "And those rascals."

Maliha wanted to deny it, but she could not. Barbara had said she loved her like a daughter. Amita was so devoted it could barely be anything else but love.

"You love me?" she said finally.

"Much as I am forced to regret it every day, since I know you will not share my bed,"— Maliha noticed a frown flicker across Constance's brow; it was not going to be a happy parting when Françoise moved on—"yes, Maliha Anderson, I love you."

"Are you sure that's not just lust?"

Françoise smiled. "Oh yes, there is the lust, of course,"— Constance was becoming a storm cloud—"but I know what that is and I can separate the lust, so the thing that remains must be love."

"What about me?" said Constance.

Maliha marvelled at the way Françoise refocused her attention on her lover, drew her into a delicate kiss and washed away all the doubt. "You, Constance, are my special and most beautiful love."

"*Aaaaaaiiiiieeeeeeeeee!*"

Lilith's scream pierced the dome like a knife driven into the heart. It was loud enough to make thought impossible and told of a pain so acute it transmitted the agony to any who could hear.

"Goddess!" It was Izak. Maliha was already moving; she had launched herself in the direction of the children the moment the scream touched her ears. It was almost as if she had been waiting for it.

She focused first on Izak. He was pulling back from the twisting form of Lilith. She was arching her back and flopping forward, her arms and legs jamming out at odd angles then pulling in. It was if she was possessed by a demon trying to claw its way from her body.

The description was not entirely inaccurate.

Lilith drifted towards the deck. Maliha used the dome to push off and intersect the girl's path. Lilith screamed again, but it was choked off halfway through, as if the muscles of her throat refused to obey her.

Maliha grabbed her as she passed and wrapped her arms about her tightly, preventing her from lashing out. Her legs were still free and the child repeatedly kicked, driving her heels into Maliha's thighs and knees. The lack of gravity did not reduce the pain.

Maliha made shushing sounds, but even if the child could hear her it made no difference to her behaviour. Maliha's shoulder crashed into the deck. She cushioned Lilith from the impact, crushing her own chest and stomach.

She continued to cling to the little girl.

"I'll fetch the doctor," said Constance.

"No, he can't do anything," said Maliha. Lilith's struggling seemed to have lost some of its strength; her muscles were probably tiring. "Help me get her back to my cabin."

ii

"Is she going to die?" said Izak.

"Yes."

"But you're the goddess."

"I'm not."

Maliha had managed to make Lilith drink a sleeping draught concocted from the pills and powders the doctor had supplied. She had been holding them in anticipation of this day.

She had sent Constance and Françoise away after they got the child restrained. They had even had to gag her at first. It was just as well the default British approach was to ignore badly behaved children, as they had passed several people.

But now Lilith was lying quietly. Her breathing was hoarse, but her muscles only spasmed occasionally.

Maliha sat on one side of the bed while Izak stood on the other.

"You said you were the goddess."

"I never did, Izak," she said, treating him as an adult. He may be young but he had already seen horrors in his life she would never witness. She had never starved on the streets the way he had. The pain she had ever suffered was nothing compared to his.

Well, no, she corrected herself, but what she had suffered could not compare to Izak or Lilith's suffering. The girl's anguished cry was a pain that could not be truly expressed.

She did not imagine the creatures of Venus reacted this way. Were these fungal creatures parasites or symbiotes? It probably varied. But Lilith's reaction to this one, whichever it was, did not seem to be in the best interests of the fungus either way. It was uncontrolled.

Probably because our bodies did not react the way a victim should.

"It was other people who said I was a goddess," Maliha continued, as if she had not left minutes between her sentences. "It was a man in India. A man with his own agenda, who wanted to create a goddess to oppose the French and the British. To throw them all out of India. It was not my idea."

"You said we could call you Goddess."

"Because you would not stop." She wanted to shout at him, but it was not his fault. "I even thought it might be a good idea." Foolishness. What could she possibly have hoped to achieve?

The enemy was not Terence Timmons, his industrial empire or his fleet of slavers. The enemy lay before her, squirming and growing within the body of her child. Monstrous.

What kind of enemy was it that made you kill the ones you loved in order to destroy it?

"What will happen to her, Goddess?"

Maliha looked up and stared at him. He held her eye, steady, serious.

Despite being unconscious from the drug, Lilith convulsed and cried out in pain.

"The pain will get worse. The thing within her will escape and fill the air with its spores. It will infect you, me and everybody on this vessel. Then we will also die."

"Can you stop it?"

She hesitated and then nodded. *I can take away the pain; in fact, I have no choice. I cannot allow the fungus to run the full course of its infection. I must prevent it.*

"You will end her life?"

Maliha felt her face muscles tighten in prelude to the tears that came. She hated low gravity for forcing her to wipe away her tears. She wanted to demonstrate her grief, she wanted the tears to streak her cheeks, but in this place they would not.

"I have a knife," said Izak and pulled out a small pointed blade he must have stolen from someone.

She shook her head. "We cannot do that. If we do, the monster inside of her will still infect us all."

"Then what will you do, Goddess?"

"Make her sleep so deep she cannot wake up."

Maliha took a deep breath. She felt numb. No part of her body wanted to move—it was so unfair. Why was life like this? Why did an innocent child have to die? Why must she be the agency of that death?

Because she had the power of life and death over not only Lilith but everyone else. She was the only one who understood that all life on Earth now hung in the balance. She was the only one who had the power to warn them, who would be able to save them.

But only if she killed this one child.

Like an automaton she went to the cupboard and fetched the pills. Moving carefully in the low gravity, she ground the pills into powder and mixed them with water, churning every grain into the liquid until no more could be absorbed.

Lilith's cries were becoming more frequent. This was not entirely a bad thing as she would need to be at least partially awake to drink.

When Maliha turned back, Lilith's eyes were open and showed the glassy black with tiny white pinpricks where the pupils should have been. She struggled against the restraints but she was no longer complaining of the pain.

Maliha felt the tears again. She forced them back. She could not allow them now. She would weep later.

"Are you thirsty, Lilith?" she said, forcing her voice into calm. She glanced across at Izak; he still held the knife. His face was hard as stone and she saw a touch of red where he was pushing the end of the blade into his thumb. She closed her eyes, took a deep breath and opened them again. Now she wore a smile.

"I expect you're thirsty. I've made you a drink."

Maliha sat on the edge of the bed. She adjusted the straw. Lilith moved stiffly, as if her muscles no longer worked properly. Perhaps they didn't.

"Here, let me hold the straw to your mouth." She moved the cup and straw towards the girl, but the mouth remained shut.

"Open your mouth, Lilith." At the command, she did so, and closed it again when the straw touched her tongue. For the brief time her mouth was open Maliha had seen that the pink skin inside was now a dark grey. She could not even be certain the sleeping draught would work.

If it did not there was only one other solution.

"Drink."

There was a moment's pause then Lilith sucked at the straw and the liquid poured into her mouth. Maliha watched the muscles in her throat contract and swallow. Again and again. Lilith kept drinking and swallowing until there was nothing left and Maliha pulled the straw from her mouth. Lilith's mouth and throat continued to act as if the straw was still there.

Maliha put the cup to one side and took Lilith's hand in hers. It was slick and cold with sweat. Lilith tensed and convulsed; Maliha held her hand tight. "Lie back, Lilith."

The girl did so. Her eyes were closed. Maliha could almost imagine she was the same girl from Johannesburg. Without thinking, Maliha made a sound in her throat and coughed. For a moment she did not realise what she was doing. Then it came to her.

Maliha remembered her mother holding her hand the night before she was to leave for boarding school in England. Young Maliha had been so scared and her mother had not known how to comfort her. So she sang a lullaby, a song she had sung to Maliha to help her to sleep on the nights when her nightmares created monsters in the dark.

So Maliha sang her mother's lullaby for Lilith as she slipped away.

"The body will be consigned to the Void at eleven-hundred, Miss Ganapathy."

She nodded. The captain sat across his desk from her, smoking his overly ornate pipe carved from some black wood. Its double curve was highlighted by thick grain-lines, unlike anything you would see from an Earth tree.

"I am, however, somewhat at a loss as to explain how she could have died from black-eye."

Maliha had discovered there was a major hole in her knowledge. So much was happening on Venus and yet it went unremarked in Earth literature. There had been nothing in any medical literature about Venusian diseases.

Black-eye. Not common but not unknown. A danger in the torrid zones and fatal if not caught early.

"She contracted it on Earth," said Maliha.

"How?"

Because a shadowy division of the company for whom you work is experimenting with Venusian fungi on Earth. Some of it has escaped to infect animals and people alike.

"I couldn't say," she said. *Because that would mean explaining more to you than I am willing to do at this time.*

"And you did not report her illness."

"I didn't know how ill she was until last night," she said. "I knew she was under the weather, having bad dreams, but it could have been the unfamiliar surroundings."

He sighed. "You haven't been to Venus previously?"

She shook her head.

"You weren't in contact with someone who had recently been to Venus?"

"No, Captain, I told you."

He sighed and made some notes on the form he was filling in. "What shall I put as the girl's surname?"

"Anderson."

He looked at her and raised an eyebrow. "Not Ganapathy?"

"I adopted them under my real name," Maliha said. Unofficially, perhaps, but what did that matter? What is in the heart is more important than what is on a piece of paper. Now he would put it in writing and it would become the truth.

I was a terrible mother.

The captain finished writing in the boxes provided. "Are you planning to continue to the surface? You could simply wait in the station for the next flight back to Earth." He paused. "Many people do."

"No," she said. "I have business that will not wait."

"If I might make so bold, Miss Ganapathy?"

"Captain?"

"I would appreciate it if you chose a different vessel for the return journey." The smile he forced onto his face was more like a grimace. "Deaths on board a ship are counted against the captain. It's not an official policy, but sailors are superstitious. If there were to be more deaths on a vessel I commanded, it would become harder to find a crew that would serve under me."

Maliha stood up and offered her white-gloved hand for him to shake. He took it.

"I understand, Captain," she said. "I hope not to trouble you further."

She paused at the door. "How long until we reach the station dock?"

He glanced at the chronometer on the wall. "A little over six hours."

She closed the door gently behind her.

$$* \quad * \quad *$$

The ship's chaplain read a short service in the Anglican seafarer tradition. Maliha did not mind; she had put up with seven years of church on Sunday on the British coast, where there were often references to the local fishermen, their trade and their losses. In some ways it was familiar and comforting.

They were in one of the airlock antechambers. Lilith had already been placed in the airlock itself, completely wrapped and bound in a white sheet that revealed her outline.

There was only a small window through which she could be seen and, after the main part of the service had been delivered, each of the mourners—Izak, Constance, Françoise and the doctor, as the representative of the ship's crew—took a moment to look in on her.

The window was at a good height for a man and the doctor went first. He muttered *God be with you, child*, but for the three women and Izak it was out of reach. The chaplain had thoughtfully provided a box for them to stand on. They could have jumped, but that would have been undignified.

Maliha wondered what Constance and Françoise might be thinking as they took their turns. She let Izak go before her. He climbed onto the box and looked through the thick quartz glass. He brushed the back of his hand across his eyes then turned to Maliha; standing on the box, his eyes were on a level with hers.

"It is a lesson, Goddess," he said. There was a cough from the chaplain at the word.

Maliha looked at him without understanding.

"It is a lesson to you that you cannot save everyone, even the ones you love." He reached out and put his hand on her shoulder. "And it is a lesson to us that we must protect you and help you so you can save the rest of us."

She wanted to argue with him, to explain that his lessons were nothing more than a rationalisation of a bad thing that had happened by chance, but this was not the time.

He jumped lightly from the box and Maliha took his place. Her breath misted on the glass, but it evaporated almost as it formed.

There was no cure for black-eye once it had taken hold. Quinine held it at bay. If she had known this, Lilith would be alive. Quinine was easily available in the tropics; she could have given it to Lilith and she would be alive now. True, she would be leading a precarious existence in a constant battle to prevent the fungus from spreading, and it was not a perfect treatment—quinine could have terrible side effects and some people could not take it at all—but there would have been a chance.

"Give her your blessing, Goddess," said Izak.

The chaplain coughed again; apparently the reference to a goddess was annoying him.

Maliha placed her palm flat on the glass. She closed her eyes. "*Namaste*, Lilith. May you fare better in your next incarnation."

There was an ensign in the antechamber as well, responsible for the mundane and practical matters of the Void burial. He too was dressed in his best uniform and he was Indian.

"Do you wish to operate the door, Goddess?" he said.

Maliha jerked her head round to him. He had a gentle smile on his young, kind face. She nodded. He held out his hand to help her from the box, though it was hardly necessary.

He guided her to a set of controls at the side of the door. "You put your feet in the floor stirrups," he pointed to two leather loops attached to the deck, "turn this to release the air pressure and, when the red light is on, press this button." The rotating handle was marked 'Air valve' and the button was the door release.

Maliha slipped her shoes into the loops—they were very loose, being designed for men's boots—then turned the handle. Without the foot loops she would have turned herself while the handle remained motionless. There was a hiss that quickly faded and she could feel the metal of the wall between her and the airlock radiating cold.

The light came on. Maliha hit the release button with the heel of her hand. There was the whine of an electric motor and a metallic thump.

Maliha did not need to look to know that the residue of atmosphere had carried Lilith's body out into the Void, most likely, given their trajectory, to burn up like a shooting star in the atmosphere of Venus. A shooting star that no one would see.

She heard the door open and turned to see the chaplain leaving. The doctor came over and shook her hand. He mumbled his condolences, gave a casual salute to the other women and departed.

With the other crew members gone, the ensign moved round in front of her, removed his cap and knelt. He touched her feet. Maliha placed her hand on his head as her blessing, in return for his respect. Rising again, he pressed his palms together above his head and bowed, then scurried from the room almost as if he was embarrassed with himself.

"What was that?" said Constance.

"Acknowledgement of my status as a goddess," said Maliha and sighed.

Constance turned towards the door. "It's a shame we're not Irish."

"Why?"

"Because if we were we'd be having a wake and drinking more than is good for us, to celebrate the dead and the living."

"I have no desire to drink more than is good for me," said Maliha. "Besides, we're docking very soon."

Heat had been radiating into the passenger area from the inner walls of the hull for the last half hour. It had started shortly after they had broken through the high cloud cover.

The vessel was sealed against the vacuum of the Void and yet, to Maliha, it felt as if the air inside was getting damp. It was the Venusian day and the upper clouds were so bright they were difficult to look at for long. Mostly white, but there were glowing veins of red and yellow running through them: the burning clouds.

Fifteen minutes or so after the first layer of cloud, they approached a second—this one more closely resembled those she had flown above in Valentine's vessel, *Alice*. They were fluffy and mountainous, unlike the higher blanket of solid coverage.

It took several minutes for the shuttle to descend through these ones, in almost complete darkness apart from the flashes of lightning, which sometimes lasted for long seconds. The winds must have been tremendous, as the stubby-winged ship was thrown from side to side.

Unlike those on Earth, these vessels did not possess complete gravity nullification—they only had the normal Faraday Effect. They used rockets to assist their launch into orbit, and gravity to return.

They emerged through the cloud and the windows were immediately streaked with thick rivulets of water. That it was raining came as no surprise.

Venus possessed almost no seasons, since it had nearly no axial tilt with respect to its orbit around the Sun. The burning clouds never broke, so the Sun was always hidden during the day. The lower cloud levels were more like Earth's, but when they cleared, the heat at ground level increased and so did the evaporation of water from the ground.

She had read the joke about Venusian weather: "How do you know it's not raining on Venus? An umbrella can't keep you dry." When it wasn't raining, the humidity increased to murderous levels.

Waterproof boots were an essential and it was recommended that each person in a party be responsible for the condition of the feet of one other member. The war in the Crimea had been the first time medical attention had been directed to the rotting that could occur on feet that were continuously damp—and that included keeping them locked up in one's boots or shoes.

'Venus-foot' they called it. If you were responsible for your own feet, you might forget to check, or pretend everything was all right. Being responsible for another meant you were more likely to check.

There had been people selling quinine on the Void-station, in the form of tablets and drinks to be taken orally, and suppositories for the other end. And all for exorbitant prices. But the doctor's information was that black-eye was only contracted in the lowlands. As long as they kept to the highlands they would be fine.

Something large and bulbous appeared momentarily through the window, veins threading through a balloon-like bag that resembled leather. One of the floaters, medium-sized. They were hunted as easy sport but lacked any intelligence so did not try to escape, nor did they make very good trophies once they were deflated.

One of them must have hit a rotor because a lump of something fleshy splashed against the window and was promptly washed away by the rain and wind.

Maliha peered out. There were rectangular shapes in patterns of light and dark in the distance; it was hard to see anything through the deluge, but that must be the city of Regina. The British capital of the polar highlands. Although there were no seasons and the planet was hot across its entire surface, the polar regions were cooler than the tropics and the highlands cooler again.

It made this part of the planet at least tolerable. Barely tolerable, but humans had an insatiable desire to spread across any territory they could. One only had to think of the Eskimo living on the ice of the poles, or the Bedouins in the hottest deserts of the world.

Now they also lived in the wettest place in the whole of the Sun's family, short of being under water.

Inside the vessel the engines' whine increased, indicating the rotors were beating hard against the atmosphere. Maintaining ships in an airworthy condition in such a place must be a nightmare in itself, Maliha thought.

The ship landed with the very slightest bump. The normal Faraday gravity had been wonderful after more than two weeks in almost complete weightlessness, but then the steward called out that they would be going heavy and counted down from ten.

Maliha braced herself. Their muscles were certain to have weakened during their time in the Void and this was going to be difficult.

The steward reached one and Maliha sank further into the chair as she returned to full weight. Her first reaction was to pant. The crew of the shuttle were used to this and they gave the new arrivals time to adjust.

Maliha turned to Izak beside her. He looked worried. She forced a smile onto her face. "Are you all right?"

"I feel weak like a baby, Goddess."

"It may take a few days to regain our full strength," she said. "Do you think you can stand?"

He did not reply but unbuckled his belt and slid forward on the chair. His movements looked awkward and he had to concentrate to make them work. He slipped off the edge of the chair and his legs folded beneath him. She caught his arm and steadied him as he got his legs under himself properly and stood.

"Good," she said. "Let me try."

"I will hold your hand," he said in a tone that brooked no disagreement.

She undid her belt and took his hand. She grabbed the back of the seat in front and carefully pulled herself upright. The old injury in her leg ached. Did it mean that she would have to return to using a stick?

She released Izak's hand. "Let me lean on you," she said and placed her palm on his shoulder.

"Are you all right, Goddess?"

"I will be."

Together they slid out into the aisle. Around them others were getting to their feet; she saw Françoise in her male guise helping Constance. Someone was crying.

Maliha allowed Izak to guide her to the exit, where they arrived ahead of anyone else. The steward smiled. "Your first time?"

Maliha nodded.

The steward's grin expanded and he flipped a large switch on the inner wall. A grinding of machinery heralded the inner door sliding sideways as the outer one swung upwards. Maliha and Izak looked out on the bright, and very damp, new world.

v

The entire sky shone with an almost uniform brilliance. The hidden brightness of the much-closer Sun was dispersed and re-emitted from the cloud cover. What shadows there were hid beneath their associated objects. Every surface exposed to the sky reflected the same light. The effect made everything look flat like a child's painting.

Hot, moist air swept in as a gentle wind pushed it around and the air sparkled in waves of rainbow colours. Maliha gasped at the sight. It was as if the sky were full of rainbow fragments floating on the breeze. They came in waves, growing and shrinking, then dissolving into nothing but light.

"Every time," said the steward, but his voice sounded as if he was smiling. "You came on a good day."

"Rainbow breezes," said Maliha. "I read about them, but the descriptions were nothing like this."

"If you'd like to exit via the ramp and go into the immigration building over there to the right, your luggage will be unloaded and brought to you."

"Thank you."

Maliha and Izak stepped out into the sparkling atmosphere. Of course, the rainbows were always just out of reach. She understood that, because the whole sky was bright and the air was frequently full of suspended droplets of water, this caused the rainbow effect in all directions. It was not an uncommon meteorological event here on Venus, but it was one of the most beautiful she had ever seen. She could not imagine she would ever grow tired of it.

Once out from under the protection of the shuttle, they were victim to the more unpleasant aspects of the Venusian atmosphere. She could feel the intense radiant heat beating down from all parts of the sky. The clouds through which they had descended were moving swiftly away. Probably to the south, since most directions this close to the north pole were South.

They were wet through in less than a minute, not from rain but from the water suspended in the air. Being wet was something one learnt to live with on this planet. It was impossible to get away from, even here in the highlands.

Every building had a canted roof, just as they did back in England, but there was no guttering. The eaves protruded a long way from the walls and were shaped over the doors to turn any water away. The perimeter of the air-dock was marked by a fence constructed from some sort of dark wood.

There were numerous vessels of different types crammed into the space. Their sizes ranged from small passenger vehicles to big cargo vessels, but Maliha did not recognise any of the designs. The majority had large horizontal drums instead of wings or rotors. To Maliha's eye they looked ridiculous though she was aware there were other methods of obtaining lift—why this approach should be so prominent on Venus was a mystery.

They stepped out across the wooden boards that lifted them from the surface of the planet; there was a moss-like growth covering every inch of the ground she could see. Its green colour was more vibrant than any plant she had ever seen on Earth.

The boards changed into steps down from the raised area where the shuttle had landed. She glanced back and realised that even the shuttle was not sitting on the ground but was on a raised platform. Something moved in the green and caught her eye.

Where the water ran in rivulets from the higher ground to the lower, a spindly leg, reminiscent of a spider's, emerged from the depth of the green. It touched here and there, as if searching for a place to rest. In a sudden motion it plunged into the foliage. When it lifted back up, its end had pierced a soft-bodied wriggling creature like a fat worm. The leg, if that's what it was, withdrew with its prey into the moss.

Maliha shivered. It was not that she was afraid, but it was so alien. She did not know of any earthly creature that behaved in that fashion. She understood the flora and fauna of her own planet. The rules were different here.

They had moved ahead when there were raised voices from the shuttle. Maliha stopped and looked back. Several of the passengers were now following her out and down to the immigration building, but at the vessel's exit a man was protesting. A woman, perhaps his wife, was remonstrating with him, and the steward seemed to be coaxing him, but he would not leave. He turned and disappeared back into the vessel.

Maliha looked up as a flock of ... birds? ... passed overhead. They were high and there was no sense of scale against the bright sky. They did appear to have wings, but she could not be sure of the details.

"Don't look up," said a man as he passed her. She recognised him as one of the passengers. He was right; it was recommended not to look up when the burning clouds were exposed.

"Alice!"

Maliha turned and waited for Constance and Françoise to catch up. Her clothes were heavy with water and her legs were getting tired. Her thigh ached even more. She would have to get a walking stick.

"Isn't this the most amazing thing? Did you see the rainbows?" Constance was full of enthusiasm. She had shunned her heaviest dresses and wore something Françoise might have chosen.

"We should get inside," said Maliha. "It's not healthy to stay out in this heat too long."

"I thought you'd be used to it," said Constance.

"Heat combined with humidity is very taxing on the body," said Maliha. "Without the ability to sweat we overheat, and too much will kill you with heatstroke."

"Well, you're a bundle of joy, to be sure. Come on, Francis, let's leave Miss Misery-guts to her foreboding."

But Françoise stopped. "Why don't you go on with Izak and find us a place inside, *cherie*? I want to speak with 'Alice' for a moment."

If Maliha was not mistaken, a flash of jealousy crossed Constance's face, but then she smiled. "Sure. Come on, Izak. Let's give the *ex*-lovers a moment."

She headed away at a brisk pace. Izak glanced at Maliha. "Go with her, Izak. Make sure she doesn't cause any trouble." He hurried off after the American.

"Sorry," said Maliha, looking at the retreating figure of Constance Mayberry.

"She is a willing pupil," said Françoise. "Quite refreshing."

"And when you get tired of her?"

"Our break-up will be her idea."

"As long as you are all right."

Françoise shrugged. "I still have some bruises and scars that will never heal, but I am alive and I have you to thank for that."

"If I had realised earlier, it would not have been so bad. I am sorry."

Françoise shook her head. "I am grateful you came when you did. Now I understand what you went through and for that I am a better person."

"You talk a lot of nonsense, Miss Greaux."

"Hush, Miss Ganapathy, did you not know I am in disguise?"

Maliha laughed. Françoise was the only person other than Valentine who could make her laugh so easily.

"Do you have a plan yet?"

"I do have one, though I imagine you would think it impulsive."

"Whatever you need, Maliha, if it is in my power to give it, I will. This man had me tortured to make you suffer."

Maliha reached out and placed her hand on Françoise's. "Thank you. For now, if you could lend me your arm—I am not adjusting well to this full gravity."

vi

The immigration building was cooler, with significantly reduced humidity. Each room they entered that had an outer wall also contained a machine built into it that circulated the air, stripping it of both heat and water vapour.

She had taken a moment to examine one of the machines and realised, as she passed her hand over it, that it contained a novel application of a Faraday grid. Though she had no real idea how it worked, she surmised the reduced gravity might lessen the air pressure, which would force some of the vapour to evaporate.

Whatever it was, it made the environment more tolerable.

The immigration process was not stringent; they were merely required to give their names, which were checked off against a list, and the purpose of their visit. The city of Regina was a British colony and subject to British laws.

She noticed that the clerks and Customs men wore very light clothing, and all of them were deeply tanned. This would have been considered a terrible thing on Earth, their pasty skin reduced to a colour similar to the natives. It seemed that on Venus there was little choice in the matter.

From the air-dock, they intended to take a taxi to the hotel.

They stepped out into the heat once more. Maliha knew it wasn't that the overall temperature was hotter even than Calcutta—although it was usually equivalent to monsoon temperatures—it was that the humidity was always higher and the resulting effect was torrid in the extreme.

Deaths from heatstroke were common here, particularly among new arrivals, not to mention those that went quietly mad from the shadowless daylight. Perhaps the luckiest ones were those who took one look at the place and refused to get off the shuttle.

Everywhere there were raised walkways primarily constructed from a native wood—anything from Earth would perish in no time from the damp and the corrosive effects of the plant and animal life.

Why would anyone come here?

The same reason they went anywhere: there were resources to be exploited. The 'granite wood' fetched a good price, as well as all the normal minerals to be dug from the ground. There was coal to be had in abundance, along with petroleum products from which diesel fuel was distilled. And all of them available for those willing and able to work in such an inhospitable place.

Once the travellers had dealt with the relatively simple administrative details, they stepped out into the city of Regina.

Maliha rummaged in her carpetbag and pulled out two pairs of spectacles with heavily tinted blue glass; she handed a pair to Izak. He looked at her with a puzzled expression for a moment and watched as she put on her pair. He examined how the arms folded out, and followed suit. They were a little large.

Behind her glasses the world turned blue and it was much easier to see what she was doing without squinting. There were additional curved strips that prevented the infiltration of light from the sides. With this level of protection she glanced at the high clouds again. Now, rather than the homogeneous colours, she could see with better contrast how even those clouds were on different levels and flowed in streams.

The queueing area for the taxi rank was covered but open to the air. It did not make it any cooler, but she could imagine that an enclosed area would become like an oven.

"You must come to dinner," said Constance as they waited in the queue. Then she jumped and cried out as an insect with a body the size of Valentine's hand fluttered past.

The monster possessed numerous rudimentary eyes on the head section. There was the usual thorax and abdomen construction, but it had many more legs than one might expect and at least six pairs of narrow wings that spanned two feet. But its colours shone even through Maliha's glasses. She slipped them off and squinted as the creature floated back out into the light. It glowed in iridescent blues, greens and yellows that flowed across its form.

"It's beautiful," she murmured. She had seen plates in the book at the Johannesburg Consulate but had not believed the scale provided, and the printed colours did not do the real creature any justice.

"Are there more things like that?" muttered Constance.

Maliha looked at her friend almost with pity; she had clearly done no research. "I am afraid so, and some far less attractive than that one." Not to mention all the species yet to be catalogued, let alone discovered.

"I don't care what my husband wants," said Constance in a complete reversal from her initial reaction. "I won't be staying." She looked across at Françoise. "What about you?" Maliha could not mistake the sound of desperate longing in her voice. It was almost as if Constance was addicted to carnal acts.

A taxi arrived and carried away a party of three. They all moved forward.

"I am feeling quite *revigoré* … invigorated?" It seemed Françoise had taken the opportunity provided by the distraction to ignore Constance's question.

Maliha nodded. "It's all the plant life. Venus has more oxygen in its air. It has that effect." Rather than receive the medicinal benefits of oxygen in one's own home, one could simply move to Venus and have it provided for free.

Another taxi appeared; the city of Regina did not seem to have many. The arrival of a shuttle was probably their busiest time.

Since every roadway was also built up from the ground, the vehicles themselves did not need to be very different from those at home. They had four wheels, pneumatic rubber tires and were all large enough to have their own Faraday grids, which no doubt reduced strain on the raised streets.

Finally their time came and they climbed into the large interior of their ride. Maliha was particularly grateful for the reduced gravity; her thigh was aching. Porters ensured their luggage was stowed in the capacious rear compartment. The taxi also possessed a cooling unit and it was a blessed relief to be inside. Maliha gave the name of the hotel while Constance read her new address from a small, black book.

"Do come and have dinner with us this evening," said Constance.

Maliha looked at Françoise, who shrugged. "Françoise is staying with you?"

"I have employed her as my companion."

Maliha returned her gaze to Françoise whose lips crinkled into a smile. "It is a convenient arrangement, *n'est pas?* It had been suggested to me that a frontier such as Venus would be more tolerant to one with my—" her smile widened "—preferences."

"I doubt it," said Maliha. "But even if it were true, you have the appearance of a man. How will Constance's husband feel about that?"

Quite unashamedly, despite the presence of Izak, Françoise reached inside her shirt, adjusted something, and her bosom became more pronounced. She removed her tie and undid the buttons at her neck, revealing a little *décolletage.* "*Et voilà,* Francis Gray has disappeared and, with a little rouge, Françoise Greaux has returned."

Maliha shook her head. She did not think any good would come of this, but it was true that men were far quicker to assume relationships with men than women. And Constance's husband did not take a great deal of notice of his wife, which was part of the reason for her difficulties. But still…

But still it was none of her business.

The hotel was the first stop, since it was close to the air-dock. Hotel staff quickly unloaded the luggage, and Maliha checked to ensure they had only taken her trunk and smaller cases. Constance held the door open and leaned out. "Tonight at eight, Alice. Say you'll come."

"It's six-thirty local time right now," said Maliha.

"Is it? All right, nine then. Shall I give you the address?"

"I remember it."

Constance hesitated. "Of course, you do." She looked around and beckoned Maliha closer conspiratorially. Maliha played the game and drew closer. Constance reached out and took her hand. "I just wanted to thank you."

"For what?"

"You know," Constance glanced back into the taxi at Françoise then turned back to Maliha. "Introducing us. Especially as you have also *known* her."

Maliha suppressed the urge to frown and pull her hand away. Constance was trying to express her gratitude, which Maliha appreciated, but she lacked any discretion, which was less acceptable. Instead Maliha leaned forward and gave Constance a kiss on the lips—not provocative but a little more than just friends. Now Constance would have another fantasy for her bedroom.

Maliha waved to them as the taxi departed. It crossed her mind that kissing Constance that way might be considered cruel, but the woman was too self-centred to see it that way. She would just enjoy the thrill of it. After all, it had been public.

"Come on, Izak," she said. "Let's get out of this heat and see what the hotel has for us."

vii

Constance Mayberry's new residence was a few miles outside the main city and, according to what Maliha had read, Regina had a smaller population even than Johannesburg. However, after twenty minutes in the taxi, they were still driving through residential areas. If all these buildings were occupied, the population was much greater than estimated. She thought of the ships bringing their cargoes of people looking for a new life—though not this one.

As evening came on, the light changed. The hidden Sun moved round the planet until there was a portion of the burning clouds that was in the planet's shadow and no longer glowed. The light was dimmer and there were shadows. It made Venus more real.

Once they passed out of the city proper, the roads continued to be raised and in good condition. The buildings were spaced out and they had fences. The fences were noteworthy—they looked as if they were fortified to resist military attack.

Maliha was not aware of civil unrest on Venus, though it seemed there were considerable holes in the knowledge she had acquired.

"Stop!" shouted Maliha through the glass that separated the passengers from the driver. He had to be told three times, but eventually he did bring the vehicle to a halt. Maliha opened the door and stepped out onto the slick granite-wood surface.

The roads might be in good condition, but there was insufficient traffic to keep them clear of fungus and other growths.

"What's wrong?" shouted the driver.

"Nothing, I want to look at something."

"Stay on the road."

She could not place his accent. It was English but with a strange lilt that did not come from any of the larger countries, like Australia or North America. Of course, it was a Venusian accent. Or just a British Northern Venus Territory accent—perhaps merely a Regina accent.

Izak followed her out and handed her the cane they had acquired from the hotel.

She walked back along the road, taking care not to slip and trying to avoid the cracks. Who knew what lurked in the inky black between? In this place stepping on the cracks might be more than a child's game.

The steam engine of the taxi panted quietly behind them; she could almost block it out and listen to the strangeness of this barely tamed wilderness. Creatures shrieked and cooed invisibly among the plants. There were movements that could not be attributed to the breeze. Things with wings and bulbous balloons floated above her.

Two minutes later she stood looking across a hundred yards of water-logged land at the remains of the saurian monster she had glimpsed from the taxi.

She had heard Venus described as a young, primitive planet. One reason for this description was the preponderance of massive dinosaur-like creatures, some of which were ferocious in the extreme. Well-heeled hunters came in their hundreds to bag these monstrosities and bring home a trophy—usually one of their hands or feet, since their heads were far too big to carry back to Earth.

The scientists had attempted to bring back living specimens of some of the smaller species, but they had all suffocated through lack of oxygen. Given what she knew now, Maliha considered this failure a mercy.

She studied the body now lying in the green sward. She imagined it had not been dead long, since growths of fungi and mosses had not yet fully covered it. Parts of the skin rippled and moved; her stomach heaved when a gash in the skin revealed a glimpse of something large and grey moving under the surface.

Half the head remained intact, though it was in shadow, while it appeared the remainder had been blown away, perhaps by the hunter's shotgun. She removed her glasses—the light blinded her for a moment—then stared at the head. The one remaining eye was visible. It was midnight black.

She glanced at her blue-tinted glasses thoughtfully.

Izak stamped hard on something next to her foot. She jumped back as he did it again and again. There was a squashed streak of something spindly lying crushed beneath his feet. She replaced the glasses to block out the light.

"Let's go," she said and added another lesson to her mounting list of appropriate behaviour on Venus: *don't stand still too long*.

The taxi set off once more with the two of them sitting in the back. She pulled down the blinds on the window next to her. There had been no details of the makers of the glasses in the Army & Navy Stores catalogue; she had chosen these from the selection offered because they were in the higher price range but not the most expensive.

She removed and examined the glasses. The workmanship appeared to be of good quality. There was a maker's name and address along the inside of the arm, which indicated they had been manufactured here in Regina. It made sense, since only those who lived on Venus could understand what was needed here.

The taxi turned off the main road and drove up to a gate. A man approached the driver who, after enquiring, passed on her name. Maliha could not help but notice the heavy-gauge shotgun and the two mounted machine guns on each gate pedestal. She was reminded in passing of the city states of Italy. Each home was fortified and the servants must comprise the Army.

Did neighbours help one another? Were there negotiations and political manoeuvring between the houses? Marriages of convenience? Star-crossed lovers? She smiled inwardly at her flight of fancy then became more serious—perhaps it wasn't so far from the truth, with the House of Timmons controlling it all? And, if that were the case, there would be other families ready to take over.

Here the roadway was no longer built from wood but, as they headed uphill, constructed from slabs of black rock. And, though still raised from its surroundings, rested on the ground itself. As in all things, wealth determined the materials from which one's property was constructed.

They drew up at the house, which looked to be a square construction, probably around an atrium in the middle. There were no windows below the second floor. Like a castle's defences. But here they defended against the fauna, and perhaps the flora. Did fungi come under the heading of fauna? She had read two articles arguing that they belonged to their own genus because they were entirely dissimilar to plants.

The entrance was not a driveway up to the doors of the house, as it would have been on Earth, but once more it was defensive. The building stuck out on the ground floor to form a tunnel with a heavy gate at each end. As they approached, the gate swung back and admitted them.

They alighted from the taxi and, before Maliha had a chance to pay the driver, the footman had done so. They were escorted inside and Maliha glanced back to see the taxi driving away, marooning them. She exchanged a glance with Izak; he had also watched their means of return depart.

They were on their own.

viii

They were guided through to the atrium. It was not what Maliha had expected.

Rather than being open to the elements, it was covered with a construction of metal and glass, tinted in a similar manner to her glasses though not as heavily. And here were plants from Earth. There was ordinary grass underfoot, two apple trees and numerous bushes, including a rhododendron.

With the vibrant life that teemed outside the walls, one might expect these imported plants to be equally enthusiastic in their growth. On the contrary, however, they looked pallid and stunted.

"They're sad, aren't they?" said Constance from behind her. "I had hoped for something more from them when Leonard asked me to send them last year. The gardener says they're all like this—nobody can get them to grow properly."

Françoise stood beside Constance, their arms interlocked. The Frenchwoman was dressed once more in her flowing French fashions and looked as lovely as ever, even with her hair cropped short.

"Carbon arc lights," said Maliha after a quick nod to Françoise.

"I'm sorry?"

"Carbon arc lights."

"What are they?"

"There is a doctor of biology who claims plants require a form of invisible light to live," Maliha said.

"Ultra-violet," said Françoise.

"Yes, it gets blocked here on Venus by the clouds." *The same thing that turns the pale skin of Europeans brown and the reason they avoid direct sunlight whenever they may.*

"Well, what do the damned Venus plants use?"

Maliha shrugged. "I'm sure someone is studying it, but I do know that arc lights emit that form of light." She paused. "Though they do use a lot of electricity and the problem might be something else."

"But if it works they'll grow properly?"

"I think so."

Constance drew closer. "Well, don't say a word about it to anyone else—not only could we corner the market on the whole arc light market on Venus, it would give me an 'in' with the locals. I mean, seriously, from what I've heard they're a real tight bunch and hate outsiders."

"I thought your husband was a friend of Timmons', and isn't he the bigwig?"

"So I thought, but it seems like there's a whole bunch of them. Old money, new money, doesn't matter. Leonard says it took him a long time to get in with them," said Constance. "Though he says he's finally making some headway."

She checked her watch. "Need to get this adjusted for Venus time." She frowned as she did some calculations. "Yeah, time for dinner." She glanced at Izak and then stared at Maliha as if expecting something.

Maliha considered making it difficult for her, but this might be convenient. She withdrew to the side of the atrium, taking Izak by the hand.

"They don't want you at dinner."

"Because my skin is dark?"

"That and because of where you were brought up."

Izak nodded; he did not seem to be insulted. It was normal behaviour for white people, as far as he knew. Maliha and those she associated with were the exception.

"But that's good. They'll probably take you to the kitchens. Keep your ears open; see if you can find out anything about Timmons and his circle."

"Do you want me to search the house, Goddess?"

She shook her head. "I'm not sure there will be anything to find here, so don't do that unless you're sure you can get away without anyone noticing."

A maid, also of African descent, arrived and escorted Izak away.

Constance took them across the lawn, up two flights of stairs and into a series of rooms that looked out across the shadowy, but still light, Venusian landscape. "Not sure I'll get used to the way they put the living rooms higher than the bedrooms," she said.

Maliha studied the sky. It looked as if a bank of low cloud was moving in and that meant rain. On Venus, low cloud always meant rain. Towards the tropics the cloud was almost continual with the heat and humidity in lethal proportions.

They came to a small dining room designed for a maximum of twelve.

"My husband will be joining us shortly," said Constance. "Do you want a drink?"

"Water," said Maliha automatically.

Maliha had been introduced to Leonard Mayberry but, even though they had stayed in the same house for a day or so, she had never had a conversation with him. When he arrived a few minutes later he looked much older than he had a year ago, his eyes and forehead lined with worry. Or was it just the oppressive climate of Venus?

He shook her hand. "Pleased to meet you properly at last, Miss Anderson. Constance has spoken of you very often." There was something secretive about the way he said it, a strain in his voice, a stiffness in the hand he offered to shake hers. She decided not to make it easy for him.

"We were at the same table at the Mawdsley house for Alex's funeral," she said, almost as if she was offended.

"Oh, sure, you have a face no one could forget." His smile was all teeth. She could not tell whether it was flattery, insult or a racial slur. "You're the one that had his wife and daughter locked up."

Maliha smiled as sweetly as she could manage. "If I had had my way, Mr Mayberry—"

"Call me Leonard."

"—I would have seen them hang, Leonard."

"Well, you're a bloodthirsty one." He laughed, but she thought it was forced.

She scratched the back of her hand and noticed the way his eyes flicked down. He met her eyes as he looked back up.

"Strange for a person so young to use a cane."

"An accident a couple of years ago."

"Must have been bad."

"It was."

Constance arrived between them. "You two are getting along just fine, I see. I knew you would." She turned a conspiratorial eye to Maliha. "Just don't get him started on the history of warfare."

The dinner gong rang and the four of them moved to the table. They could have been anywhere in the British Empire. The Americans did not have an empire; they preferred to stay out of anything to do with Europe, though they still seemed happy to supply the Germans with helium. Perhaps they were concerned about the power of the British and that they might try to reclaim the colonies that had once been theirs.

The Mayberrys certainly did not lack for servants, with two maids serving, the butler, and plenty of activity in the kitchens below. The food arrived via a dumbwaiter placed just out of view.

Maliha apologised almost sub-vocally as her stomach made itself known. She flushed with embarrassment.

"Someone's looking forward to their meal," said Leonard quite indelicately.

However, Maliha felt quite the reverse. The flush she felt turned into a sweat and the food she could smell—she could not quite tell what it was—caught in her throat. A feeling that her stomach was about to revolt spread through her.

Conflicting emotions tore at her. The desire to remain where she was and not embarrass her hosts was at war with the need to move immediately, otherwise embarrassments would be felt all around.

She jumped as Françoise's hand came down on hers. "Are you all right, Maliha?"

Maliha did not trust herself to open her mouth lest the limited contents of her stomach came back. She turned her head and stared into Françoise's eyes, shaking her head vehemently.

Françoise threw her napkin on the table and jumped to her feet. She pulled Maliha to her feet.

"What's going on?" said Constance. "Françoise? Maliha?"

Supporting Maliha so she did not need to retrieve her stick, Françoise rushed her from the room, past the serving staff to a set of stairs. The carpeting gave way to a wooden surface.

Maliha bent over and retched several times, then could not hold back the contents of her stomach any longer. She was mortified for a few seconds as her stomach acids burnt her throat, then a wave of lightheadedness swept through her and she collapsed against Françoise.

CHAPTER 7

i

Maliha could tell from the way the sheets were pressed down on one side there was something heavy on the bed next to her. She heard the quiet breathing of Izak. From behind her closed eyes she knew it was full day, though on Venus that started any time after the equivalent of three in the morning.

The memory of the previous night caught up with her and she groaned. She just wanted to pull the sheets over her head and stay here forever. Or just die now. To become ill at her hosts' table? So embarrassing.

How did she feel now? She felt fine, though her thigh ached a little. There was something about Venus that disagreed with her old injury. It reminded her of the tales of old sailors who could tell the changes in the weather from the way their joints ached. But she was barely twenty. And she was hungry.

What had that been last night? She went cold at the possibility that perhaps her precautions with Lilith or the attack on the ship had failed and she had become infected. There was no way she could know until later. The mere smell of quinine, when Dr Lemming had shown her, turned her stomach and made her retch.

Perhaps that would be a fitting end, as long as she could exact her vengeance on Timmons and his cohorts.

Did Leonard Mayberry know that he had been directed to fetch his wife just so that she could be implicated in a murder? Did he care? Was it some initiation ceremony into Timmons' inner group? Did Timmons even have his own clique?

Was it just a coincidence? She shook her head, she had been over this before. It could not be a coincidence, not when the Spencers, Françoise and Constance had all been on the ship.

Why had she not asked the steward for his reasons? Why had he allowed himself to be infected? Why was he so willing to die? What was wrong with her? She had become forgetful, inefficient, and had almost failed to save Françoise when she had had the answer.

If she was going to be this forgetful perhaps she should begin to make notes.

She checked to ensure she was wearing night clothes. Silk. Constance would have nothing less. She slid out from between the sheets. Izak lay fast asleep. The clock on the mantel showed the time to be around five-thirty.

She found her clothes in a dressing room, along with her walking stick. Beyond the dressing room was a bathroom. She washed and dressed. Then she woke Izak and instructed him to clean up; no one had told him to undress and it was not something he did automatically as yet.

She was not sure whether it would elicit a response, but she rang the bell anyway. It took a few minutes before one of the kitchen staff arrived at the door. Maliha instructed her to fetch some bread and water—her stomach felt normal, but she did not trust it—and see about arranging transport back to Regina.

The girl curtsied and left.

It took five minutes for Izak to emerge. He had not removed his shirt to wash and it was wet around the collar and cuffs.

They were on the middle floor and the windows of their room gave out onto the atrium. Nothing moved. There was not the slightest breeze, since it was enclosed, and there were no birds, nor any chance of the flowering plants or apple trees becoming pollinated, since no native insects had been brought here.

They should have at least had a beehive. That would have helped.

With Izak, Maliha left the room and made her way downstairs to the main entrance. Several of the male staff had been roused from their beds and were preparing a steam carriage while holding back yawns.

"Where are you going in such a terrible hurry, *cherie?*"

It seemed that Maliha's instruction not to disturb the Mayberrys had been obeyed, but she had not mentioned Françoise.

"We need to get back. I have forgotten something."

"You?"

"Don't laugh at me, Françoise."

"I am not laughing," she said, drifting in wearing a diaphanous dressing gown that hinted at the elegant body beneath but showed nothing. Maliha could imagine what the male servants were thinking, and the female ones as well—though they would be less complimentary. "I am worried about you."

"There's no need."

"I do not know whether to slap you or to kiss you."

"I seem to recall you enjoyed both," said Maliha.

"Oh, you remember that. So your rememberings are selective?"

"I have forgotten to do what I do best," said Maliha. "There are questions I have not answered."

"And I said I would help you in all things."

Maliha took a step that closed the gap between them. She put her arms around Françoise and pulled her in close. Françoise seemed initially surprised, but Maliha felt the slim arms reach around her waist and shoulders. She rested her chin at the base of Françoise's neck.

Making her words as quiet as possible, she whispered. "Then make sure you mention, in front of Leonard, that I seemed very ill and that there was something wrong with my eyes."

Françoise pushed her back and held her by her shoulders. "This is what you want?"

"It's important."

Françoise nodded. "As you wish." She hesitated for a moment and then planted a kiss on Maliha's lips. They had an audience, so it was not as passionate as Maliha suspected Françoise would have preferred. But it would no doubt be the talk of the staff quarters for some time. And would distract them from what had really just occurred.

"Don't forget," said Maliha.

"It seems I am not the one who has been forgetting things," said Françoise. "But do not fear—it shall be done."

Maliha gave her another peck on the cheek and extricated herself from her ex-lover's arms. Without Valentine, Maliha felt that perhaps she would not mind being back in those arms. But that was all in the past. Things had changed.

A wave of heat flooded through the door when it was opened for Maliha and Izak to pass through. Maliha paused to turn and wave, but Françoise was already gone.

ii

The journey back to the hotel was without incident, though the sky went black at one point as a cloud of creatures passed across. She had seen huge flocks of starlings in the autumn in England—enough to know that this was a flock of something that twisted and folded through the sky—but they were too high to see precisely what they were, and so numerous they must number in the millions.

The moment Maliha entered the suite, she knew something was different. She had left her carpetbag closed by the chair. It was open. She shook her head—what if she was wrong? What if she was misremembering?

No. If she could not trust her own judgement she was completely lost.

She would look at the bag in a moment; the first thing to be done was to check the rest of the suite. She cautioned Izak to take care, though truthfully she suspected he would be better at survival than her if confronted by a thug.

However, the rest of the room seemed untouched, which made her doubt herself even more. Who would touch only her bag?

Timmons played games, lethal ones it was true, but games nonetheless. This would be his doing. Something in the bag. Cautiously she examined it and saw the offending item sitting right there on top. A book.

She took it out and perched on the armchair. *Through the Looking Glass* by Lewis Carroll. She had read both books and enjoyed their outrageous flights of fancy. There was a bookmark at the end of Chapter Six; she knew the text without looking, but read it anyway:

"'Oh, how glad I am to get here! And what IS this on my head?' Alice exclaimed in a tone of dismay as she put her hands up to something very heavy and fitted tight all round her head.

"'But how CAN it have got there without my knowing it?' she said to herself as she lifted it off and set it on her lap to make out what it could possibly be.

"It was a golden crown."

This was the point in the story where 'pawn' Alice is promoted to a queen in the crazy chess game when she reaches the eighth square. What could it mean? Did it mean anything? Was it a game within a game simply intended to distract?

Maliha tossed the book away onto the bed. She was not interested. There was proper work to be done. But first she really did need some breakfast.

* * *

Room service delivered promptly and she ate voraciously. Izak was more circumspect, and practised the use of his eating utensils. He sawed his food into small chunks and used the fork for each piece.

Maliha knew he was lonely. Lilith had been his only family, even though they were probably not related. Separation from loved ones was something with which Maliha was acutely familiar. Those first years at the school had been like Dante's Circles of Hell.

At least Izak did not have to put up with the hate and the abuse.

She knew it had changed her.

"When I was a child in India," she said, "my mother and I used to play games. Would you like to play a game?"

Izak looked up from his plate. "I want you to bring vengeance to the one who killed Lilith, Goddess. I am not a child."

She nodded. "Very well, Izak. But when this is over, you and I will play games."

He went back to his food and Maliha wondered whether he was cutting food or slicing into his enemies.

Maliha dressed for the Venusian day in a loose-fitting dress that permitted the circulation of air and still managed to cover most of her skin. Izak's male attire was similar in style and purpose.

The early explorers of the planet had suffered badly from rotting skin conditions and preventative steps had had to be taken, the most disgusting part being the application of Vaseline to the feet before putting on stockings and long, waterproof boots. It had been found to be the most potent protection available, since it prevented the ingress of water and spores.

Maliha handed the outdoor glasses to Izak and picked up her own. Then she snapped off one of its arms.

"Oh dear," she said. "I appear to have broken them."

That, at least, brought a smile to Izak's dour face. His past on the streets of Johannesburg had given him an appreciation of subterfuge. Maliha placed the broken glass on her face, with the one remaining arm over her earlobe.

"Come, Izak, let us go in search of a repairer of spectacles."

They stepped out into a downpour. Umbrellas on Venus were a whole size larger than those typically found in London or Manchester, but their uniform black colour remained the usual. Maliha erected hers, though her clothes were already wet through from the few seconds of exposure.

The temperature seemed to rise by the minute as they plodded along the raised walkways. Since Regina had been built from scratch, the town planners had taken the trouble to separate pedestrian traffic from mechanical.

The walkways were higher than the roads themselves, creating a delicate spiderweb through the buildings, which now possessed access on two or three separate levels. Both pedestrian and mechanical paths were built from the ubiquitous grainless, black granite-wood bound together with steel hawsers. The metal seemed to be holding up well against the wet environment and she assumed it was made from the new 'stainless' alloy.

Even so, the flora and fungi of Venus were trying hard to infest the city: Along the walkways and across the buildings greenery was taking hold everywhere. It gave the place a curiously soft appearance, somehow more natural than a city usually looked.

Signposts marked every junction and, as instructed by the hotel staff, they followed the route towards the city market. This was a relatively new construction funded by the benevolence of the rich merchants. The walkway they were on widened out and descended to a four-storey building.

Great rotating doors gave them access to the interior, where Maliha furled her umbrella. The grand market was a single open space with broad skylights to illuminate the interior. Around all four sides were three levels of wide balconies housing shops of all sorts, and on the floor of the building were demountable market stalls.

Maliha frowned. A cacophony assailed their ears—the ebb and flow of thousands of people laughing, shouting and negotiating their bargains. The most prominent smell was tobacco smoke, with underlying scents of bread, herbs, cooking meat and other things completely unrecognisable.

But so many people. The sheer quantity emphasised her concerns about the extent of the suburbs. It made a mockery of the official estimates of Regina's population, which was said to boast no more than ten thousand people at the last—admittedly imprecise—count. For every one person here there must be ten or twenty that were elsewhere in the city.

That would mean the population was more likely to be fifty thousand, perhaps even twice that.

She walked forward and leaned on the ornate ironwork of the rail overlooking the market. The air had the bluish haze of tobacco smoke. There were native flying creatures twisting and looping near the skylights.

The humidity was far less in here, but the heat was more intense than outside.

Izak moved up beside her.

"Someone follows us, Goddess."

Maliha did not turn. "Are you sure?"

"Yes."

"Is it just one person?"

"Just one."

"Come along."

She wandered without any urgency along the balcony. The shops here were jewellers and watchmakers. She paused to look in at each window. Every now and then she would point out something to Izak. In the reflection of the glass, she caught more than one glimpse of a working-class man in tall boots and dungarees, with a white shirt but no jacket. He had a peaked cap that cast a shadow across his face. She could not think what his trade might be.

Having established the man, she walked into a watchmaker. She discussed adjustments to her watch and swapped it for a temporary replacement already adjusted for Venus time. She asked for, and received, a pen, some paper and an envelope. She wrote out a set of instructions and put them in an envelope, which she placed in one of her own pockets.

She thanked the watchmaker, who informed her the watch would be ready that afternoon.

She and Izak then continued their promenade. She jumped as a deluge of rain thundered onto the roof. Looking up, it seemed as if a wave had landed on the building and was slowly dissipating. Thin streams of water cascaded down into the market below.

The concept of a cloudburst existed on Earth, but she was aware the Venusian equivalent was similar to tipping a bucket of water onto a sandcastle. Everything here was so much more extreme.

She sighed and moved on.

They approached the first corner and, scanning the shops ahead, she saw on the next lower floor a sign with the name of the spectacle-maker she wanted. A double flight of steps, busy with shoppers and traders, led that way. As they went around the first bend in the stairs, she resisted the temptation to glance up at the man but instead pulled out the envelope.

"Take this, Izak, and hide it about your person."

His years of pickpocketing made it disappear in a moment. She doubted the man would have seen anything of their transaction.

"When we get to the shop I'll give you a shilling for a couple of pies; you go to the market and fetch them. I will head back to the entrance after buying new spectacles. The man will follow me. You bring the letter back to spectacle-maker and give it to the person behind the counter. I will have forewarned them of your arrival."

"Yes, Goddess."

Maliha pulled out her purse and took out two shillings instead, just in case the prices here were inflated. Izak might not be able to read, but he knew his numbers, at least when it came to money.

She watched as he ran off into the crowd. She felt a pang of fear, like any mother seeing their child heading into the unknown, even though he had a far better chance of survival than she would have had at his age. Besides, there was no reason to suppose there was any danger.

The door to the shop was open, but there was no one behind the counter. The sound of the market faded a little as she entered. The floor was polished wood and an electric light illuminated the cramped space. Dozens of completed spectacles lined the walls. All of them had the tinted blue glass, though some were of a deeper hue than others. One or two were completely black.

There was a handbell on the counter. Maliha picked it up by its wooden handle and gave it a gentle ring. The sound penetrated the place and moments later a woman with magnifying goggles pushed up to her forehead stepped out from the back, holding an unfinished pair of frames.

"Can I help you, miss?"

Maliha held out the broken glasses. "I broke these."

The woman took them. Her fingers were thin and delicate; they almost seemed too large for the rest of her. "Why?"

"I'm sorry?"

"You say you broke them," she said with a tone of accusation. "My frames do not snap like this."

"I…" Maliha did not feel she could tell the truth but nor could she lie. Her voice trailed off. "…need a replacement."

The woman looked as if she was going to argue but then relaxed. She peered at Maliha's face then turned to a rack behind her. "You need something less heavily tinted," she said. "Trouble with buying from the catalogue, you can't have them properly fitted." She pulled a pair of finished glasses from the rack. Maliha could see the blue was less intense and allowed in more light.

"Why do I need ones like that?"

"Your eyes are already very dark, sweetie. Being Indian you're already used to sunlight—not like us pasty types, blue eyes, can't take the sun. Leastways not in this place."

"Oh."

"Here, sit there while I fit them." She indicated a chair in the corner. Maliha sat and the woman tried them on her. She tutted, took them off again, went into the back and returned with a pair of round-nosed pliers that she used to bend the end of the arms slightly more.

Maliha wondered about the time. It would not take Izak very long to find something to eat.

"Do you make the glass as well?" asked Maliha as the spectacles were once again placed on her nose. She could feel the arms gripping her ears a little tighter.

"My husband."

"Can you do special commissions?" Maliha was staring ahead, looking out the door. The man who had been following her was looking at her in the reflection in the glass just outside the door. He did not seem to realise that if he could see her then she could see him. Still, he was definitely out of earshot.

"What sort of commission?"

"I am after something quite unusual, like Muller and Fick?"

"Can't say I know them."

"Your husband might."

"He might," she said and stood back. "There you go, those are properly fitted. If you look after them, and don't break them, they'll last just fine."

Maliha got to her feet. "Thank you. How much do I owe you?"

"Two and ten, love." The woman took the white fiver from Maliha and got her change from a drawer.

"A boy will come by in a minute," said Maliha. "He's got the details of what I want. If you can tell him whether you can do it and how long it will take? Or if you can't do it," she said. "But it's very important and I'll pay whatever you ask."

The woman put her head on one side. "All right, dearie. Whatever you say."

Maliha thanked her and headed out. She turned left, back the way she had come, just as if this had been her sole destination—which it had been—but her shadow was gone. She returned upstairs and waited.

iv

Izak handed her the second pie then offered her the change almost as an afterthought, but all she said was, "Keep it."

She bit into the pie as they headed out. The rain had stopped, but the heat was still intense, with the water that had fallen now evaporating and saturating the air.

They took a cab. She gave the driver the address she recalled from the passenger and crew lists the captain had supplied.

"Did you deliver the letter?" she said between mouthfuls. The meat in the pie was unrecognisable.

"She said they would do it," said Izak.

"By tomorrow?"

"Evening."

"That's good."

A wave of sickness hit her like a wall and she barely managed to hold back her stomach's contents. She almost threw the pie back to Izak and then she sat back in the seat, willing her body under control. She would not embarrass herself again by vomiting in a taxicab.

She closed her eyes. No, that was worse. She focused on the city passing by, watching buildings slowly moving in the distance. There was no question: Regina was significantly larger than official estimates back on Earth.

They passed the main business centre and moved out into an area filled with modest dwellings. Focusing on the details helped to distract from her rebellious innards. If there was one thing she noticed about the towns and cities of England, it was how crammed together everyone was.

They tended to repeat the same pattern wherever they went but not here. From the pictures she had seen of the United States, this place was more like that frontier land, where space was so plentiful that everything was spread out.

The people must have engaged in major deforestation to build these endless roads and walkways, not to mention the buildings themselves.

The cab pulled off the main road and down an incline to an area not unlike a railway platform. Maliha and Izak disembarked into the heat. The cab had used some cooling system for its interior. She paid the driver and found several unusual coins in the change, including a half-crown that should not exist. There was a picture of Edward VII on one side but on the obverse, instead of Britannia or St George, was a semblance of the goddess Venus in the Roman style.

She was not aware that Regina and the surrounding territories had been given permission to mint their own coins. It was possible it had not been reported in a newspaper she read, though that seemed unlikely.

However, there must be an ideal quantity of coins per citizen to allow a country to function. And if one had a higher population than expected, one might need more coins, and that might be noticeable.

Maliha wondered where to go next but saw there were clear signs indicating the various residential streets. The road they had come along ran parallel to a river cut deep into the rocks below them. After the rain, the water was plunging through it at a tremendous rate and was close to the top of its gorge.

Their walkway crossed it at a height of twenty feet and then descended by a series of wet steps to only five feet from the ground. Everywhere was the same dense covering of moss and grasses. Rivulets cut through it, joining and separating as they went tumbling to the edge of the gorge and over.

She caught a glimpse of a thin and sinewy skin winding through the water and plants, stopping and starting every now and then. Its body was wider than her hand with a length of at least ten feet. It had a mottled green and black skin. She shook her head. Snakes were common enough in India. When you found a cobra, you sent for the man to collect it and take it away.

The buildings here were small—only a single storey, on piles to make them stand out from the water and with perhaps four or five rooms each—but, as she had noted before, each one was separate. A far cry from even the most opulent Georgian crescent back in England, where every house was attached to the one next to it.

She reached the number she remembered. The house of Ignatius Hammond, the recently deceased steward serving aboard the *Atacama Sea.*

The front door had two layers. There was an outer door frame covered with a thin gauzy material; it gave slightly when Maliha pressed her fingers against it and there were a couple of small insects caught in its weave. Behind it was the actual door.

There was a knocker made of wood to the side of the door. Maliha rapped it against the frame twice.

The trapped insects—similar to flies but with more pairs of wings—buzzed intermittently. Someone laughed in the distance and an unknown animal made a sound, somewhere between a dog's bark and the caw of a crow. She turned and looked along the houses, which stood in two rows facing one another. The walkways ran in parallel in front of each row, with a crosswalk every third house. It was all very neat and ordered.

The unlatching of the door brought her back. She glanced at Izak, put her hand on his shoulder and leaned on her walking stick. Her new glasses hid her eyes.

"Yes?"

The speaker was a woman of about forty, the right age to be married to the murderer. Her face was slack, her hair greying from its original brown, and her eyes lacked interest.

"Mrs Hammond?"

"Yes."

"Your husband is Ignatius Hammond?"

Interest appeared in the eyes and she stood a little straighter. "Who are you?"

Maliha toyed for a moment with using her alias but decided against it. "Maliha Anderson."

There was a flicker of recognition. "You and your boy better come in."

She pulled the main door further open and unlatched the outer one. Maliha stood back as it swung outward, then stepped inside. She had to walk past Mrs Hammond, who shut the outer door after Izak had entered.

The room was sparse. There were basic furnishings: a table, chairs, shelves with a few books and ornaments. Most noticeable by their absence were any sort of soft furnishings; there were only a few cushions and no carpet or rugs. One might put this down to a lack funds for such luxuries, but Maliha suspected the climate of Venus was more likely the culprit. Soft products would rot quickly and provide places for plants and fungi to grow.

The native environment imposed itself on everything.

She could hear the regular thump of a small steam engine; she guessed it to be driving the fan that circulated air in the room. It was not as effective as a dehumidifier, but it was better than nothing and reminded Maliha of Barbara's home in Ceylon, with the steam *punkhawallah*.

"I have been told my husband is dead," said Mrs Hammond; the sheet had said her Christian name was Elise. She did not invite Maliha to sit, despite the fact she was leaning on her stick.

"Yes, I'm afraid so."

"They didn't say how he died. Do you know?"

"I was there."

"Let me see your eyes."

Maliha removed her glasses and the woman peered at her face. Then she looked away, glancing at a photograph on a shelf. The aggressive tension seemed to leave her and she deflated.

"You know he had black-eye then," said Maliha. She felt awkward standing up, so, without being invited, she went to the table, pulled out a chair and sat. Elise Hammond followed suit, as if she had been waiting for permission.

"He wrote that he'd been infected," she said. "How did he die?"

Maliha could have wrapped the truth in euphemisms, but it would have had less impact. "He shot himself."

Maliha was surprised at the lack of shock Mrs Hammond expressed at the news. There was no reaction beyond a tensing of her muscles. Instead she said, "And had he done the job he was supposed to do?"

Maliha was not sure of the answer to that. He had murdered two people and almost killed another with torture. What would drive a man to do that?

"Did he?" She was almost frantic at Maliha's delay in answering.

"Yes." *If his job was to attract my attention and then infect me with black-eye.*

"You don't look like you have it."

"There probably hasn't been time for it to show yet," said Maliha. "I keep being sick, my clothes have become tighter and I have passed out more than once." For some reason it seemed that her being infected affected the woman's happiness: if Maliha was infected that was a good thing.

"All right," said Elise Hammond. She stood up and went into what Maliha surmised to be the kitchen. The fact that the woman was satisfied Maliha had the disease from the description of her symptoms was worrying. Perhaps she had not been able to prevent infection from Hammond or she had picked it up from Lilith, who was at least as far gone as the man, if not further.

Elise Hammond returned, carrying an envelope. She handed it to Maliha. It was oily in texture to protect it from the damp and thin enough to only contain a single folded sheet. Maliha's real name was written in traditional copperplate hand on the exterior.

Maliha sighed. Once more he was ahead of her, but if she had not turned up on the Hammonds' doorstep then the letter would have remained undelivered and all else would be the same. It was not any form of prescience, it was simply preparing for all eventualities. Maliha tucked it into her reticule.

"What did they promise you?"

"That I could go home."

"Earth?"

She nodded. Maliha found that unconvincing. Would a man commit murder, inflict torture and then commit suicide simply to allow his wife to go home? She said as much and Elise looked scared.

"They said you mustn't tell me," said Maliha.

Elise nodded.

Maliha glanced at the photographs, which showed young men, women and children in stiff poses.

"They said they would kill your family."

The woman's eyes became wide with fear and she looked around as if someone were listening.

"What difference do you think it makes, me knowing this?" said Maliha. "The reason they forbade you to tell me was to demonstrate the power they have over people such as you." She stood up. "Let me explain something: Mr Terence Timmons has gone to a great deal of trouble to prove that he has greater power than I do. I have been his nemesis since even before I knew I was. I have interfered with his plans and he finds that difficult to accept from a woman. To that end he has concocted a disgusting and murderous plan to show me that I do not have any power."

She paused to take a deep breath.

"It is possible that he has successfully infected me with black-eye. It is entirely possible that I will die a painful death." She leaned over the woman. "But I tell you now, Elise Hammond, that I will avenge the deaths of all those he has tortured and murdered. And that includes your husband."

v

The light was failing as they reached the centre of the city once more. They had had to walk for some distance before reaching a small market area where they could order a taxicab to collect them.

Maliha found herself to be more tired than she expected and her corset, though not laced tight, still clenched her middle as if her waist was expanding. Hammond had mentioned his clothes being tight. As the fungus grew beneath the skin the body expanded. It had happened to Lilith.

All the while the letter waited in her reticule. She had resolved not to look at it until she had eaten and rested. She was looking forward to removing her boots, which were pinching around the ankles.

The taxicab came to a halt outside the hotel. Maliha paid the cabby and they made their way upstairs.

Maliha placed the letter on the occasional table near the door and went into her room, after directing Izak to remove his boots and clean his feet. The humidity in the room was at a comfortable level— she realised she was thinking of the weather in terms of humidity rather than temperature.

In her room she stripped off her clothes, glad to rid herself of the clinging and heavy fashions. Next to the wardrobe was an airing closet designed to dry clothes that had been worn during the day, should the occupant wish to wear them again.

She did not, but she hung up the clothes to dry anyway. She unlaced the tops of her high footwear and forced first one then the other from her feet. They sucked as they came free and she found it useful to push a finger into the ankle part to break the vacuum seal made by the Vaseline.

The greasy material was unpleasant, but her feet were as pristine as they had been when they went into the boots. She located a towel and wiped her feet clean of the gunk. Her encased feet had become very hot and it was pleasant to have the cooler air on them.

She threw herself back onto the bed, happy to just lie there. The day had been exhausting and her ankles throbbed having escaped their confinement. She closed her eyes.

* * *

Valentine leaned over her. She could feel his naked body. He pressed his lips against hers.

She jumped at the knocking on the door. "Goddess?"

Confusion filled her for a few seconds. A dream. A glance at the clock on the wall told her she been asleep for nearly an hour. The door handle turned and the door opened a short distance.

"It's all right, Izak," she said. "I'm fine, I fell asleep. Don't come in!"

The door stopped.

"I'll be out in a minute."

The door shut.

Maliha sighed. Hammond had said something about headaches and bad dreams, but that had not been a bad dream, just one of longing.

She dug out a nightdress and threw it on, then covered herself further with a dressing gown. Finally she untied her hair and let it hang loose so the air could get to her scalp.

In the sitting room, Izak was seated on the settee. He had a pencil and was scratching away in a notepad. The movement of his hand indicated he was shading.

"Are you drawing something?" asked Maliha as she picked up the letter from the table and crossed back to the armchair. Izak nodded. "Show me."

With a touch of reluctance Izak slid from his place and brought the pad over to her. She took it gently and smiled at him.

"It is not a good picture, Goddess."

She looked at what he had drawn. There was a flat horizon, the ground part shaded with tight strokes in the distance and much wider ones close up. A tree stood a little to the right. It resembled the banyan in the square in Johannesburg where they had first met.

The silhouette of a woman in what could have been a sari stood against the horizon. And, halfway to the horizon, there was a small figure also in silhouette. Maliha could not tell whether it was walking into the distance or approaching. Perhaps it did not matter.

"I like this very much, Izak," she said. "You are very skilled. Can you tell me about it?"

"This is our tree," he said, pointing, "and this is the goddess."

Maliha pointed at the smaller figure. "And who is this?"

"Lilith."

Maliha found she could not speak and was weeping once more. She sniffed and rubbed the back of her hand across her eyes.

"Where is Izak?" she asked when she could finally get the words out.

He turned to look into her eyes. "I am drawing the picture, Mother."

Maliha fell to her knees and flung her arms around him. She sobbed into his shoulder. After a few moments of holding himself stiffly, his arms went round her tentatively, and then in a sudden move he embraced her back. He clung to her and she heard him crying too. The first real emotion he had shown since his sister died.

After a time they both ceased crying. She held him as long as he needed to be held even though her knees and thigh ached at the strain. Finally he pulled away and she wiped the tears from his eyes with the cuff of the nightdress.

With an effort she stood and fetched a kerchief. She handed it to him. "Blow your nose and you will feel better." Inside she wondered when she had become her mother.

She picked up the notepad, smoothed some bent corners and returned it to him. "Keep drawing," she said. "And when I can I will find you better materials, something especially for drawing."

"What materials?" He sounded out the word carefully.

"Special pencils and paper."

He nodded and looked at what was in his hands. "I like these."

"Then when you have used them up, I will buy you more of those."

She found the letter, which had fallen between the cushions, and sat down again. Izak lay on the floor and started another picture.

Maliha used her nail to break open the envelope as she did not have an opener to hand. She unfolded the letter.

Dear Miss Anderson,

It is customary to commence such a letter as this by stating the sender's hope that the recipient is in good health. Such a statement seems redundant and, perhaps, insulting where we are concerned.

By now you will understand the consequences of daring to interfere with my business. Your health is no doubt far worse than you would have hoped and is deteriorating.

I would very much like to meet you in person before that becomes impossible. If you would be so kind as to make arrangements to travel to Timmonsburg—

"Timmonsburg!" Maliha exclaimed. "The man thinks a great deal of himself."

"—Timmonsburg. It is not to be found on any common map and you will find it necessary to contact…"

She stopped reading and crumpled the paper in her fist.

"Of course, Mr Terence Timmons, I will be delighted to meet with you."

vi

She did not know how efficient the Regina postal service was but the following morning after breakfast, she composed a letter to

Timmons' agent, indicating that she wished to travel to *Timmonsburg* the following day. She found the word so offensive she had some difficulty in writing it.

She sealed the envelope, addressed it and then called for a bellboy to put it in the post.

She sat back in her chair and drank what passed for coffee on Venus. The more she thought about it the more she felt there was something off about the timings.

In his letter Timmons had implied that she should, by now, be aware of the illness that infected her. This was problematic for two reasons: First, she was reasonably confident she had avoided infection from Hammond; and second, even if she had contracted black-eye, she would have done so earlier than expected and would therefore be in a much worse condition than she actually was.

That there was something wrong with her seemed clear enough. Her forgetfulness, the fainting, sickness, bloated abdomen and ankles (as they had been that morning), the way she cried at the drop of a hat and, not least, her inability to think logically unless she concentrated—these all indicated some long-term illness. However, several of these symptoms had manifested before she met Hammond.

There *were* the two earlier occasions she had been exposed to black-eye: the child in the diamond mine and the man at Mama Kosi's house. But if she had contracted it then, she would most certainly be showing symptoms as bad as Hammond's by now. Her eyes would be black.

All evidence pointed to the fact that she did not have black-eye, despite any similarity in the symptoms she was experiencing. Perhaps it was a different fungal infection? Who could say what was in the air when the scientists were packing up in a hurry back in Johannesburg?

She sighed and looked across at Izak, who was once again lying on the floor and drawing. He was halfway through the notepad; she hadn't asked to see any more but she would before they were parted.

It did not matter whether she had black-eye or some other infection. This time she was going to die. She was heading into the maw of Hell to meet with the very devil himself.

If she did not die of fungus-induced illness, he would kill her. And if he did not kill her but simply imprisoned her for his own amusement, then she would kill herself.

Or she would kill him. That was the preferred alternative, but she had no idea how she was going to achieve that. It was a certainty she would be searched, and a gun was out of the question even if she concealed one successfully. She had been lucky to hit the window on the Voidship and she knew it.

She felt calm. She knew she would find a way. Izak rolled onto his side and smiled at her. Smiled. Since the cathartic release yesterday, he had relaxed.

"How are your feet, Goddess?"

She smiled too—he had remembered about being responsible for her feet, just as she should be responsible for his. Of course, she was responsible for his entire life, just as a mother should be.

She held up her feet and wriggled her toes. "My feet are in excellent condition, although my ankles are a bit swollen. And how are yours?"

He rolled back onto his stomach and bent his knees so his feet went up. Maliha gave them a long appraisal. "They look healthy, very good."

She took in a deep breath through her nose and blew it out through her mouth. "We have to go out," she said. "Where's the Vaseline?"

To avoid the compression of her body she chose something a little looser today and more in-keeping with the styles worn by the city dwellers of Regina. She and Izak applied Vaseline to each other's feet and helped each other into their footwear. The boots were still too tight, but they did support her ankles.

They exited the hotel in the middle of a downpour and took a cab back to the Mayberry residence.

They entered the main hall after Maliha made it clear to the cabby, this time, that she intended to return and required him to stay. She was not going to be marooned again.

Constance threw her arms about her. "Sweetie, I was so worried about you when you left like that."

"Sorry, Constance, but there's was something I really had to do."

"Well, you're back and just in time for coffee. Real coffee."

They sat in the atrium, light pouring in from above. A new metal gantry was under construction at the far end, though no workmen were in sight.

"I had them start work on your arc lights straight away," said Constance, following her gaze. "I'm already hungry for some real green, maybe even an apple or two."

"Not for a while."

"Well, we'll see."

"I thought you were planning on leaving as soon as possible?" said Maliha.

Constance looked guilty. "Yes," she whispered, "but I haven't told anyone."

Françoise came through from underneath an arch. Maliha admired the way she held herself; she was always so elegant. She did not, however, look very happy.

Maliha stood and they kissed on both cheeks, but Françoise held her when her mouth was out of sight of Constance.

"Get me out of here," whispered Françoise. "I'll do anything, Goddess."

Maliha frowned. Françoise didn't believe that nonsense, but clearly things were not going to plan for her.

"Coffee, honey?"

And they sat. With Maliha's only prospect a horrible death—and Françoise desperately wanting to escape what Maliha guessed to be tedium punctuated by very brief and unsatisfying bouts of sex—they drank coffee and even had a game of cards.

Constance chattered about the house, the weather, the plants, the heat, the humidity and the staff, to the point at which Maliha found she had stopped listening.

"You must be having a horrible time," said Maliha, interrupting Constance's flow of describing in detail the events of the storm during the night.

Maliha saw Françoise glance up to see if the comment was to her, but Maliha's attention was directed at their host.

Constance cut off her stream of verbal minutiae with her mouth open. She took a sip of coffee then upended the cup and drained it in an unladylike way. "I can't stand another day. I hate it here. I hate him. I hate everything. I wish I had never come."

Maliha smiled. "The next shuttle lifts tomorrow morning."

"I can't do that."

"Why not?"

"How could I?"

Maliha shrugged. "You just do it."

"But … Leonard."

"You just said you hated him, were you lying?"

"I … I don't know." She poured herself another coffee and knocked it back. "Yes."

"Yes you hate him, or yes you were lying?"

"I don't hate him," Constance said in a small voice. "But I can't stay here."

Maliha looked over at Françoise; her face was still marked from the beatings and burns she had received from Hammond. There was a cigarette burn on her cheek that would never go, though she could disguise it with make-up.

"You saw what happened to Françoise." It was not a question.

Constance was forced out of her own world for a moment and into someone else's. She looked at Françoise. "She looks much better."

Françoise kept silent, though she no doubt objected to being spoken of in the third person.

"You're lucky it wasn't you."

"I know."

"You were only invited on that vessel with me in order to be murdered, or perhaps framed for murder, which amounts to the same thing, since you die in both cases."

"But Leonard wouldn't do that…"

"It's possible he did not know Timmons' true intention in having you travel on that particular vessel," said Maliha. "But he did it because he was told to, not because he wanted you here."

Maliha fell silent to allow Constance to stew on that thought.

vii

"What do you need, Maliha?" asked Françoise. Constance glanced up and looked as if she had disembarked from an atmospheric at the wrong station.

"Would you enter the jaws of death with me?"

Françoise's eyebrows creased then relaxed. "Of course."

"Would you enter the jaws of death *instead* of me?"

Françoise smiled and hesitated before answering. "I believe I would," she said. "But I do not think that you would ask me to, Goddess."

Maliha mirrored her smile. "No, I wouldn't."

Constance looked from one to the other. "What is this?" Her voice trembled as if she feared that Maliha would demand a terrible price of her.

"I need you to take Izak with you back to Earth, Constance, and deliver him to my home. There's someone there who will look after him."

Izak had been sitting on a large chair with his pad and pencil, which he had been sharpening with a small knife. He looked up at the sound of his name. He said nothing, but he nodded to her.

"Oh," said Constance, unable to disguise her relief at such a simple request. "Of course, if that's what you need."

"I'll leave him with you," said Maliha, "and I'll send his clothes ahead. Do you want me to pay for his ticket?"

"No, I can do that," said Constance. "It's the least I can do. If I'm already getting two, another won't make a difference."

"I will not return with you," said Françoise. "I will stay with Maliha."

Constance gave a little cry. "You can't! I *need* you."

Françoise shrugged. "*Cherie*, it is not *I* that you need, it is just *someone*." She sighed and placed her hand on her lover's. "This is not the way I had intended us to part, Constance. If I tell the truth, not one part of this journey has been the way I originally desired. I have enjoyed our time together, but it could never have been forever."

Constance pulled a kerchief from her sleeve and dabbed at her eyes. Maliha was not sure she was really crying. So much of Constance was just for show.

"You made me feel wonderful," she said.

"I know, *cherie*, but there are many people in the world who can do the same for you."

"But how will I know the right one?"

Maliha decided her act was getting out of hand. "That's enough, Constance, you are a grown woman not a schoolgirl."

The words were a slap. Constance jerked back and straightened in her chair.

Maliha continued. "If you really think that finding someone suitable to satisfy your desires is a genuine problem, I will write a letter to Amita. She will vet appropriate candidates and provide you with one, or more than one. Male or female, whichever you prefer."

Constance opened her mouth as if to speak and then shut it again without uttering a word.

"Shall I do that for you?"

Constance nodded, still too surprised to speak.

"Good. That's settled." Maliha looked at her watch; the Venusian day was a little shorter than Earth's but there was sufficient similarity to maintain the same count of hours.

"I have to go to the watchmaker to pick up my watch, and then do some additional shopping, so I should be going."

"I can be ready in half an hour," said Françoise. She stood immediately and went off into the house.

"Does your husband have any modern maps?" asked Maliha.

Constance shrugged. "I don't know. He's got a library."

The library was cooler and drier than any other part of the house. Maliha spent the next ten minutes going through the books while Constance fidgeted by the door. She was probably already working herself up into a state of nervous excitement over the prospect of having no sexual release at the hands of a lover for several weeks.

"What are you looking for?" she asked as Maliha scoured the index of another atlas.

"Timmonsburg."

Constance laughed out loud.

Maliha glared at her. "What's funny?"

Constance suddenly stopped laughing and put her hand to her mouth. "Oh, I'm not supposed to know. He could kill me."

"You're leaving the planet and, besides, he's invited me there."

"It can't even be real," she said. "Perhaps it was an in-joke and I misunderstood."

Maliha closed the atlas and slid it back where it had come from. She straightened and walked over to face Constance.

"Just tell me."

"It's a flying rock."

"What are you talking about?"

"I heard them talking," said Constance, "about flying up to Timmons' Mountain."

"It could just be a house on top of a hill. Why say it's flying?"

"Because one of them said it was over the tropics at the moment."

"His exact words?"

Constance nodded.

"Perhaps it's just a Void-station."

"No, because they said they were hunting snarks."

Snarks were huge floating predators in the upper atmosphere preying on other balloon creatures. They had defensive quills that could pierce metal and moved like snakes through the air using stiff vanes that protruded from their upper and lower bodies.

Maliha paused. The nonsense poem 'The Hunting of the Snark' came from *Through the Looking Glass*. It could not be a coincidence, but what did it mean?

She recalled what Khuwelsa Edgbaston had said about the crystal with Faraday qualities. What if you could energise an entire mountain of the material? You would still need power to keep it in the air but, yes, you could have a mountain that flew.

But how would you find it?

"And this is something you overheard in the last couple of days?"

Constance nodded. "Are you saying it's real?"

"Oh yes," said Maliha. "I do think it is real. Timmons Mountain. *Timmonsburg*."

They made their way back to the atrium and met Françoise; she only had three cases. With two staff moving her luggage, they made their way to the front door. The taxi was still there, puffing quietly to itself.

Maliha knelt down in front of Izak and was transported back to that moment at the dock in Pondicherry when her mother and father had put her on the boat to England. At that time there few many passenger fliers and those were only for the very rich. So eleven year-old Alice Anderson had had to take a berth on a ship for three months with one of the older staff to attend her.

It had been late afternoon and the Sun was casting long shadows. The harbour bustled with people and machines. Smoke rose from the single funnel of the steamer. It had seemed huge to her at the time, though by the end of the voyage it resembled a book one had read a thousand times and knew every word. And not a very good book, at that.

Her father had kept his emotions locked inside, while her mother had hugged her and wept. She had not wanted Maliha to be sent away; that was her father's decision. But in the end his resolve cracked and he too hugged her and wiped away a tear when he thought she wasn't looking.

Maliha clung to Izak and wept.

"Do not cry, Goddess," he said. "I have a drawing for you."

She let him go and he handed her a sheet of paper torn from his notebook. She wiped her eyes. The picture was similar to the first one she had seen. There was the horizon and the tree, but this time the tree was tiny, barely the size of her nail. And the goddess reached from the bottom of the sheet to the top. She had been rendered better than in the first picture and she was still a silhouette, except she was white against the dark ground and even darker sky. The final flourish was the stars. He must have spent ages filling in the sky while leaving gaps for each of the stars.

"The goddess is very big," she said.

He simply nodded.

CHAPTER 8

i

Françoise stared out into the rain-filled atmosphere. The cab was forced to drive at a reduced pace in the deluge as they returned to the city.

"Why would someone follow me and then not follow me?" said Maliha.

Françoise tore her attention away from the misty, grey landscape and into the electrically lit interior. "Perhaps you scared them away."

Maliha appeared to consider the possibility. "The fellow did not run—he simply ceased to follow." She shrugged as if at an internal thought. "Perhaps it was just some ordinary criminal and nothing to do with Timmons at all."

"Do they have ordinary criminals here?" said Françoise trying to suppress the edge of humour in her voice.

Maliha directed a stern look in Françoise's direction, so she smiled coyly and then added to make amends, "Perhaps he had seen everything he needed to see."

Maliha nodded. "It's the only thing it could be."

"What were you doing at the time?"

"Buying new glasses."

"Meaning you broke your others?"

"Yes."

Françoise gave Maliha a thoughtful look. "Deliberately?"

"You know me too well, Miss Greaux."

"And we're heading to the market building now?"

"To pick up the order, yes."

"And you'd like me to do that."

"Yes."

Françoise narrowed her eyes. "Did you have all this planned from the commencement?"

"Not at all, I had no idea Constance would be desperate to return to Earth, or that you would be keen to leave her so soon." Maliha sounded sincere, but Françoise did indeed know her well.

"But if that had not been the case, you would have arranged it thus."

"I'm sure Constance would have felt it her duty to escort Izak back to Earth."

"Especially when you reminded her you saved her life."

Maliha shrugged again in imitation of Françoise.

"And you knew I'd follow you."

"I thought you might."

Françoise sighed. "I still hold you in my heart, Miss Anderson, and I am very sad you will not share my bed any more."

Maliha smiled and put her hand on Françoise's wrist. "Things have changed and, besides," she said, "I recall it was you who pointed out I should be with Valentine instead."

Françoise bit back her comment that Valentine was dead. Instead she looked out into the rain. The ground just beyond the raised roadway was awash; only the tops of the taller grasses could be seen. It was as if they were driving across an infinite marsh.

After a long time the cab entered the city. It traced its way up and down the labyrinthine aerial roads until it came to a halt by the central market building.

"I will never again complain about the rain in Paris," said Françoise as she held the wide umbrella over herself and Maliha, who paid the driver. The beat of the falling drops played a persistent drumming on the taut fabric, and water poured from the angled surface in a constant waterfall.

Maliha stood up and wrapped her arm under Françoise's.

"I do not even know why we bother; we are wet through even with the *parapluie*."

"Perhaps because the air is so thick with water it would be possible to drown as one walked?"

They splashed, ankle-deep in flowing rainwater, across the arrival area. Françoise could feel the current pulling at her feet as the water tumbled away. They reached the covered area before the doors and stepped up into the relative dry. Françoise looked back at the cab driving away, throwing up a great wave of water as it did so. She shook her head, sending drops of water flying from her hair like a dog.

Françoise shook out the umbrella while Maliha brushed the surface water from her own clothes.

"Come, Miss Greaux, let me introduce you to the wonders of the market."

Once inside they approached the balcony overlooking the floor and the other raised galleries. A group of players occupied the middle of the main floor, enacting a play of some sort.

Maliha pointed out the optician's shop.

"Won't they be expecting you?" said Françoise.

In reply Maliha pulled a thick envelope from her reticule. "Just give them this. It contains a letter of introduction and money."

Françoise took it and tucked it inside her dress. "Where will you be?"

Maliha nodded in the direction of the businesses on the opposite side of the market at this level. "Talking to one of the travel agents. But come with me and we will play-act a disagreement. In case we are being observed."

As they walked further from the entrance the floors became drier, but Françoise and Maliha still dripped.

The constant drumming in the background—which Françoise had not previously noticed due to its pervasive and constant nature—stopped abruptly. The drop in noise levels was reminiscent of one's ears popping after riding an atmospheric or an unpressurised balloon. All the sounds became clearer.

Françoise glanced up. The remains of the downpour slid from the glass roof and the burning clouds pierced the dark. She looked away quickly.

Maliha led her past several travel shops until she came to one she seemed to like; Françoise thought it looked disreputable. The frontage was dirty and several large, dead insects lay behind the glass. The name of the previous owner had not been removed but had been covered by a limp sheet of card with letters that had run. It was like a caricature of a badly run business.

Françoise did not find it hard to work up a disagreement with Maliha about entering. She had no desire to meet the proprietor, who would no doubt leer at them both; it was a habit of men Françoise found particularly distasteful.

"Very well then," said Maliha. "You find something to amuse yourself while I discuss our travel plans."

"Whatever you decide," said Françoise. "I will not go on any journey arranged with these people."

As she flounced away she wiggled her hips provocatively to remind Maliha what she was missing. Constance sighed. She needed to find another woman who was willing to dominate her in bed. The memory of Maliha's actions brought a healthy flush to her cheeks. She pushed the memory away. She could not think that way. Maliha had made her decision, but perhaps she would come back to Françoise when she no longer grieved Valentine's loss.

She was so deep in thought she missed the stairwell and had to backtrack. She found the shop easily enough. There were two other people there waiting to be served. One looked to be a local by his loose and casual dress, and his boots were not new. The other's boots were pristine and he looked uncomfortably wet.

The woman at the counter smiled. "Can I assist you, madam?"

Françoise extracted the letter, now slightly damp, and handed it over. "I am here to collect an item."

The woman took the envelope but did not open it. Instead she disappeared into the back. There were three chairs; neither of the other two customers was using them, but Françoise sat down and felt the damp seep through to her behind. It was quite unpleasant. One advantage of staying with Constance had been that Françoise had had no need whatsoever to leave the house and so remained completely dry for two days.

On her return the woman had a case for glasses, which she handed to the tourist in return for a couple of British pound notes. She dug into a drawer behind the counter and counted out some change. Françoise had struggled with British currency; it was so complicated—francs and centimes were so much more logical.

The local pulled a particularly heavy pair of glasses from the rack. They had large blinders on each side, as well as lens material so thick Françoise could see nothing through them.

Both customers left and the woman disappeared briefly into the back again. She was carrying a small package when she returned. She made to hand it over to Françoise, but she held on to it so they were both gripping it.

"You know," she said, "they used to think that black-eye was caused by staring into the burning clouds for too long."

"Did they?"

"Now they know it is a fungus that eats into the fibres of the brain and the eyes."

"That is unpleasant," said Françoise hoping the woman would stop talking and release the package.

"I hope your mistress knows what she's doing."

Françoise met her gaze. "As do I."

The woman finally let go of the package and Françoise tucked it beneath the folds of her dress.

ii

Françoise reached the travel agent just as Maliha was emerging. Her face was grim. Françoise was about to ask what was wrong but did not get the chance.

"Come on," Maliha said and whirled away towards the exit, with Françoise trailing behind.

The air outside was already intensely hot and it was like breathing underwater. Françoise shook her head; the sooner she was off this planet *dégoûtant*, the better she would like it. She would never criticise the monsoon again.

They found a cab, Maliha gave the name of the hotel and they climbed inside. Once more they were dripping wet and this time it had not been raining.

"What is wrong, *cherie*?"

Maliha glanced at the driver's compartment; the sliding glass door between them was closed.

"Men."

"*Oui*, they are very infuriating, *n'est pas*?"

Maliha glanced at her and raised an eyebrow. "He wanted to discuss the trip with my husband."

Françoise laughed. "Perhaps I should don my disguise once more."

"I managed to persuade him."

"Tell me what you did to him."

Maliha sat back. "I bribed him."

"*Mais non*! You did not emasculate him with your tongue?"

Maliha hesitated then realised what Françoise meant. "I doubt he had the wit to understand my insults." She sighed. "But he did understand my money."

"Why did you choose such a stupid one?"

"It was your comment about criminals that made me think of it," said Maliha. "Although Timmons controls much of what happens here, there must be a class of criminals that are not in his sway. After all, Timmons is part of the legitimate establishment."

"So you wanted someone criminal who did not report to Timmons."

"As you say."

"But why?"

Maliha glanced at the driver. "I'll tell you later. Did you get it?"

Françoise tapped the place where the package was held safe at her waist. Maliha nodded then turned to watch the passing buildings.

Back at the hotel they explained the change in arrangements at reception and then followed the porters upstairs with Françoise's bags. A letter had arrived for Maliha, but she did not say what it was.

Once they were alone Françoise extracted the package and handed it over. Maliha said she had to send a reply to her letter, so Françoise headed into the bedroom. She threw off her clothes and extricated her feet from her boots. She spent a great deal of time wiping the disgusting unguent from her feet with a towel.

She got the unpleasant feeling she was being watched and the muscles behind her ears tightened as if she had heard something. She turned to see Maliha standing at the door, watching her. Unaccountably she felt embarrassed at her nakedness.

"How long have you been watching me?"

"A while."

"I do not think that is your 'cricket'."

"Not fair play? Why?"

Françoise pouted. "Because I have a very adorable physique, just as you do. You can see mine while I cannot see yours."

"I will not sleep with you, Françoise."

"Who said anything about sleeping, *cherie*?" she said. "I am only concerned with the cricket."

"Fine," said Maliha and came into the room. "You can help me undress and get my feet clean."

"You have delightful feet."

Once she was naked, Maliha grabbed her dressing gown and wrapped it around herself. Françoise frowned. "A dressing gown is cricket?"

Maliha sat in the chair by the dresser. "Do my feet."

Françoise grinned and gathered up the towel.

"And no funny business."

Françoise expressed innocence, then crouched down and set to work wiping Maliha's feet and ankles, working up her calves and massaging the muscles.

"I would call that funny business."

"But we are not laughing."

Maliha pulled her leg from Françoise's grasp. "Seriously, Françoise. I cannot."

"*Will* not."

"Don't be upset."

Françoise sighed and shook her head. "You do not know what you have done to me, Maliha. I am the schoolgirl with the passion." She stood up and sat back on the bed. "All I want to do is hold you and kiss you."

"I am engaged to Valentine."

"He is dead, *cherie*, you have told me yourself."

It was Maliha's turn to sigh. "I know."

"Did you promise him you would never touch another?"

"No."

"Would he expect you to never love again?"

"I don't think so."

"So?"

"It's too soon."

Françoise went to her bag and pulled out her own dressing gown. She slipped it on. "There," she said. "You see? I understand. But…"

"But what?"

"When it is no longer too soon, will you promise to be with me?" The pleading tone of her voice surprised even Françoise. Her desire, her love for Maliha was stronger than anything she had ever felt and yet she was willing to put it aside.

Maliha opened her mouth to speak.

"No," interrupted Françoise. "No, do not say anything. Do not make a promise. It is unfair of me. It is not cricket." She sat facing Maliha. "*Merde*, what have you done to me?"

"Made an honest woman of you?"

"I very much hope not, *Mademoiselle* Anderson. I do not believe I could live with myself if I were honest."

Maliha laughed. "I do not think I could love you if you were, either." Then she paused and became serious once more. "There is something I need to tell you."

"Do not say it," said Françoise. "I already know."

"What?" Maliha looked horrified.

"You are a man in disguise!"

Maliha shut her eyes. "No, stop it. I am being serious."

"You cannot be serious, we have nothing to drink," said Françoise, standing up, "and I am hungry."

"What do you suggest?"

"Oh, I do not know? Here we are in a hotel where there is a restaurant where they serve food and wine, *peut-être*," said Françoise as she strode across the room to her luggage, stripping off her dressing gown as she went. "Here is a good idea: we will put on some clothes and go to dinner."

*   *   *

Maliha found the meal satisfying, though Françoise said the wine was indifferent. It did not travel well and had come all the way from Earth.

"It is not likely they will ever have their own wine," said Françoise as she put down her empty glass.

"Too wet," said Maliha.

"*Oui*, one cannot grow grapes in this, they will rot on the vine."

"You can make gin out of anything."

Françoise shuddered. "Mother's ruin. Yes, no doubt they will make that. In this dismal place everyone will need to drown their misery."

The waiter cleared away the dishes from the main course. Maliha was feeling better. She had avoided any tight clothing and the meal had not been a trial. She had noticed the glances from the men in their direction.

Two years ago such looks would have had her scurrying for a hole and left her with such anger. Only two years. She had changed so much. She felt lightheaded and looked at her empty wine glass. Two years ago she would not have touched wine, but between them they had drunk a bottle. Françoise seemed unaffected, but Maliha knew her own faculties were diminished.

"When I left school in England all I wanted to do was run home and hide," she said suddenly.

Françoise looked at her. "And now you are a goddess."

Maliha shook her head. "Don't." She picked up the dessert spoon and looked at her distorted reflection. Her nose looked even bigger than it was normally.

"I have a big nose."

"Maliha Anderson, I do believe you are drunk."

"The condemned ate a hearty meal."

"And drank too much wine." Françoise reached out and put her hand on Maliha's. "It would be easy to seduce you now."

"I wish you would."

Françoise shook her head and released Maliha's hand. "No, *cherie*, you do not and you would despise yourself in the morning."

"No more than I usually do," she said and felt tears welling up. "I'm going to die, Françoise, and I'm going to kill you too. Don't come with me tomorrow, you shouldn't die."

"You are talking nonsense."

"No, we are going to hunt snarks and boojums, but they are going to eat us."

Maliha jumped back in her seat as Françoise stood up. She thought she might hit her, but she did not. Instead she hooked her arm under Maliha's and dragged her to her feet. Maliha staggered.

"There's something wrong with the Faraday," Maliha muttered. The room did not want to keep still and each time she tried to focus on something it slid away to the left. And then the floor decided to come up to meet her.

iii

Françoise was in her nightclothes when Maliha opened her eyes. They were back in the bedroom and it was behaving like the restaurant had: sliding away to the left when she focused on something. Maliha had an unpleasant taste in her mouth.

"Have I been sick?"

"Oh yes."

"Sorry."

Françoise shrugged. Maliha looked at her arms—she was also in her night things. The room was becoming steadier, but the taste in her mouth was disgusting.

"Did you undress me?"

"Of course."

"Sorry," she said, then her mind wandered and she had a thought. "You know the men in the restaurant fancied us."

"Is that supposed to impress me?"

"No," said Maliha, "but it impressed me."

"I know what you're saying," said Françoise, coming over and sitting beside her. "Let me ask you a question."

Maliha draped herself on Françoise's shoulders and rested her head there, breathing in the scent of her hair. It was damp. Everything here was damp.

"Maliha?"

"What?"

"You're not listening."

"I think I might be a little bit inebriated."

"On half a bottle of wine?"

"Drinking alcohol is against my religion," said Maliha, "both of them."

"I am trying to make a point."

"Sorry."

Françoise pushed Maliha off her shoulders and brought their faces close enough to kiss. "Do you think I would love just anyone?"

"Truthfully?" said Maliha.

Françoise pursed her lips. "Very well, perhaps that was not a good example. What about Valentine?"

Maliha shook her head, and regretted it. "No, he would not love just anyone."

"But he loved you."

Maliha could not suppress the sudden outburst of tears and sobbing. She felt Françoise get up and move away.

"Sorry," said Françoise. "This is the wrong time for that."

Moments later a kerchief was being thrust into Maliha's hand. It took her a few minutes to get herself under control.

"What was it you wanted to tell me earlier?"

"Can I have some coffee?"

"I didn't think you drank coffee."

"I don't."

Françoise paused. "I'll get them to send up a good, strong pot."

* * *

When room service knocked it was Françoise who went to the door and brought in the trolley. In addition to the coffee, there was a selection of light sandwiches, toast and boiled eggs.

Maliha munched her way through toast and drank the coffee. There was no milk, but that was no loss—she had not had milk until she went to England and she avoided it as much as she could, though milk-based puddings had made regular appearances on the school menu. No animal that gave milk could survive on Venus unless completely coddled, which made it a very rare and extremely expensive commodity.

Maliha felt better and the lack of order in her thoughts withdrew as she consumed more. There were no fruits either and the bread tasted strange; Maliha assumed it must contain local replacements for the difficult-to-acquire ingredients.

But the local food supply must be sufficient to feed the population which, as she had established, was far larger than expected.

"They cannot be importing it all," Maliha said out loud. "There are not enough ships coming and going."

"What are we talking about now?" asked Françoise.

"Food," said Maliha, taking another bite out of her slice of toast. There was something on it that could not be butter. "This is bread that is not bread, and butter that is not butter."

"Foreign food always tastes strange."

"Is that how you felt about Indian food?"

"This," she held up a sandwich, "I do not know what this meat is, but it is a good sandwich. In India, no sandwiches. No proper bread unless I demanded it."

"What would it be like to be born and grow up here?" said Maliha. "With your government millions of miles away."

"I suppose there must be children who have never known anything else."

"They would be Venusians; they would hate Earth if they visited. They would resent being at the mercy of men so far away." Maliha thought again of India. The British had always ruthlessly suppressed any hint of rebellion, especially since the mutiny of '57.

The resentment was there. It bubbled beneath the surface always. It was the reason she was now called a goddess, all because one priest had thought it would be clever to name her thus. He wanted a figurehead people could rally around. Perhaps he thought a woman would be easy to manipulate, but Maliha was not interested in playing his game.

The name had stuck anyway.

"The Indian Mutiny was caused by the East India Company," she said.

Françoise shook her head. "What is the subject now?"

"If you ran a business more powerful than most governments, with more money than most countries, and someone told you to stop what you were doing, would you do it?"

"I think I would ignore that person."

"What if you were told to do it by the most powerful country in the world?"

"I suppose I might do it."

"What if you secretly owned a fleet of Voidships more powerful than anything in the world?"

Françoise put her head on one side. "I think you have had too much to drink and have been reading too much Jules Verne, or your H. G. Wells."

Maliha ignored her. A planet with a large population that had reached self-sufficiency. A fleet of ships—who knew how many—that possessed almost complete nullification of gravity without the Rutherford-Tesla device. Those whose families had been part of the EIC were still powerful back in England; they were lords and commanders of great trade empires—just like Timmons.

For a moment she thought about the scale of it: not just Venus but perhaps Mars, mining operations on Mercury and perhaps further. What about the remains of the planet Phaeton, and beyond—all while the great and good of Earth took their little health tours around the Moon.

"But none of that matters," she said.

Françoise pulled a face and poured herself another coffee. "Is it always like this around you? I do not remember you being so like a … butterfly."

Maliha smiled. "No, I was not. I have had some ideas. They may be nothing, just a fancy, as you say something Verne or Wells might have dreamed up." *Especially Herbert George, who is always so keen on social reform.*

An ache had started up in her temple, but it was only a pain and an improvement on her earlier inability to think in a straight line.

"Françoise, I am going to ask you to do something," she said.

"I will do anything."

Maliha held up her hand. "No, listen, I will tell you what it is and then you will decide, not before."

"I will say yes whatever it is."

"Please stop arguing with me."

"Yes, Goddess."

Inside, Maliha screamed. Françoise had a way of needling that always got under her skin.

So be it.

iv

Françoise strolled into the disreputable travel agent at nine o'clock the following morning in her gentleman's outfit. There had been a rainstorm, but it had passed quickly and the temperature had soared.

"Morning, sir," said the man behind the desk. He was dressed in a jacket and trousers that were too small for him, over a shirt that needed a wash. He did not move from his position with his feet up on the desk, lounging back in the chair that looked as though it ought to collapse under his weight.

"My name is Francis Gray," she said. "You are expecting me." Françoise had a voice with a naturally low pitch and, coupled with her male appearance, it gave the impression of a slightly effete man. She had discovered that women found this to be less threatening, making it all the easier to make their acquaintance and get them into bed. By the time they discovered she was not a man they were usually past caring.

True, it was deceitful and she knew Maliha would not approve. That is why they did not discuss it.

The man brushed off his hands and climbed to his feet. The chair creaked as his weight lifted from it.

"Ferdie." He stuck out his hand to shake; Françoise was not happy about that, but she was wearing grey gloves so she did not have to come in contact with his skin. The man's hand was soft and his grip was weaker than hers.

"No time to waste, we'd better be off," he said and walked out of the shop. Françoise followed. He did not seem concerned with security and did no more than shut the door after turning over the sign to 'Closed'. There was no lock.

"Do you want a gun?" he asked as he led the way to the stairs.

"I am armed."

They climbed the stairs and he said no more, but she could hear him wheezing as the steps took their toll. Françoise wondered how he fared in such a damp environment—surely he must have difficulties with his lungs?

He walked slower as they went along the next floor, not in the direction of the taxi rank for the public but through a door between two stalls and into a narrow corridor that led out to a private service area.

"Borrowed this," he said. They approached a small, three-wheeled, diesel-powered carriage that had clearly seen better days. Its exposed metal was rusted and the suspension springs looked worn through. "Doesn't look like much, but it will get us there."

Fully open to the elements, thought Françoise. "If we don't drown." She fetched her dark glasses from an inner pocket and put them on. She glanced up at the burning clouds. The earlier storm was already gone from sight and only a few small, low-level clouds remained.

He fired up the engine—at least it was quicker than steam—as Françoise settled herself in the cracked leather seat that may have once been red but now had a layer of green mold. She shook her head.

The carriage shook as the engine caught and its vibrations threatened to throw her out. She grabbed the side of the vehicle to steady herself. *It will probably be better when it's moving.*

It was worse. The wheels were almost bare of their shock-absorbing rubber and every bump and crack in the road was transmitted through to her seat. It must be like riding an old velocipede over cobblestones.

She had no idea in what direction they were heading. The light came from all directions in the day and there were no landmark buildings for orientation.

The machine rattled along the wooden road. It seemed to be a major thoroughfare, because of the other vehicles of all sizes, including large omnibuses and lorries, but it did not compare to the traffic of a major city back on Earth.

Finally she recognised the air-dock. The shuttle on which they had arrived, or something similar, sat on its raised platform and there were other landing areas further out. Her driver took them on a side road that led around the dock, until they slowed and turned off into the private yard.

Françoise clambered from the vehicle. Her body still felt as though it was being shaken by the vibration of the machine.

"Good little thing, eh?" said the man, laughing and slapping the front of the carriage. "Looks like nothing, but it goes well."

She managed to force a smile onto her face. "Good, yes." Maliha had given her an envelope stuffed with notes. Françoise pulled it out and held it out.

The man snatched it and ripped open the seal. He spent a minute counting the notes, twice, then looked up with a smile and nodded. He separated out a wedge of notes and pocketed it.

"Where are the flyer and the pilot?" she said, suddenly nervous they might be betrayed. She put her hand on the gun in her pocket. She saw his eyes follow the movement of her hand.

"Don't you worry, mate," he said. Françoise could not place his accent. "Your friend wanted things nice and secret, that's what it's all about. I got you a pilot who can do the job you need—no questions asked."

"No questions asked?"

He looked suddenly serious. "None."

The yard they were in was bordered on one side by a solid, wooden fence along the road, and a building on the other three sides, as if someone had built a stable, forgetting there were no horses on Venus.

Ferdie headed to a door and hammered on it. "Reggie's a bit deaf," he said by way of explanation before he started up hammering again. The door opened beneath his fist.

"Orright, Reggie, job's 'ere."

Françoise was expecting a face to appear about the level of Ferdie's, but instead it appeared a good foot and a half lower, a pale face, peering out from the shadows. It stared at Françoise and then looked up at Ferdie. "Gots da leaf?"

Ferdie handed over the envelope. Reggie stepped out. He was dressed head to foot in grey leather that was old and torn in places. It matched Reggie's wrinkled skin, though whether that was an indication of age, Françoise was not sure. His face was in shadow under an equally tatty helmet. Reggie counted the notes.

"Good leaf, you garn."

Ferdie shook hands with the diminutive Reggie and headed back to the carriage. "See ya, mate," he shouted to Françoise as he re-ignited the engine and climbed into the driving seat. Françoise shook her head as he pulled round in a tight circle and thundered out of the gate.

Her attention was yanked back by the screeching of wood on stone as Reggie pulled open one of a pair of double doors.

Reggie pushed both doors back until they were wide open. Françoise could see nothing in the interior; electric lights did not seem to be much in use on Venus. The hotel had them, as did the immigration building and the Mayberry house, but most other places did not.

How could any civilised place work without electricity? The answer was simple enough: they could not. Venus was a very great distance from being civilised. What was it Maliha had talked about last night? Would these Venusian hordes descend on Earth and go the way of the Roman Empire?

An engine spluttered into life in the dark beyond the double doors.

What emerged, bumping out into the open, did not look like anything that could fly. It had neither balloon nor wings, and there was no horizontal rotor for lift, but there was a vertical one at the rear for forward thrust. It was not much bigger than the rusted machine she had arrived here in.

It did, however, have what looked like wine barrels. There were four of them: two mounted at the rear and two at the front. They might have been thought of as wheels except they were far too wide and did not touch the ground. In the middle of all this was a small enclosed space for the pilot and an engine behind.

Tiny Reggie was leaning against the frame and pushing it out into the space. He stopped when he had it more or less central. "You in."

Françoise looked at her watch. They were still in good time; Maliha's transport was not going to leave for fifteen to twenty minutes and they needed to be ready to follow.

"You in!" shouted Reggie. He had moved to the cage in the middle and was holding open a door. Françoise raised her hand as if to deflect his ire. She headed forward and stared into the compartment. It was not large. The pilot sat at the front; the space available for a passenger was almost sitting atop the engine.

It was just as well she was being a man; it would have been impossible to climb into the space in women's clothes. She pulled herself in as the light levels dropped and water tumbled from the sky.

She had not been paying attention and had not realised she was not standing on a raised platform. The yard was stone-flagged. Within moments it was inches deep in water, which was rising fast.

Reggie did not seem concerned. Françoise glanced back to the engine thudding beneath her. Water steamed off the casing as it struck. The ceiling withstood the onslaught of rain without leaking, though the racket it made was deafening.

Reggie climbed up in front of her, splashing water everywhere, and slammed the door shut. He sat and threw a couple of levers. Something ground painfully against something else. The metal barrels whipped into motion, spinning faster and faster. Water flew from them.

Françoise looked out at the yard as the water continued to rise. She could see it pouring in through the doors of the buildings. She shook her head; this was not a world she wanted any part of.

She felt herself lighten, not the fully powered gravity reduction of a modern flyer but something less. The water had reached the bottom of the door and was seeping in as Reggie increased the power of the engine. The drums spun even faster and the strange craft wobbled into the air.

The worrying lurches of the vessel evened out as they gained altitude, but there was an intense vibration from the engine and the rotating drums that jarred her teeth.

Françoise relaxed the death grip she had on the back of Reggie's chair, then grabbed it again as he powered up the thruster and they moved forward. The whole vehicle tilted to the left as they turned in that direction. Françoise had never felt so unsafe in a flying vehicle and she considered herself a seasoned traveller.

The rain was still pouring and the ground below was almost invisible through the grey, waterlogged air. But Reggie seemed certain enough as to the direction, so she tried to relax and sit back, leaning against the back of the compartment. There was no backrest.

The letter Maliha had received at the hotel gave instructions for meeting with a vessel that would take her to the 'mountain'. The plan was that Françoise would follow and land there too. She, however, was not to interfere with Maliha. She had her own instructions.

Françoise sighed. She had agreed, of course. She was unable to fathom what it was about Maliha that made her so compelling. Françoise had always been the one in control: she knew she was beautiful, and men would do anything for her in the hope she might bless them with a kiss—or something more—and women almost always fell before her and were grateful.

But Maliha? Françoise had not even seduced her; Maliha had kissed Françoise first. Maliha had come to her bed unbidden, though she had been distraught and in need. It was Maliha who saw through Françoise's lies and dominated her. And it was Françoise who had sent Maliha away to be with her true love, despite wanting to keep her.

Françoise looked out into the grey. Maliha was the better person and Françoise would be happy to be half the woman she was. Even if she *was* reckless and impulsive.

Maliha believed she was going to die today and yet she still went.

Françoise brushed back a tear. There was no point making this water-world any wetter than it already was. She leaned forward and put her mouth near to Reggie's ear.

"How long?"

"Five and five." Reggie lifted his left hand from the controls and opened and closed his gauntleted fist twice.

"Ten."

"Five and five."

Françoise sat back and glanced at her watch. What did he mean?

A few minutes later they burst from the wall of water. The light of the burning clouds flooded the cabin with light. Françoise blinked behind her glasses. It was as if they had broken through a curtain.

She looked back at the plummeting rain, which looked more like a waterfall stretching into the distance. Coruscating rainbows danced through the air, moving to the song of the wind. This planet may be appalling, but when it chose to show its beauty it poured it out by the bucketful.

Her watch showed five minutes had passed. Is that what he had meant? That it would be five minutes in the storm and then five more? How could he have known?

Looking down, she saw they were already beyond the perimeter of the city. In fact, there was not a single building in sight, though with the light coming from all directions it was hard to make out anything. The ground itself appeared to be a flat plain of green except where the water reflected the brightness of the sky.

Like Earth there were copses where trees grew close together. In each of them, always near the middle, was one larger than the others, almost as if the smaller ones were children gathered around a parent.

The surface was generally flat, or at least it appeared so in the strange light, and the expanses of water must be level. Further towards the horizon, she could make out undulations in the terrain, as well as storms pouring their abundance onto the surface.

Then there was a road; it cut in from their left. Reggie flew across it but turned to parallel its course. It was the only way she could judge their height and she estimated they must be at least two kilometres up.

Movement nearer the horizon caught her eye. She turned her head in that direction and stared. A herd of lilac monsters, legs like tree trunks, heads the size of houses, bodies bigger than the carriage of an atmospheric, ponderously splashed across a shallow lake. There were perhaps twenty large beasts and a dozen more young ones that moved faster and—it was unmistakable—played with one another. One of them had a branch or a root and two others were pulling on it, trying to take it.

As they passed out of sight it was their lilac colour that seemed to stick with her.

She felt her stomach sinking hard. The thruster had reduced its speed but the lifters were now running faster and they climbed into the sky.

vi

Somehow Reggie had known precisely where they were and how far the edge of the storm was. Françoise shook her head, it was impossible. She studied the back of Reggie's neck—she could see skin between the flying hat and his threadbare shirt.

She clenched her fist as she recoiled at the strangeness. His skin was the dark colour that she saw in his features, but, rather than the soft continuous surface she expected—or even skin that had been become brown and cracked from exposure to the horrors of Venus—it was leathery, with darker lumpy nodules and green moss growing on it.

Françoise sat back and stared at the back of his head. She wondered what was under his hat. Perhaps she did not want to know.

They were still climbing. The road they had been following had become little more than a line winding through the luminescent green. Though it was hard to make out, a hill that had been blocking their view no longer did so and behind it several buildings came into view.

In the spaces between them were flying vessels. She could make out people walking between the buildings and one of the machines. Whether one of them was Maliha, she could not tell. She thought Reggie's flyer must be visible, but then anyone looking would be staring at the burning clouds and nobody wanted to do that for very long.

She cried out and grabbed the chair as Reggie threw them to the right. Fleshy ropes floated past them on the left. Françoise leaned against the window and peered up.

A writhing mass of tentacles drifted a dozen feet above them, above which a bulbous, veined balloon rippled in the wind. "What is it?" she said breathlessly.

"Kraken," came the grating voice with the unplaceable accent. "Small."

Françoise estimated the balloon to be twenty metres from end to end.

"Lost," was Reggie's final word on the matter.

It was lost? It was a nightmare.

Below them one of the fliers had taken off and was heading ... Françoise had no idea. It was heading away from them. Reggie engaged the thruster and the little vessel accelerated after it.

Françoise tried to relax, but the seat was very uncomfortable. It had been designed for someone smaller. Did Reggie have a wife? Or was Reggie female and had a husband? Or a wife? Françoise shook her head.

What would Maliha do in this situation?

Nothing. She would just observe. *Well*, Françoise thought to herself, *I am not her. I am in a vessel I don't understand, being flown by something that does not appear to be human, to a place I don't know, on a planet where I do not belong.* She shivered. She had not been so afraid in a long time.

"See," said Reggie. He waved in the general direction of forwards.

Françoise looked out and down. The green of the land was coming to an end; it had an edge. As they moved across it the surface changed, no longer the flat mossy green with trees but a torrent pouring from the flat highlands. As far as the eye could see it was the same, one long cascade tumbling over the edge. The slope descended for over a kilometre until it met another body of water, churning with waves.

They had reached one of the oceans—or was it all just one ocean? She could not remember.

And then they were past the strange coastline. Now there was just the sea. The waves and swell reflected the light of the burning clouds with the same brilliant yellows and reds. She closed her eyes against the glare.

* * *

She awoke to a jerk from the flyer. Through the windows, the world was dark grey and water streamed across the panes. Another storm. Françoise lifted her wrist to check her watch, but it was too dark to see. Her neck and legs ached with stiffness. She tried to stretch, but there was no space.

"Where are we?"

"South."

Françoise remembered Maliha saying something about every direction being south when you're at the North Pole.

"Are we still over the ocean?"

"Yes."

"In another storm."

"Yes."

"How do you know where to go?"

"Follow."

"But you cannot see anything!"

"Follow good."

Françoise closed her eyes. She just wanted to be out of this damned ship. She wanted to be on solid ground or, better, on *dry* land, if such a thing existed on Venus. She wanted to be on Earth.

She clung to the seat of the chair with both hands as panic swept through her.

The grey outside and the growling of the engine were constant. The back of Reggie's head was unchanging. Her heart thumped in fear. She was far above an infinite ocean in a storm.

"Nearly there."

Reggie's words were like a balm on her electrified nerves. She relaxed a little, much to her own surprise.

"How long?"

"Six."

A hoarse laugh exploded from Françoise's throat, as if it had been put there by someone else. "Six," she whispered and giggled. "How long before we come out of the storm?"

"Not."

She absorbed the meaning of that. They would be reaching the mountain before they came out of the storm. She had no alternative other than to trust him, but another wave of fear gripped her.

The journey continued. At first Françoise tried to count, mouthing the numbers to see how much time had passed, but she gave up when she realised that she was counting too fast. And she did not know how long Venusian seconds were.

She peered into the fog, hoping to be able to see what Reggie could see, but there was nothing but constant grey. She could only see as far as the ends of the lifting drums. Then the grey directly in front of them became much darker.

Reggie reduced power to the thruster and the vessel tilted to the right as it turned, though the only real evidence of the turn was that the dark shadow moved around to their left.

This must be the mountain, she thought.

Her stomach lifted into her mouth as Reggie suddenly dived and turned in towards the mountain. The shadow went across the top of them. Françoise saw lights, electric lights, through the mist and against the shadow.

Françoise swallowed. The mountain was flying. Somehow it made her hate Venus even more. How could mountains fly? Perhaps it wasn't a very big one.

Reggie did not stop beneath it but flew straight until they came out of the shadow, then up the other side. Now the shadow was on their right. She was about to ask how they were going to get onto the mountain, when he turned in towards it and accelerated.

Françoise screamed as the approaching blackness resolved into a solid wall of rock.

vii

Maliha recognised the advanced Faraday effect she had felt in the *Pegasus* with Sellie and Johannes. So, a mountain *could* be made to fly if it were made from that material. It would still need power to make it stay up—rotors most likely—but it was only a matter of scale.

They called it a mountain, but she wondered how true that really was. In the mind of common men it would only need to be five or six times the size of a large vessel to qualify. And with the additional gravity reduction, the power to keep it up would be proportionally less.

The flyer that had brought her was of a standard British design, with four rotors, each of which could swivel from horizontal to vertical.

However, the cabin of the vessel had been designed for comfort. It resembled a small drawing room with sofas, armchairs and occasional tables, though each item was firmly attached to the floor and each seat possessed a restraining strap.

She climbed out of the armchair. She had not been tied up and there had been no attempt to disguise their direction of travel; not that that meant anything, since their destination could move. It must, however, have a fixed flight plan so it could meet other vessels. The logistics in keeping it supplied with fuel alone must be quite challenging.

The cabin had air-cooling, which had made the whole journey quite comfortable. Today she had chosen to wear a sari. Her choice of costume was partly one of convenience, since it was designed for hot and sweaty climates. The other factor in her choice had been more complex.

She had woken with a dry mouth and an aching head. She remembered every part of her drunken behaviour the night before. It might not have been as excessive as some she had witnessed—it had only been half a bottle of wine, but that was far more than she was used to.

It was in that moment of contemplation she felt she knew at last who she was. She would never be a European. They would never accept her. To them she would be, at best, a second-class citizen. At worst she would be sub-human.

No. She was Indian. And they could accept her as that, or not at all. She had ceased to care. Françoise had not commented on the sari, though there had been one or two sidelong glances.

The main passenger cabin possessed a kitchen, which was not stocked, and an adjoining toilet and W.C. She retreated to the convenience before her contact, a man called Andrews, returned to take charge of her.

She made use of the facilities and washed her hands thoroughly. She took pleasure in the pure hot and cold running water; it was a style of living she might have enjoyed if she had ever had the chance. She dried her hands on the towel and looked into the mirror. The dark glasses hid her eyes. She removed them.

It was still her face that looked back at her: the lightly tanned skin, deep brown eyes, her hair, in need of a brush, but there was no time now. She reached into her reticule and removed the package the spectacle-maker had provided. She undid the outer wrapping and pulled it open. Inside, padded with cotton wool, were two small leather pouches.

She pulled open the ties on the first and slid out a very thin piece of black glass. Its curve made it look like a piece of an egg that, if complete, would be about an inch and a half to two inches across. The other pouch contained another.

Being careful not to touch the inner surface, she ran a fingertip around the edge. It seemed smooth. Nothing to catch or scratch. While the glass was very thin, it was coloured so densely it was difficult to see anything through it. The two pieces were not circular but mirrored one another. Each had a straighter section on one side and extended deeper 'below' the straight part than above.

"Where are you?" shouted a voice from the other side of the door.

"I am utilising the convenience," she said with enough penetration to reach him.

"Hurry up."

"Some things cannot be rushed," she said. *That should embarrass him into silence for a while.*

She picked up the first piece, the one for the left. She took a deep breath, pulled her lower left eyelid out between finger and thumb and pressed the glass between eye and lid. She blinked furiously and had to stop. She had known, intellectually, that placing a foreign object in her own eye was going to be difficult. She had intended to practice, but the drink had made her forget.

Her eye was watering. She took another deep breath and held it. She willed herself to calm and slid the bottom into the lower part of her eye. She suppressed the panic and lifted her top lid. She found she had to move the lens even deeper to get it under the eyelid, but then she was able to move it back.

"If you don't hurry up I'll break down the door."

"Your master would not like you to damage his vessel. I will be ready shortly."

The second lens was easier in some ways—at least she knew she could do it—but more difficult because her body's natural resistance fought even harder. But she overcame it and the second lens was soon in place. Both eyes were leaking tears that crawled hesitantly down her face in the very low gravity. She let them be. Crying was a symptom of a weak female in men's eyes.

Maliha tidied and flushed the packaging down the toilet, while the pouches she put in her reticule. She adjusted the *pallu* hanging over her left shoulder, then pulled a fold over her head and eyes.

She unlocked the door, forcing the bolt back so it made a solid sound. She did not want to surprise him; he had a gun.

She paused in the open door.

"I am ready."

viii

If she had not known she was on a flying vessel—they had flown underneath it—Françoise would have sworn they were in a cave on the ground. It definitely was a cave: the vehicle had shot through a small hole and ended up in a stone-walled room with pipes running through it.

As her eyes adjusted she could make out a sealed door to one side. It was hotter than hell in here. But she had no time to consider. Reggie was climbing out of the ship and he waved at her to follow.

Her aching muscles and stiff joints did not want to obey, but she forced them to move. Reggie held out his hand to steady her; without thinking she took it and felt the knobbly skin she had seen on his back and neck beneath his glove. She snatched her hand away. He didn't seem to mind and still offered his support.

What would the goddess do? Françoise really needed his help, so she let him take her hand. She clambered down and stretched. Reggie headed off towards the door into the gloom. She followed. The pipes set into the wall radiated heat so intensely it felt as if it would sear her skin.

Reggie turned a circular handle on the door several times until it swung open. A blast of freezing air poured through and the cave was instantly filled with mist, along with the sizzling sound of water landing on intensely hot metal.

A calloused hand grabbed hers and pulled her through the door, which was slammed behind her. There was more light here, but it was so cold, like the deepest freezing winter in Dijon. She shivered and tried to look around.

"Help," said a weak voice beside her. She turned to see Reggie on his knees. He reached out to her. His face was as pitted and calloused as the rest of him. And his eyes were a dark and alien red. She gasped as he fell forwards.

Françoise could feel her damp clothing freezing. It cracked as she moved. She hesitated. It was unnaturally cold in here and it would probably kill her if she stayed put. Reggie had already succumbed; he might be dead.

She grabbed Reggie by the back of his jacket, which was slippery with ice, and pulled. Getting him moving was hard; the cold was draining the strength from her, but gravity here was like it had been on the Voidship.

Ahead was a passage. She took it, moving as fast as she could. It led up a short slope into another room of pipes, but in this one her frozen breath joined the crunching frost on the floor and the icicles hanging from every surface.

Another door. Breathing had become painful and the cold dryness tore at her throat.

She dropped Reggie, then, using her sleeves to protect her skin, she turned the slippery handle. It took a while to get the door fully unlocked, but she managed and pushed it open. Another cloud of mist went up as the freezing air met the warmer air beyond the door. She pulled Reggie through and pushed the door shut. She gave the lock a few turns for good measure as she shivered in the warmth.

It was another corridor. She left Reggie's body where it was and sat against the opposite wall. She felt the warmth seep through her clothes and into her skin. She swore she would never complain about the heat of Venus ever again.

As she recovered she looked around. There was a sign on the door in English: 'Heat Exchange'. She shook her head. What had possessed Reggie to land here? More importantly, perhaps, how had he even known about it?

She looked at the prone body. Previously Reggie had been rigid, frozen in the position that he had originally fallen. Now his joints were relaxing and he collapsed to the floor. She had seen someone revive a frog that had been put in ice. Perhaps Reggie was like a frog. There were definite similarities: He was very ugly.

And not human. Another secret.

Maliha had talked about the human population being much bigger than was expected, though Françoise was not sure how she knew that. But here was a frog man. A real Venusian. From what Françoise had gathered from people talking here and there back on

Earth, there was no intelligent life on Venus, just creatures that resembled primeval man.

But Reggie was living in the city and Maliha's disreputable travel agent knew all about him. Used him. Paid him.

Françoise shook her head; it did not bear thinking about. She hoped Reggie really was like the frozen frog so he could fly her off this floating rock.

She had warmed through, though she felt as if she might have caught a chill. She laughed inwardly at the mere idea of catching a cold on Venus. She stood and moved along the passageway. Maliha had given her a specific task: to gather any intelligence she could from the offices of Timmons while Maliha was distracting him.

She wanted information about the scale of Timmons' activities and any of his colleagues. Meanwhile Maliha would take steps to eliminate Timmons completely. That was the word she had used: "eliminate". Françoise assumed Maliha meant to kill him. She was certainly angry enough to do so, though Françoise was not sure how Maliha could possibly achieve that without any form of weaponry. After all, she was not actually a goddess.

She was deep in thought as she walked into the next chamber and found herself staring at the back of a man bent over some instruments. She froze.

He had not noticed her entrance and continued to study a panel of dials. He tapped one and sighed. He stood up straight and turned. His shock at seeing Françoise surpassed her surprise at walking in on him.

"Who in God's name are you?" He tensed, though Françoise could not tell whether that was because he expected to be attacked or because he was going to attack her.

"*Pardon?*" Françoise crinkled her brow in a semblance of confusion and attempted to look as innocent as possible. "*Je suis perdu. Je cherche Monsieur Timmons.*"

He frowned as he looked her up and down. Françoise had completely forgotten she was in men's clothes. That did not work very well with the helpless female approach. The next door was closed. He was on his own, probably only an engineer and not a guard.

So she fainted.

ix

The air-dock in which the ship had landed possessed doors that completely excluded the atmosphere of Venus. The entire space looked big enough to accommodate a vessel of considerable size, at least five times the length of the one that had brought her. The lenses over her eyes made everything so dark it was difficult to make out any details at a distance.

She wondered briefly whether Françoise had been able to follow. The storms would probably make it almost impossible. She shook her head a little as she descended to the deck. She had her walking stick and leaned on it, although there was no need in the light gravity.

They crossed the deck between two other vehicles of a similar design to hers; on one was painted a heraldic lion and on the other, a unicorn running. She frowned and turned back to look at the vessel they had left; it too had a symbol, a stylised sun with eight flames. She shook her head. It meant nothing. She noted several other smaller vessels sitting on the deck. It was a pity she had never learnt to fly else she could have escaped in one, perhaps.

The walls and ceiling glinted at her as she moved. She recognised the hexagonal crystalline structure as resembling quartz, but these crystals were so much larger. Each was at least three feet in diameter, extending from the floor to heights of thirty or forty feet. It was as if they were in some subterranean cavern rather than floating thousands of feet above the ground.

The crystal walls were interlaced with rooms hacked from the rock and panelled with the ubiquitous granite-wood.

They passed into a corridor. She reached out and touched the crystal. It was warm to the touch and slick like oil, though it left no residue. And, if she was not mistaken, it possessed an electric quality.

It was as Sellie had said, a form of rock with the power of a Faraday grid, yet much finer in resolution, hence providing a vastly improved barrier against gravity itself.

Though she had been unable to see the mountain from the outside, she knew that it must possess rotors and thrusters of enormous size to keep it aloft and propel it from place to place, which meant it must be supplied with power to drive them. Water was plentiful, so they would just need something to boil it.

This told her three things: They had a level of industry sufficient to build the machines; they had a production and transportation capacity to keep them supplied with fuel; and Timmons had monstrous arrogance to engage in such a level of conspicuous waste. He must possess an arrogance that exceeded all the fools of Christendom combined.

Good.

They proceeded along the passage. There were junctions here and there leading off who knew where. She sighed inwardly. The place was enormous—how could she possibly bring it to ruin?

Her friends were right. She was impulsive, reckless and her plans were half-baked. In this instance the plans had not even been given time to rise. She had no idea how she could possibly succeed. There would be no cavalry to rescue her at the last minute.

Finally they reached a pair of double doors. Again these were far bigger than they had any right to be. They were constructed from wood and had been carved with intricate patterns that were reminiscent of the Doric style but included the same sun symbol as the ship. So he saw himself as a Roman? An emperor perhaps? The Sun itself?

She was stopped several yards from the doors while her escort went forward and used an electrical signalling apparatus located in a hatch by the door. She did not attempt to see what he was doing; his body hid his actions and escape was not something she was seriously considering.

From a corridor behind there was a murmuring of voices. Someone laughed and she heard the words "the old walrus" quite distinctly. It was drowned out by more laughing.

She sighed. Why would people here not consider themselves the normal ones? They were privileged and served a man of great power. They might not even know of his murderous machinations.

Her eyes were sore from the lenses and they watered constantly. Tears dribbled slowly down her cheeks.

A grinding sound and the pumping of machinery filled the air. The doors swung back, inward. The chamber within was brightly lit, with electric lamps in the form of multiple chandeliers hanging from a high ceiling.

She frowned—the place looked wrong. Her escort gestured for her to enter. She moved forward, using the stick as if she had no choice. The floor of the hall was a chequerboard of huge white and black slabs, and columns flanked the walls. She could not determine the length of the hall. It looked very long indeed.

At the far end a massive dais rose from the floor and atop it was—to make no bones about it—a throne with a giant man sitting in it. The pedestal was flanked at floor level by two other chairs and, again, these were occupied by huge men.

Incongruously, they all wore simple but well-tailored suits. In a hall of such majesty and grandeur she would have not been surprised by royal robes of ermine and crowns on their heads.

She stopped inside the doors and heard the machinery closing them behind her. They closed with a thunderous crash that echoed through the chamber. The room still did not look right, how could Timmons be a giant? Assuming that was him. She put her head on one side and squinted at the chandeliers. They were very large but the further ones looked curiously distorted as if they were bigger.

Optical illusion. She hid her laugh with a cough. The whole room was constructed to appear to have parallel walls and a flat floor. Instead it closed in on itself and made the furniture and the individuals at the far end appear to have enormous size.

Trickery, illusion. Smoke and mirrors.

Mirrors? *The Looking Glass* again.

She could also play games. She walked forwards, counting the chequerboard squares.

x

An elegant collapse to the floor was easily achieved in low gravity, and Françoise was not even bruised. As she hit the floor she thrust her hand into her pocket. She affected a low moan, closed her eyes and went limp.

The fellow would either realise she was a woman or he would think her a womanly man. Either way, he would no longer see her as a threat. She lay there with her eyes shut, willing him to come and examine her.

To calm herself she counted frog men.

She reached ten and had heard no movement. She was wondering whether she dared open her eyes when a shadow crossed them. Curiosity must have got the better of him. She could hear his breathing now. It came closer; he must have crouched. She moaned and rolled slightly to free the hand in her pocket.

The man touched her cheek—one might wonder what that was expected to achieve—and then tapped it in some ineffectual attempt to revive her. She rewarded him by fluttering her eyelids and then opening them a little.

He was close enough that he could not see what she was doing with her hand.

She smiled gently. "*Merci, monsieur*," she said in her most alluring tones. He smiled back. She moved her small gun to his belly. "But now, step away or I will be forced to shoot you. And please", she added, "do not make any movement that might arouse my suspicions because that too may result in your death."

The smile on his face was replaced by fear. She watched him carefully as he stood and moved back. His eyes flicked to her hand, as if to satisfy himself her threat was not empty.

"Please put your hands in the air, also."

He complied. Françoise pushed herself up into a kneeling position, never taking her eyes from him and keeping the gun pointed in his direction. She stood.

"That is excellently done, *monsieur*. Now, if you will remove your belt and then take out the laces from your boots, we can proceed in ensuring you do not meet with a fatal accident." He did as he was told. Françoise used the laces to tie his wrists behind his back and used the belt to tie his ankles to a very cold pipe.

There was a movement behind her and Reggie appeared. He was moving with slow steps and using his arm to balance himself against the wall. He really did have the appearance of a frog. His eyes did not protrude, but they were large.

"So you are recovered?"

Françoise caught her prisoner staring wide-eyed at Reggie. She knelt and planted the gun against his temple. She had his full attention.

"Why do you stare?"

He glanced at Reggie and stuttered his reply. "You have it trained."

"Trained?" she said. "Yes, it is, and why does that surprise you?"

"They are ignorant beasts."

"This is a particularly clever one."

Maliha wanted her to gather information; this was very valuable. She stood, pleased with herself. "Come along, Reggie."

She headed for the door but came to a stop when she heard a thump and a weak cry. She did not want to turn. Reggie, now fully recovered it seemed, moved past her. There was something liquid and red on his hands. Françoise went to the door before she looked back.

The engineer lay unmoving. His eyes were open and blood leaked with inexorable slowness from his temple.

When she turned back to the door Reggie was in front of her.

"Why?" she breathed.

Reggie moved his shoulders in a manner that so resembled a shrug it could be nothing else. "Dey not know."

It took Françoise a moment before she understood his meaning. It horrified her. She hoped that Reggie would not decide she was his enemy. And also that they would not meet anyone else. It was not that she was squeamish, but to be defenceless and then killed in such an offhand way had no … honour?

However, they did not meet anyone else. She explained to Reggie where she wanted to go and he led the way. Sometimes he would stop for a several seconds, sometimes a minute, then he would move on and she did not know why. It was almost as if he could see around corners. On one occasion when Reggie stopped, she heard murmuring voices echoing along the crystal corridor. After a few moments he backtracked and led her a different way.

They climbed some stairs and walked along a smoothly cut passage that stretched for two hundred metres. There were no doors on either side, but there was an opening on the right about halfway.

Reggie flattened himself to the floor and squirmed his way past the gap. Once he was past it he stood and waited for her. He did not make any sign, but Françoise assumed he wanted her to do the same. She got onto her knees and crawled.

When she reached the opening she saw a set of steps leading down from the gap, with benches on either side like an auditorium. It was a huge hall and she could see Roman-style pillars on the other side.

A voice echoed from within. "Miss Anderson, welcome to my humble eyrie."

Françoise froze. She wanted to look. She needed to look.

Reggie gestured at her, another very human mannerism carrying urgency and concern.

Maliha's voice floated clearly through the air. "It is very impressive." Then she coughed and the coarse sound echoed through the room.

Hearing her speak pushed Françoise into action. She moved forward to the safety beyond the gap and stood. She flattened herself against the wall and edged to the opening. She peered out, moving as slowly as she could.

There was a double door at the end of the room; a black and white criss-cross pattern on the floor closed inward as she moved forward until Maliha came into view. She looked like an old woman, leaning on her walking stick with her head down and the sari covering it.

"You brought me here, Timmons," she said. "What are you going to do with me?"

"How many friends have you lost, Miss Anderson?"

"Do you mean how many have you had murdered?"

There was no response from the other end. Françoise waited.

"I have lost too many people," she said.

Françoise almost laughed out loud. Maliha had not answered his question. She was playing with him. Perhaps she had a plan after all.

"And does it hurt, Miss Anderson?"

"Why?" she said. "Is the pain of others the only thing you can experience?"

"Not at all," he said. "I merely wished to demonstrate to my colleagues how thoroughly you have been brought down."

"Valentine, the Spencers—though they were hardly friends—Françoise, Constance Mayberry. What have they ever done to you that you should make them suffer?"

"Now, now, Constance Mayberry she is not dead," he paused. "Though she will be when the law catches up with her, since her husband lies poisoned by her hand."

"What?" Maliha sounded genuinely hurt and angry. "You did this even though you already had me?"

Reggie pulled at Françoise's sleeve, distracting her. She turned and put her hand to her lips. Reggie almost climbed her arm to get his mouth to her ear. For a moment she thought he was attacking her.

"Child," he hissed into her ear.

She screwed up her face. "What?"

"She child."

Realisation struck Françoise like a thunderbolt.

xi

Maliha tried to focus on the game she was playing here. Was she trying to get information or bring about Timmons' death? Both, really, and the latter option was still vague. He would be absolutely certain he was in control; it was time to chip pieces out of his confidence.

"Which square am I standing on, Timmons?" demanded Maliha.

"What?" said Timmons.

One of the other men stood up. "What's she going on about, Terry?"

"Nothing, Jeremy, she's a woman. You can't expect any sense from her."

Maliha raised her voice. "You didn't answer my question, Timmons."

"That's because you weren't asking anything intelligent." He laughed and the other two men joined in, though Maliha felt their participation was forced.

"Your associates don't share you confidence, Timmons," she said. "They're worried. You bring me into this great hall of yours, with its tricks to make people feel small," —in fact, since the optical illusion would work in reverse, she probably did look small to them—"but I am not cowed, Terence Timmons."

"You are irrelevant."

"Is that why you spent so much energy on bringing me here?" She barked out a laugh. "Why did you not just have me killed? It would have been easy enough. Although," she paused for effect, "even a fall from a Voidship failed to kill me."

"You were lucky," he said. "And your William Crier was dealt with afterwards. You have been amusing to toy with, but you have no significance."

"Why?" she said. "Because you think I cannot stop you and your friends from dominating the Earth?"

Then he really did laugh. It was so genuine Maliha felt her blood run cold. How wrong was she?

"Your mistake, Miss Anderson," he said and climbed to his feet, "is in thinking we do not already control it." He paused. "Are you not going to ask me how that can be?"

But she already knew. Once he had claimed it, she had raced ahead and grasped it in all its detail. He was not planning any sort of invasion—he had no need of it. Still, the longer she kept him talking the more he might reveal. "How can that be?"

"Trade," he said and, though she was not looking at his face and she continued to keep her face down, she knew the smile he had. She had seen it in every man who was happy to demonstrate his superiority. "My associates and I—"

"The East India Company."

"We were that once and hold that title to remember our heritage," he said. "But we are so much more now. We control more wealth than any nation of the Earth. We stand above presidents, kings and emperors. We have the power to do anything we wish."

"It's not enough though, is it?"

There was a moment of silence that stretched into seconds.

"You like to play chess, Timmons," she said. "That's what this was, wasn't it? A game where you had every move covered. Where nothing I could do would change the final outcome."

"It has been a diversion," he said. "But hardly chess, more like dangling a fish on a line and waiting for it to tire before reeling it in and smashing its head on a stone."

Behind his words she could feel the cold of complete dissociation, as if he no longer considered others to be real. When you could fulfil your slightest whim, what remained? Only the inflicting of pain, because all you can feel is the agony of others. He expected her to suffer.

"On the contrary, Timmons," she said. "It is chess. After all, look where I am standing."

He laughed again, but there was uncertainty there. "Raving again. No wonder women belong in Bedlam."

"Count them, Timmons. What square from the door am I standing on?"

He said nothing.

"Come on, Timmons," she said. "I'm sure you can count. What about your associates? I would call them your friends, but you have no friends and neither do they."

There was a pause. The man who was not Jeremy spoke. "The seventh."

"That's right," she said. "I am on the seventh. What chess piece am I? A bishop? A knight? A rook?"

"Ha! If you were a chess piece, Miss Anderson, you would be nothing more than a pawn. You have done everything exactly as I planned. You are nothing."

"Well," she said, "that's fine. You see, I am entirely happy to be a pawn."

The one called Jeremy piped up. "At least she knows her place. We could have some fun with this one, Terry."

Maliha shivered at what she imagined his idea of fun might be, but that didn't matter—the game was not over yet. She stepped forward onto the black square in front of her and laughed. "Now I am on the eighth, I expect you know what that means?"

There was silence.

She pulled back the fold of fabric from her head and stood up straight, no longer leaning on the stick. "I have been promoted from pawn to queen."

A new voice broke the silence, the man who had not spoken before. "Black-eye! She has black-eye. You said she would only die of that if she was too afraid to come."

Maliha stared at the triumvirate of businessmen. They were all on their feet. Timmons faced her from the dais, but the other two shuffled back. They looked massive but it was all illusion.

"Stay where you are, you cowards!" shouted Timmons. "Or I'll shoot you first."

They froze and stared up at him.

Not them, Timmons, me. "Shoot me, Timmons, and you'll be infected too."

There was the distinct sound of a gun being cocked. "You're too far away, Miss Anderson. I can kill you and we'll be away before there's any chance of infection." He lifted the gun and pointed it at her.

The sound of movement on the balcony to her left distracted Maliha for a moment and she turned to see someone launching themselves into the hall. A gunshot echoed round the hall. She was surprised not to feel the impact, not even the burning pain of a graze.

She turned her attention back to Timmons. His gun was pointed directly at her. He had missed.

He fired again and she flinched. She heard the bullet ricochet from the stone floor behind her. And again. And again. The sound of shots was deafening in the enclosed space.

She remained standing. There was no sensation of pain. Nothing.

"What the hell's wrong with you, Terry?" shouted the one who had been hysterical about her black-eye. "Kill her!"

Someone landed on the ground beside her. "You can't kill her, Timmons, she's a goddess."

Françoise. Maliha was annoyed. Why could she not do as she was told and get information from Timmons' office while she had him distracted?

"And who's this?" The excitable one's voice was getting higher in pitch.

"This is Françoise Greaux," Maliha said clearly. She let it sink in. "You had her killed, if you recall, tortured to death."

"No, this is a trick." Timmons stepped off the dais and drifted to the deck. He strode towards them, closing the distance in long strides. He did not intend to miss again.

But Maliha smiled. Timmons was backed into a corner. He had been unable to shoot her, probably due to the visual effects in the room, and someone he had supposedly killed was back from the dead. If she didn't know better she might have been convinced of her own godhood.

"I am Françoise Greaux and the goddess brought me back. She killed your torturer by casting him out into the Void. She died and she came back also."

Maliha thought that final flourish was a bit too much. She was right. Timmons raised his gun and shot Françoise as he approached. She went down with a cry and a moan, with her hands clutched to her stomach. Maliha resisted the temptation to run to her and continued to face Timmons.

The sound of a distant crash penetrated the hall from behind her, followed by sporadic gunfire. The two other men looked at one another. They hesitated, waiting for the other to act, and then together beat a retreat behind the dais.

"Don't leave!" she commanded and they froze. "I want you to witness his failure."

With her smile broadening, Maliha took a step towards her adversary.

"Do you know who I am, Terence Timmons?"

He jumped as there was another, louder crash from behind the doors.

"Who am I?" she shouted, dragging his attention back to her.

"Anderson, Alice Maliha Anderson!"

He raised the gun.

"Shoot me now, Timmons, and you will die of black-eye." She
took another step towards him.

The gun clicked. He pulled the trigger again and again.

"It's a six-shooter, Timmons, and you had an empty barrel for
safety."

Out of the corner of her eye she saw Françoise move and the
glint of something metal.

"I am the avatar of vengeance, Timmons. I am the Durga Maa."

The metal flashed at her; she turned her head and intercepted
the gun Françoise had tossed. She turned back to Timmons.
Whatever was crashing towards them was just beyond the doors.
Maliha knelt on one knee, and bowed her head.

There was a tremendous crash and splintering of wood. The air
filled with clouds of dust. In the noise and turmoil, Maliha extracted
the lenses from her eyes. Powerful diesel engines roared and the gale
from the rotors tore through the hall.

She blinked with relief and rose like a demon with her sari
whipping around her. Timmons was staring over her shoulder and
backing away. She did not look. She did not have to. The engines
idled and the noise reduced. She still had to shout.

"Timmons!"

He looked at her with amazement as he realised her eyes were
no longer black.

"You killed people I knew and loved. You killed people I did
not know. And for all of them I claim vengeance, Terence
Timmons."

She lifted the gun, aimed for his chest and pulled the trigger. In
the almost non-existent gravity the gun kicked hard.

He stood there with blood seeping from a graze in his shoulder,
staining his fine suit.

Maliha tutted and tossed the gun aside. "Valentine," she said and
gestured towards Timmons, "if you wouldn't mind."

"Are you sure?"

"What?"

"You won't be annoyed at me?"

"Just do it!"

A shot echoed through the hall. Timmons clutched at his chest, his gaze wavered and he collapsed to his knees. The spell the scene had cast on his two associates broke and they fled.

Maliha walked up to Timmons and knelt on one knee beside him. Blood was pumping from his chest under considerable pressure; something important must have been badly damaged.

Good.

"I'm glad you weren't killed outright, Timmons," she said, "because it's important for you to know that you have failed utterly."

She met his eyes. She could see the agony in him and she felt no pity.

"It's not just your failure, Timmons," she said. "By playing this game you have shown me the hand that you and your associates are playing. I know the scale of your empire. More than that, I know your mistakes and the horrors that you are going to unwittingly inflict on the people of Earth."

"I ... don't ... care..."

"No, and that's the problem." She sighed and stood. "But anyway, you're going to die and I, a mere woman, have killed you."

"Not ... stop ... us ..."

"No, I know that, but your associates have seen me bring you down and that will slow them."

She felt someone come up beside her. A hand she knew came into view, holding a gun. He pulled the trigger and shot Timmons through the head.

"Was that entirely necessary?" she said. "I hadn't finished."

"Oh, I expect you would have been melodramatic, just walked off as his life's blood seeped away. Then someone would have come in and rescued him. Besides, we need to get out of here before reinforcements turn up. Too much jabbering."

Maliha turned to Valentine. He looked older. She rested her hand on his arm for a moment and then crossed to Françoise. She carefully lifted her body, went across to the flyer and handed her up to Valentine, who had climbed aboard.

"*Alice through the Looking Glass?*" she said.

"It was the best I could come up with in the time, what with lions, unicorns, snarks and boojums," he said. "Come on, we need to go."

Bullets ricocheted from the hull fired by Timmon's guards. Valentine climbed into the pilot's chair and brought the engines up. Maliha sat next to him.

"I think I'd better teach you to shoot," he said as they turned in the confined space. He gunned the thrusters and the crew of the stronghold dived out of the way as he rocketed along the corridor towards the dock.

"And fly," she said.

Valentine used the guns mounted on the flyer to wreak damage on the other vessels in the dock, before turning them on the locks and hinges of the main door until, as the rain poured in, he burst out into the storm.

They had landed at a small town, close to where the highlands dropped off to the sea in the endless coastal waterfall. A doctor had treated Françoise's wound; it was unlikely to be fatal as long as she was kept under normal temperatures and humidity.

The vehicle Valentine had commandeered possessed both of those qualities, being one of Timmons' personal vessels. There was not a great deal of room, but it would do for them for the time being.

Once Françoise was settled Valentine took them into the air again.

"Where are we going?" Maliha asked.

"The goddess has a mission."

"Kindly refrain from using that term."

"As lovely as ever, Miss Anderson."

She felt a rage explode inside her. "You dropped me out of an airship with no parachute at several thousand feet!"

"It wasn't that high, one thousand at most," he said casually. "I saved your life."

"I thought you were dead. They told me you were dead."

"I may have implied that someone else was me."

She hit him on the arm just above the elbow.

"Oww!" He rubbed the spot. "What was that for?"

"Because I love you, you impossible man."

He turned his smiling face towards her. "Really?"

"Don't fish for compliments," she said and crossed her arms, pointedly ignoring him.

They flew on. The flyer made good speed, but it was late in the evening when they touched down on the outskirts of a small town. A high, thick wall surrounded it, while a network of wires criss-crossed above it.

They climbed into the rear cabin. Maliha checked on Françoise, who was sleeping. Valentine was rummaging in some bags. Maliha frowned.

"Is that my luggage?"

"You're not going back to the hotel."

"No, I suppose not, but you brought my luggage?"

"And Françoise's. Ah, here it is." He stood up, pulling out a rectangle of cloth covered in a green and yellow pattern: Riette's *kanga*.

"You found him?"

"Assuming he's still alive."

"I really do love you."

"So you keep saying, but I might be more convinced if you refrained from hitting me."

Maliha wrote a note for Françoise and attached it where she would be able to read it when she awoke.

Valentine held the umbrella as they walked along the raised wooden walkway to the small house. They were wet through, of course, and Maliha clung to the *kanga*.

As Valentine knocked, Maliha realised she was trembling.

A young man answered the door. He was clean-shaven and dressed in the loose-fitting clothes all Venusians wore. He frowned when he realised he had no idea who they were.

"Marten Ouderkirk?"

"I am he," he said and the Boer twang was evident in his voice.

"May we come in?"

"Who are you?"

Maliha glanced up at the rain and the half-light. He stood back and allowed them inside, where they dripped on the wooden floor.

"My name is Maliha Anderson," she said. "I met Riette." She held out the *kanga*, allowing it to unwrap slightly so the pattern was clear. The *kanga* that Marten had bought for her.

He did not move at first and then he reached out and took it from her. He clutched it to his chest and turned away from them so they would not see him weep.

* * *

"Are you sure about this?" asked Valentine as they climbed back on board the ship with Marten following.

"Yes."

"You collect people."

"I know, I'm sorry."

"I imagined we might go somewhere and be alone for a while."

"After killing one of the most influential individuals in the solar system and scaring two others?"

He powered up the rotors and they lifted off smoothly.

"They'll go after Amita and Barbara to try to get to you," he said.

"Amita already has her instructions, they'll be fine."

"How could you have known this would happen?"

"I didn't know it would, but I knew it could. Timmons isn't the only one who can make contingency plans."

They were silent for a while.

"Don't you need to rest?" she said.

"We have appointments to keep," he said. "You're not the only one who makes contingency plans either."

"We're going back to Earth?"

"I thought that would be best."

"Yes, it is," she said. "We'll have to intercept Constance and Izak when they arrive, but I think I know someone who will help with that."

She glanced back through the cabin door to where Françoise lay, looking back at her with a grin on her face. The revelation that her symptoms were not caused by any form of Venusian fungus had been both a relief and a concern. Françoise had been happy about it though.

Maliha turned back to Valentine. "And when we get back the first thing we have to do is get married."

"Yes," he said. "If that's what you want. I didn't think you were in a hurry and there will be a lot to do."

"We have to."

"Have to?"

"Yes."

There was a short pause.

"Oh."

~ end ~

Thank you for reading the Maliha Anderson series. It's been quite an adventure for everybody—myself included.

If you enjoyed them please write a review on your favourite website, and you don't have to have bought a book from Amazon to review it there.

There will be more about Maliha Anderson but in the meantime you can read the other books in the same setting by going to http://bit.ly/steve-turnbull

And, to be sure you don't miss any future works, why not join the mailing list at http://bit.ly/voidships.

Steve Turnbull was born in the heart of London to book-loving working-class parents in 1958. He lived with his parents and two older sisters in two rooms with gas lighting and no hot water. In his fifth year, a change in his father's fortunes took them out to a detached house in the suburbs. That was the year *Dr Who* first aired on British TV, and Steve watched it avidly from behind the sofa. It was the beginning of his love of science fiction.

Academically Steve always went for the science side, but he also had his imagination—and that took him everywhere. He read through his local library's entire science fiction and fantasy selection, plus his father's 1950s *Astounding Science Fiction* magazines. As he got older he also ate his way through TV SF like *Star Trek*, *Dr Who* and *Blake's 7*.

However, it was when he was 15 he discovered something new. Bored with a maths lesson, he noticed a book from the school library: *Cider with Rosie* by Laurie Lee. From the first page he was captivated by the beauty of the language. As a result he wrote a story longhand and then spent evenings at home on his father's electric typewriter pounding out a second draft, expanding it. Then he wrote a second book. After that he switched to poetry and turned out dozens, mostly not involving teenage angst.

After receiving excellent science and maths results, he went on to study computer science. There he teamed up with another student and they wrote songs for their band, with Steve writing the lyrics. However, they admit their best song was the other way around, with Steve writing the music.

After graduation Steve moved into contract programming but was snapped up a couple of years later by a computer magazine looking for someone with technical knowledge. It was in the magazine industry that Steve learned how to write to length, to deadline, and to style. Within a couple of years he was editor and stayed there for many years.

During that time he married Pam (who also became a magazine editor), whom he'd met at a student party.

Though he continued to write poetry, all prose work stopped. He created his own magazine publishing company which at one point produced the subscription magazine for the *Robot Wars* TV show. The company evolved into a design agency, but after six years of working very hard and not seeing his family—now including a daughter and son—he gave it all up.

He spent a year working on miscellaneous projects including writing 300 pages for a website until he started back where he had begun, contract programming.

With security and success on the job front, the writing began again. This time it was scriptwriting: features scripts, TV scripts and radio scripts. During this time he met a director, Chris Payne, who wanted to create steampunk stories, and between them they created the Voidships universe, a place very similar to ours but with specific scientific changes.

With a whole universe to play with, Steve wrote a web series, a feature film, and then books all in the same Steampunk world and, behind the scenes, all connected.

Join the mailing list at http://bit.ly/voidships